I0730182

AMNANDI SAILS

THE KHUMALO TRILOGY BOOK TWO

ZIG ZAG CLAYBOURNE

AMNANDI SAILS

Obsidian Sky Books
Detroit, MI

ISBN 978-1-7322980-5-7

First Edition: August 2025

Cover art, map, and interior design by
Jesse Hayes, anansihayes.com

Dedicated to Deb, who could have journeyed so much more,
and to every instance of Black Girl Magic
of which far too many are unaware.

AMNANDI WRITES

The young woman, at times described as a wash of colors seeking rest, at times a stone soul, at times a witch, reached into a pocket of timespace, pulled her small journal from its air, and wrote while curtains of raindrops cooled the open space under her family's covered patio. She had spent more time in the shade of the patio's ornately carved roofing and columns than in the house itself. It was still the home her mother and grandparents napped in whenever she and her mother needed deep rest. Whether weary, haggard, sometimes injured, or simply ready, beautiful Insheree always welcomed them, leaving Amnandi Khumalo the perfect time for writing.

Perfect times necessitated thinking.

She and Unina Ayanda, her mother, had been home for two weeks.

For Amnandi, thinking was no hardship. Contemplation was bliss, particularly when accompanied by the heavy rains of the wet season. Water couldn't help but be a thousand stories told.

A tale involving a child details growth, she wrote. *It should be noted that we are all children of a certain age. I have decided that at some point in the future my writings will be made available. You will not take offense if I do not concern myself with to whom. Know this: every word is accurate. Know because it is about friends and written by myself.*

As for why these words will find their way to you, it has been said by the poet Thao, A tale is always safest within the teller, but that is not what a tale is for. *I don't write as often as my mother does. That may be a failing, but I openly admit I don't frequently write my own accounts of things because I prefer to live them. It's one selfishness I enjoy. However, the first time one sees the world alone is important. Certain feelings demand words. Certain questions. Many actions. And memories. Words can become home when home—* Amnandi twiddled the pen in her long, strong fingers as she glanced at the delightful reliefs of goddesses and planets on the yuffa tree columns around her, each telling Erah's story in their way.

When home, she wrote, *sleeps quietly.*

"A trickle of rain," she said aloud to her pen which needed to be dipped again, a sign a story was ready to be told, "invites a memory."

She dipped it. *This is not truly my story, but it* is *my story.*

Her trained ears listened for patterns in the rain. Shortly after resuming writing, she heard her mother's soft, slow footfalls stirring in the kitchen as Unina prepared tea. Amnandi tucked pen and pad away for later, preferring to join her.

ZIG ZAG CLAYBOURNE

INTRO TO DIVING

All witches are sea witches. What a wonderful thought. No matter where Amnandi Khumalo was, the sea was there. The arms of the goddess never closed.

The young witch stared downward from the top of a mast, a mast she'd scaled many times, had even stood on the very tip many times, at turns for duty on this merchant ship, at turns to get away. The aged post was wide enough for both feet.

With a final measured, deep breath, she pushed off as if sprung.

She arced high over the ship, clearing its port, tucked into a somersault, and angled her arms and legs the way the old divers along the Afrelan coasts had taught her. A blink after leaping, Amnandi arrowed inside a pod of awaiting dolphins.

The dolphins hadn't requested she dive. *That* had been a challenge from a captain who had promised Amnandi's mother to present such tasks to the esteemed witch's growing daughter whenever useful opportunities arose.

The challenge here was to enter the water so smoothly, the dolphins didn't disperse.

This particular pod had followed the *Bane* between islands, primarily because ship's carpenter Sarantain fed them from the larder master's daily catches.

Not one moved away as Amnandi entered the water. She barely rippled. Immediately, the dolphins circled her underwater and followed her to the surface, their clicking conversations overlapping into the consensus *Do it again.* Dolphins had only recently decided humans were sentient, always curious to see what the land things would do next. A human might toss half a net's catch overboard, or play baleful music during a lull atop the smooth sea, or even—as now—create true art. The bubble trail Amnandi formed was flawless in its curvatures, spatial relations, and duration.

She even, at the perfect moment, merged with her art, seamlessly dipping to perform a twisting flip that threaded her through her own trail.

Sharp claps pulled the dolphins' attention to the ship.

A woman sitting precariously atop a rail brought her brown hands together. Her lively skirt, festooned with feathers, echoed the congratulations with each lifting breeze. She whistled, then waved a beaten wide-brimmed straw bonnet.

"Well done!" shouted Captain Maab Pinyasama.

Amnandi waved back. "Are the dolphins pleased with me?"

The feathered woman nodded. "They barely knew you'd entered!"

Amnandi met the eyes of the dolphin nearest her. It seemed to agree. She hadn't yet learned to communicate with as many species as her mother had, but there was no mistaking joy. The dolphin nudged her hand and she knew it meant for her to take hold of its snout. As she did, it dived, twisting with her in a stream of collaborative bubbling before leaving her spinning. It then followed her upward.

Amnandi rotated slowly within their circle, showing respect to each. "All communication is a matter of intent," her mother had given as a language lesson or another during Amnandi's childhood. "*Intent* must flow outward." She missed her mother. And even though the sayings were woven into each of Amnandi's seventeen years, she missed those, too. She missed the scent of her mother's hair during hugs.

She treaded water. A proper witch knew that missing those you loved was good. This journey would see her back in her mother's arms soon enough. She would be a better witch for missing her mother and, she hoped, a better human. She had encountered few better teachers than the petite captain of this teardrop-shaped merchant ship.

Amnandi swam to its scratched and scarred lacquered hull, caught the knotted rope thrown down, and climbed up. This ship had seemed vast to her on her first voyage on it seven years ago when Unina had allowed her to travel alone under watchful supervision for a short island run. Amnandi climbed its side now as though ascending a simple staircase, and when she reached the top and hauled herself over the railing, her tall body stood a full two heads above Maab.

"Permission to drip on board, Captain?"

"Granted. You even get a mop." Pinyasama's eyes beamed. There was no mistaking joy. "You remembered the angle of your feet this time."

"And my hands," one of which she ran over her shorn head. The feel of stubble against her palm never failed to delight her. It was like feeling the electricity directly from her brain. And wet? Paradise. The dolphins would get sick of her this trip! She already considered the next dive.

"Permission to get out of those wet wraps as well," said the captain, her singsong Myyrai accent clipping the words into crisp bits. "You look like you're being prepared for burial."

The gray cotton cloths Amnandi wore under her usual robes covered her from torso to knees. She beamed at the captain's joke. "Drop me overboard for my own burial at sea and I'll dive as perfect as ever," said Amnandi.

The captain clapped her on a shoulder. "Go, woman. While the wind takes its rest, we'll continue ours. Dry and bring your koka. I feel like singing."

***

There being no reason to expect danger on this voyage, Maab didn't mind a bit of diversion.

She couldn't sing to save her life. This did not deter her.

And because she didn't sing on board often, her crew of twenty-seven souls rarely complained. She somehow made bawdy songs sound romantic and sad songs hopeful, always with a tremulous quality to her voice that said, *I have done things so that you don't have to.*

As the *Bane* bobbed, she sang "The Lovelorn Dance."

"I know to whom my heart is bound,
I know 'tis bound for you.
I know to whom my heart is bound,
I lash myself to you.
And should we part, I'll send my heart,
To search all worlds for you."

Amnandi's vibrant orange-and-blue tunic matched the paint of her koka, an instrument that could not help but sound beautiful.

It was the perfect song to sing to a ship on its way "home," and though the crew claimed lineage to at least a dozen lands, any port was home. The strings of the koka dutifully rode the rises and clefts. It was a simple tune, mostly twangs and stops, but

Maab's voice was expressive, so Amnandi's fingers wandered and improvised in accompaniment.

Maab caught the eye of her first mate, Patrice Skye, who thought the crew had rested a little more than needed this time out. People waiting for orders to be given got sloppy. But this last hour on calm waters had lulled even her.

The two women exchanged a nod.

While Maab sang, Maab strolled. Few truly noticed how studious the captain was when she relaxed. A respectful crew always knew the sea was unpredictable. A sailor's lull was merely a nap with one eye open.

Maab observed the state of knots, the morale of troublesome or troubled crewmembers, how evenly crates were stacked, the dryness or wetness of the deck, and sundry minutiae as kept a ship a ship.

"I know my love does not yet rest—" She met eyes with carpenter Sarantain, whose love, Grucca (waylaid off this voyage by a common yet highly perspicacious illness), awaited them at port. Waterfall. Where Maab and Amnandi's adventure first began so many years earlier. The journey thus far from the northwestern coast of Afrela to the northeastern coast of Eurola, with sundry stops in between, had been fruitful but, more importantly, uneventful.

Sarantain gave a playful hardening of his eyes to say *He had better be at rest.*

"I know Grucca pines for you." She and Amnandi strolled onward, eventually stopping to sit near three crewpersons playing a new card game they'd barely learned at last port, leading each to attempt to bend the rules to their benefit without outright cheating. Captain Maab Pinyasama did not allow cheating of any sort on her ship. The *Bane* had sailed for over a decade without a single choking, stabbing, slitting, or fight that wasn't over and done the moment it was broken up.

She made her way belowdecks.

"And in the hold," Maab sang, nodding in succession to midnight Dedoura and snowy Niss, former acolytes of some goddess or other (Maab couldn't remember; there were too many), sworn to acolytic compassion and honesty. If they had to break an interloper's arm, it was guaranteed they'd set it apologetically afterward. *"Dedoura and Niss, quietly watching over"*—Maab gestured expansively at the empty space and few crates or barrels still there after the *Bane*'s most recent dropoff—*"all this."*

"She's improvising," said Dedoura.

"Child sister," Niss said to Amnandi. She always called Amnandi *Child sister*. "Run."

"We would simply cross paths again," Amnandi said, forgetting the existence of humor for a moment while acknowledging quite literally that they were on a boat.

Maab warbled onward. *"Onboard I am both captain and mother to our traveler of the witching ways. See? She stays and plays! But Niss receives double watch today. Let us see now what she has to say."* This with a full set of eye twinkles above her smile at the warrior woman, whose own soft smile never truly completely left her leathery face.

"I'll be satisfied," said Niss, "to see us make it home," and she finished with automatically drawing a circle over the veins on her left wrist with her right thumb, a prayer beseeching the goddess's favor.

"Have we been away so long?" Sometimes, a captain's sense of time differed wildly from the crew's.

"I've people I need to see in Waterfall," Niss allowed, accompanied by that faraway, soft smile.

"Which is precisely my song!" said Maab.

Amnandi immediately played a recurring motif that, to the ear, became the workings of a clock, moving the mind—and time—decidedly forward.

Captain Pinyasama ventured further. The *Bane* was well sized and properly proportioned for each of the things it had to be: a courier of goods, a fighter when needed, an explorer at its best. The umber tang of sawdust pulled her toward Sarantain Hiver's workshop.

Sarantain's assistant—needed in Grucca's stead—currently stacked unsalvageable planks from various areas of the *Bane* to see how many she could chop with an axe in one go.

"Amis, you'll hurt yourself," said the captain.

Amis Dotrig, champion against boredom and friend of Amnandi forever, paused. She looked to the captain, then Amnandi. But stayed on Amnandi.

"Yes?" the young witch prompted.

"Waiting for you to add *again*," said the short, multi-bandaged, unkempt friend from Waterfall, still freckled where Niss was weathered.

Amnandi somehow made the koka sound like a sneer, then tucked the instrument at her side.

As the pale girl came around the stacks to show proper honor to the captain, the full-fledged, highly trained witch of the world of Erah threw a portal which Amis couldn't avoid stepping into, and from which Amis exited decktop right beside the card players, who shrugged and continued their game.

"Again," Amnandi said. She loved doing that to her.

Maab roared with laughter. "How many is that this week?"

"Three," said Amnandi.

"I've no doubt of at least ten by the time we port," said Maab.

Moments later, Amis Dotrig marched down the creaky wooden stairs, saying not a word to anyone. When she reached the carpentry workshop, Maab said, "Frankly, I can't see how you don't expect that by now."

Amis huffed upward at Amnandi. "At some point, I'm going to go off on an adventure all my own."

"You do that," said Amnandi.

"I plan to."

"No, I meant that I *want* you to experience all wonders."

"Oh." Amis was only a year younger than Amnandi. A year, at times, felt like ten.

"I'll refrain from porting you without your permission for the remainder of this voyage," said Amnandi.

"Come," said Maab Pinyasama, having seen that her woodworking and repair crew's needs were solidly met. "I can rhyme for at least two more verses. The cook deserves no less."

The ship's cook and backup physician hated Maab's singing and had no problem telling her so. Her name, Leena, meant *bitter*, which as far as Maab was concerned was entirely accurate. She was kin by marriage to Maab's sister.

"*I know of where—*" Maab paused to nod to Leena's apprentice (every duty aboard a ship being apprenticed to full redundancy). The apprentice hauled two pig-sized sacks of rice, one on each shoulder, toward the ship's massive cast-iron pot. Boiling lent the warm tropical air a bit more humidity.

The galley's cross-breeze ports were wide open. Amnandi, while playing, studied the duo of sea and horizon through one.

Maab continued her song. "*I know of where my heart is bound. Is bound for stew.*" She stopped, studying a massive chopping board's lines of onions, carrots, fresh-caught fish, and beets. "No heat in today's meal?" she asked her sister-in-law.

"Not everything requires spice, sister."

"Carry on."

To the captain's back, the wiry chef said, "I won't ask the same of you!" with a whack of a sharp knife to a green fish's head.

"Enjoy this rest!" Maab shouted back, then sang louder.

***

A dash through the berths and rowing station below, then

past the heavy drab curtain of the captain's small quarters, up the stairs foreship.

The soft wind had shifted a bit.

Several crew members who'd been spread out when Maab went below hovered close at the prow, backs to her approach. Their voices quickly rose. One turned to shout for the captain's presence but snatched it back when he saw her, instead directing her attention over the side.

The sea within two strokes along the side had gone inky black.

"What's our perimeter look like?" Maab called out. Crew from various places rushed to sides. Voices following one another gave the same report.

A sailor's rest.

It appeared a drop of ink had fallen from the sky above the sky, bobbing with the barely drifting ship.

"This is why we don't stop," someone muttered, hoping Maab wouldn't hear.

The miasma spread surely outward until the diameter equalled that of the length of the ship. Maab made sure Amnandi was still in tow as she raced about. The ink neither stained the hull nor adhered. Merely sat atop the water and lapped the *Bane's* hull like mercury.

The *Bane*, for all intents and purposes, became the pupil of a black, unseeing eye.

"Oars," Maab said to the first mate as the muscled woman came into view. Within moments of Mate Skye relaying the order, slots opened low in the ship's belly at port and starboard. Rows of long oars speared out.

"Straight on," said Maab calmly.

Witch stuff or god stuff.

For Maab Pinyasama, barely a shrug.

Skye gave the drum beside the wheelhouse two rapid whacks, an order which carried through the wooden pipes leading to the oar master's station below and his quickly assembled crew of rowers.

Maab heard two sharp strikes in acknowledgment.

The ship moved forward.

The ink didn't hold them, nor did it go away, being their shadow as though cast from directly above.

"Again," ordered Maab.

Skye gave two strikes.

Two strikes answered, straight forward again.

The shadow remained.

"We are espied," Maab said to Skye. "Hold."

Skye beat the drum once.

"Bring me an oar," Maab said to Amnandi.

***

Amnandi threw a portal, stepped through, relayed the captain's wish to the nearest rowing duo, who expertly removed the long oar from its mount. She threw the return portal and, with the help of the young rower holding the other end of the oar stepping through behind her, presented the waxed wood for inspection.

Unina had often told her that rest invited appeals from spirits.

Not a speck of ink, just slightly glistening wood, perfectly shaped and balanced. "You wouldn't have fetched it if you'd sensed harm," Maab said. "Or had it simply been wood and water. Speak on it."

"There's spirit in the wood but not of the wood." No need to guess. There was unmistakable power there. "This is goddess work."

Maab nodded after stepping closer to the oversized oar and inspecting it herself. "Return it."

Amnandi glanced over her shoulder to be sure the rower was

ready. At his nod, she settled her end of the oar in the crook of an arm, threw the portal with the other, and led the way, hearing Mate Skye anticipate her captain. "Everyone on deck?"

"Aye."

Mate Skye clanged a bell that focused all eyes on the open space the captain moved toward. Amnandi elected to walk up the stairs with the rowers, the galley crew, and sundry others belowdecks. Up top, she searched for Amis.

The sun shone crisply and clearly.

A mystery.

Or an opportunity.

For Captain Maab Pinyasama, there wasn't always difference between the two.

"The captain thinks we've sat long enough to be noticed by the gods," said Skye, setting the stage for the curious.

Pinyasama hopped a crate for height. She nodded to one of her crew. "Keep watch on it." All the various feathers stitched to her sarong flapped in a sudden gust of wind. She raised her voice. "Being chosen is nothing new, but that doesn't mean we don't have good fears. I fully expect, acknowledge, and embrace yours. We drop anchor and remain here overnight until we get clear guidance. If no guidance, we leave."

"We can't sit a solid two hours without some goddess getting it into her head to waylay us?" someone groused.

"These feathers come at a price. The sea always knows where I am. Its needs are our needs. Aye?" Another gust shimmered the feathers.

"Aye," most grumbled. The gods did make their needs known— this was common knowledge—but not with the frequency at which Maab Pinyasama encountered them. Over the course of five years, Amnandi's mother had relayed news to Amnandi from Maab of five missions from the gods. Usually the goddess.

"We've got an eye," said Pinyasama. "We've got a sudden wind telling us we must not rest. Our young witch was in the water not an hour ago, communing by grace of the goddess." She hopped off her crate. "We wait to see what's revealed." The captain headed aft, where she planned to stand, sit, or slouch for as long as necessary. "Amnandi," she said, everyone knowing that somewhere in the crowd, the young lady would've put herself within easy hearing. "With me, please."

When Amnandi caught up to her captain, Maab looked her over. "You well? What're you feeling?"

"Uncertain." Then, quickly realizing that could be interpreted numerous ways, Amnandi added, "I feel that I'm uncertain, not that I'm uncertain of what I feel. I...don't like the feeling."

"Ayanda hasn't taught you some witchy saying about uncertainty being a path to enlightened thinking or some such?"

Amnandi shook her head.

"Then neither will I," said Pinyasama. "Each voyage of this ship is a promise that I will bring everyone home. Be certain of that. An intercession by the goddess is not a trivial thing. Be certain of *that*."

"I am."

"Good. Explain the wood, please."

"My breath caught briefly while holding it. I felt immobile."

"Stuck," said Maab.

Amnandi nodded.

"As we are. You had no sense of anything amiss while in the water?"

"None."

"Caprice is rarely random. Apparently, we are indeed meant to wait. A preparatory period before diving into the unknown?"

"Which one cannot prepare for. I should meditate for clarity and solutions," said Amnandi.

Seventeen years old yet speaking with so much of her mother's timbre.

"May I ask you to chronicle our possibilities?" Maab said. "Your unique insights will add the details I'd most certainly overlook."

Amnandi reached inside her tunic and pulled out a sturdy bound notebook magicked to be waterproof. "I will begin now," she said.

THE EYE

We watched in shifts all night. The sun didn't reflect off the black circle during the day, and at night torches and the slender moon lit our space but not the disc. I felt no danger from the circle, and the captain took that to mean she should feel no danger either, leading to the crew feeling no danger. This is not meant to disrespect them, but this was foolishness on their parts. What is not dangerous to a witch may be highly dangerous in deeper ways to someone else. Perhaps I could not sense that yet. Perhaps they remain in danger. It is nearly time for first mess. This crew does not dismiss or disdain goddess work. How could they when the captain's luck is itself a boon of the goddess? But if people can question, make mistakes, or be foolish, they will.

I probed during my shift at watch but received nothing. Dorsals and the tips of tails lazily circled us. Large ones. Silent ones just out of range of torchlight. Sharks. I was the only one to notice them, but felt no need to raise an alarm.

The great beasts made not a single audible disturbance of water, more evidence of the goddess.

And now the sun. The black circle unchanged. The captain and I will lower in a dinghy for tests. May it prove interesting.

* * *

"You still feeling all right?" the captain asked.

"I am," said Amnandi.

The captain gave the drop signal to the two crew holding the dinghy aloft. Rope slid smoothly through their practiced hands, dropping Maab and Amnandi steadily but cautiously. The small boat landed atop the dark water with a *whumpf* as though atop bedsheets or fine fabric. Maab raised a curious brow. Water did not *whumpf*. "Row us out a bit," she said.

Amnandi dipped her oars into the circle, which bobbed with the sea but didn't churn beneath her strokes. When the oars slid into the black, they may well not existed beyond the wood visible above the water.

Under the water, however, there was a reassuring push, and the boat moved forward.

"One stroke past the perimeter," said Maab, "then turn about. Stay prepared to heave away."

The dinghy obeyed silently. Amnandi held it steady when they once again faced the *Bane* and the circle. A narrow ribbon of clear water ran between the dinghy through the black.

Maab rolled up a linen sleeve and dipped fingers into that clear ribbon. Then the hand to the wrist. After that, the arm to the elbow.

The sea was the sea, full of warmth, active with currents.

Amnandi followed suit, resting her oars and pushing a wide orange sleeve over a shoulder.

The sea was indeed the sea, electrical, alive, so vocal it constantly vibrated, so inviting it both slowed and quickened her heartbeat. It broadcast a million messages to her bones from around the world, and her bones could only smile.

The expression on her face remained stony.

Life for a witch generally mimicked the sea: there was abundance. Emotions, potentialities, contradictions, balance, all held at arm's length for the clarity of intimacy. Yet the black hole? Nothing. It was an absence more than absence. It was refusal.

Of what? Amnandi asked it.

She had not yet touched the black.

"May I?" she asked the captain, who shifted forward and took hold of the oars even as she assented.

Maab gave a slight row. The boat touched the edge of the black.

Amnandi leaned out, her long fingers scant inches from the mysterious surface.

"Describe everything," said Maab.

The witch's fingertips met the surface and dipped through.

"I don't feel it," Amnandi said. "No resistance, no temperature." Taking a deep, centering breath, she closed her eyes for several heartbeats. "I hear it."

"What's it saying, luv?" said Maab.

"...crying."

"For?"

Looking over her shoulder with eyes closed—somewhat unnervingly—Amnandi said, "You."

Which was not what Maab Pinyasama wanted to hear.

Yet she'd made her life upon the sea. Debts were meant to be paid. "I accept its need," she said.

The depthless black pimpled into a shifting mass of points as though an ancient whale hummed a lonely baritone below it.

Amnandi yanked her arm away.

The entire surface shimmered in place, tiny spikes rising and falling so fast, it appeared the mass was hyperventilating.

And then, exactly after a very deep breath, the sea spoke, deafeningly wordless. Hands flew to ears in the dinghy and everywhere on the *Bane*.

A goddess's voice overlay their reality.

For five long seconds, brains and stomachs churned. Tears flowed freely. Regrets intensified.

When silence became a welcome, no one looked at each other.

The crew of the *Bane* glanced down at their captain. The black circle was gone.

A flotsam of feathers surrounded Captain Maab Pinyasama and Amnandi Khumalo.

***

It took all hands and the better part of the day to gather all the feathers. Maab insisted not a single one be missed. They filled three empty wine barrels, which Sarantain drilled holes in to aid the plumes drying.

The feathers were slightly larger than normal, each tipped bright blue, being the feathers of searavens, three-fingered, shapeshifting sprites who traveled from land to land, claiming small bodies of water as their own.

Maab was convinced those who'd owned these feathers were dead.

Skye was insistent with her counter. "Perhaps the goddess intends a different interpretation. Perhaps aid is required."

"If they're dead, aid is required. If they are injured, aid is required. If they require us, we go," said Maab.

"Yes, but it's *how* we go that presently concerns me. There's fire in your eyes, Captain."

"There's always fire in her eyes," said Amnandi, who had yet to leave the captain's side.

Skye took the interruption gently. "Not of this type."

"You're thinking of Penshek," said Maab.

"Penshek was foolishness," said Skye.

"Yes, it was, and I'll not repeat it," said Maab.

Penshek was on the southern tip of Afrela. Maab's own homeland of Myrrai was an archipelago mere days' journey from northern Afrela. Maab had often wondered if she and Ayanda had crossed younger paths unawares.

There was an entire colony of spirits at Penshek. No one knew from where.

"Are you perhaps familiar with Penshek's recent history?" Maab asked Amnandi.

"No."

"Then I will let you stay that way. Skye," Maab said, "there will be no foolishness. I pledge this ship on it." These were binding words.

"Witnessed?" Skye said to Amnandi.

"Witnessed."

"There's an island blue-tips have claimed. Little more than a volcano, really," said Maab.

"Northeast of us," said Skye.

This surprised the captain. "You know it?"

"I've heard tales," said Skye.

"Gods, I love tales," said Maab. "Two days' journey from here. One if the wind is kind."

"Plot the course?" asked Skye.

"Aye. Unless we hear from the goddess otherwise."

THE SHIP

Next stop: Blue-tip Island.

The *Bane* sped. Its full sails gulped air and strained their reach. Maab remembered being five and racing to every area, chasing the spray. Old sailors found unsolicited baths annoying. Maab, then as now, delighted at every splash.

Even at that young age, ships were nothing new to her. Hers was a matrilineal family of seafarers. There was never an attempt to deny the communion of feet upon wood upon water. No matter a voyage's intent, that communion remained.

Those who were blessed to feel it journeyed that much better. That was fact.

The ship's hull, as richly tawny as any horse's yet as weathered as a healthy tree, had been crafted in the fashion of the best swimmers' bodies: full-chested, straight and strong-middled, tapering gracefully to a point at the rear. A wooden teardrop halved along the horizontal.

Her ship had gone through three names, handed down from mother to child as per Myrrai custom. Grand Elder Pinyasama, finally able to sail at the age of fifty after saving all her life for the shipbuilder's commission price, had built the ship and named it *Myrrai Blood*, a nod to her familial determination. When she turned the ship over to her only daughter, Maab's mother being a secret poet of a woman rechristened the ship *Love and Gain*, which inevitably became *Love Again*, then simply *Love*. Fifteen years later, after this racing, perfect teardrop of a ship had gained a reputation among traders and couriers as being the one to beat if other ships hoped to feed their families with sea wages, Maab—twenty and cheekier than a treemunk—gave it the name it now tacked toward Blue-tip under.

There would be no children to Maaboth Pinyasama, a declaration as certain as fact. Lovers who had attempted to ply her with blessings of motherhood were gentle fools. The *Bane* either swam like a dolphin or flew like a bird. There was no in-between and way too much fun being had. There were more than enough for whom children were a wonder, and both Grand Elder and Mother remained fine with the eventual fate of the ship: a massive party and bonfire upon the vessel's rest.

Maab spied Amnandi doing her best to appear engaged but actually looking for someplace to be alone. The girl exerted excessive levels of control over herself but never pretended to be an expert of witch matters.

Amnandi was her daughter. Amis was her daughter. Every person on the ship grew with her until they decided to go on their own or go home.

One couldn't ask for a better crew or a better sky for a quest: enough blue to hope, and the right people to make worthy decisions. Wind caught the sails steadily; there was barely a need to steer.

Maab ran her fingers down her flapping sarong. Each varied

feather was a gift from the goddess and existed to remind her of the purpose of life: softness. Softness of thought, being, and the contact of one life upon another. Softness was a mystery by itself to embrace in a hard, biting world; it was an adventure to undertake. She had on her ship a young woman who, as a child, had been forced to take a life to protect another. Maab had seen that wound in others often enough. It did not heal. Softness helped. That was a fact.

And just as there were all kinds of people, there were all kinds of softness. Another fact.

Facts, facts, facts. The ship: bound for the opposite of facts. Amnandi, having found her private spot, now sitting cross-legged in total meditation, had been taught that witches dealt in reality, and that the speed of thought was to be continually tempered lest the brain go its infinite separate ways and be lost.

Maybe Ayanda had meant that specifically for her daughter's brain? Amnandi was already capable of magicks unlearned from someone else. Many of these she kept to herself, but Maab compared what she had witnessed mother Ayanda *could* do and what Amnandi *did*. Maab's gut told her Amnandi was forever on a cusp, whether in this world or myriad others.

In many respects, Amnandi, too, either swam or flew, rarely giving the appearance of true rest. Maab imagined if she whispered the girl's name, she would spring up ready for duty.

Yes, the effort to seem at ease was likely extreme.

Maab resisted the urge to go to her to tuck a loosened edge of Amnandi's bright yellow headscarf back behind the girl's ear. It took strength to meditate like that, knowing how many lives flashed by, intersected, or constantly bounced off you. There was no point interrupting her.

Blue sky, high clouds, and wide-open sea.

As the ship raced toward the unknown, other darting teardrops caught Maab's eye here and there in the water. The dolphin pod hadn't left them. A good omen.

"Whatever comes," she told her ship, "we've sailed through worse. You know how this goes."

OTHERS

"I thought I was going home," Amis said during that night's watch which she and Amnandi pulled. She scratched the wild broomstick that passed for her hair. Cracker crumbs fell out. She had no idea how that happened.

Stars glittered as though only lovers were awake. Amis didn't know exactly what she was supposed to watch for, despite First Mate Skye slowly prowling the deck stem to stern, the tall woman's eyes checking ropes, crew, the sea, or nothing which meant everything. The Mate had clearly learned vigilance from the captain. There wasn't a mistake made by Amis which the captain didn't at some juncture point out.

Which Amis loved. She'd issued herself a challenge in joining this voyage: be more the Amis she wanted to be, someone who took correction as learning (like her friend did) rather than punishment.

"Don't get me wrong," Amis said. "I'm just...ready. You know?"

"It would be good to see Bettany and Gita again," Amnandi agreed, flicking one of Amis's crumbs from a fresh tunic, ending with characteristic finality. "First this."

"Don't pretend you know what 'this' is."

"I don't."

"Well, I wish you high-flying dogshit would. What's the point me having a witch for a friend if she isn't divining mysteries?" She hoped Amnandi would warm to the teasing.

"The goddess wishes you to marry and have far too many children."

"Hoo, the disappointment in her future is five pigs big," said Amis.

"All will be well," Amnandi assured.

"It's never well for everybody involved."

"True."

Amis scanned the passing waters courtesy of Sharda, Erah's moon. Even with the moon's brightness, her eyes barely processed more than the liquid flow of night. "What if this is simply a test? Like the old stories of gods succumbing to boredom."

"My gods had words with those gods. There are no more tests."

"Are you being serious?"

"Usually."

"Do you think insects think of us as old gods?"

"I could ask if they have tales." Amnandi thought a moment for likely candidates. "Probably the bees." She scanned the waters with deeper inward sight than Amis would ever have. The water felt like water. Life below its surface formed the usual mosaic of moving pieces. Night watch in general was a lesson in meditative acuity, whether the crew knew that was Captain Maab's intent or not.

Amis wondered if this watch in particular was honing Amnandi before reaching Blue-tip. Every continent on Erah had tales of gods needing the sharp-eyed, sharp-minded assistance of its population from time to time.

Amis let things get quiet a moment. A *plip* of water broke the silence, so she did too. "Gita's father is still inventing things. Got a whole stockpile for you to see. Even been fiddling with Gita's automatons." Another *plip*. "Are you listening to me?"

"No." Amnandi moved several paces away. "Hush."

Something unseen repeatedly surfaced and dove sure as a knife, easily pacing the *Bane*. The fact that it now made noise for them to hear was disquieting.

Amnandi cast illumination from her eyes and channeled twin beams outward for Amis's benefit.

This trick was new to Amis. A bit unsettling, her friend's eyes suddenly bright as a cat's and lancing the dark, but more important things took precedence.

Amis wished a harpoon was handy.

At the next *plip*, Amnandi's head twitched. Light caught something sliding into the water, supple as an eel.

"Torches!" Amis shouted. People, having been attracted by Amnandi's show, were already on the move.

Amnandi dimmed her eyes in preparation for dousing them entirely.

"Keep those peepers hot," said Mate Skye, then issued orders to rouse the captain and light all lanterns. "What'd you see, ladies?"

"Part of something stalking," said Amis.

Maab rushed forward, blue silk robe flapping around her plain sleep linens, her bare feet tiny handclaps against the deck. "Speak on it! What graces us?"

Skye gave the nod to report. Amnandi, eyes still on the water, said, "A swimmer has made itself known."

Amis noted the captain said nothing about Amnandi's eyes, so neither did she. "Nandi suspects it's been following us a while," she said. She knew Nandi enough to know her suspicious mind.

"Anything that suddenly pops up tends to be an excellent

hunter," said Maab. "You heard nothing, saw nothing, till now?" she asked Amnandi specifically.

"Correct."

"Nothing swims quieter than the Mer. We know them only as they decide we should know," said the captain. She gently brushed Amnandi's shoulder. "Eyes off, luv."

"Even for witches?" asked Amis. She hadn't come across much on Erah that got the better of a witch.

They all glanced to Amnandi, who gave the apparent answer. "Even for witches."

"Could be a simple beast," said one of the crew, bearing a torch closer.

"And could be my gran finally come to take this ship back," said Maab. "What's more likely under Sharda's watch this particular night?"

"I've never encountered Mer," said Skye. She noted Amnandi still focused unwaveringly on the water. "I take it our young lady hasn't, either."

"No," said Amnandi.

"Should we cull speed?" Skye asked Maab.

"No, that'd be a sign of disrespect. Quiet and fast is the Mer default. Matter of fact, let's get a little more tack out of this wind, see if our ambassador acknowledges our parlay. If this one tries to speak I'll hold up a fist meaning everyone"—a separating hand on Amnandi's shoulder—"should sing. Doesn't matter what, but if they can work off each other's tune, the better. Mer talk grates on the brain."

"Should we not give it till daylight?" said the Mate. "If it's followed thus far..."

"Nocturnal folk," said Maab. "Sensitive to light."

"Aye," Skye assented. "At some point, Captain, you'll educate us on what you *haven't* met."

"A dragoon in a dress," Maab muttered, her attention hard

on the glassy water, before she quickly moved along the railing. "There." She grabbed a crewperson's hand and directed his lantern far left. A torso and two appendages that mimicked arms popped above water and smoothly did a half-circle before disappearing. The swimmer seemed made of the water or the water of it, both being pitch as the night and fluid as oil.

And no slap of a tailfin.

For several moments, only the soft rush of wind past their ears. The *Bane*'s pops and creaks traveled alongside the water the ship displaced.

Then the slap of meat against wood. For them to hear it, it must have been halfway up the hull already.

Maab ran aft. All followed.

"May I?" she said to the light-bearing crewperson who'd kept up with her. The young man handed the lantern over. Maab dimmed it as low as it could go without killing the flame, then held it aloft for her crew to mimic. All light levels aft softened to a ghost of a whisper.

Sharp, belabored reports traveled upward. Maab leaned over the railing and swung the lantern. The illumination was barely better than the moon's but provided enough to warm the dark hull and cast a brief glint off that wet part of the wood that climbed up, creating a quiet, broken approach of something sinuous, eyeless, and slick.

"Get the crew belowdecks and get them singing," said Maab. "Make that an absolute order. I don't care what, but sing they will." She focused attention on Amnandi while Skye hustled off. The girl could handle what was to come. "Want your first taste of Mer speak? With me."

❋❋❋

Darkness slid into the spaces left by the crew's departure. In quick time, only two bodies and a few safety lanterns remained, with those lanterns spaced so widely as to be lonely little stars, still dimmed to their lowest setting.

The slow, laboriously hard slap of the Mer's appendages grew louder.

Maab peered over the side again. "You afraid?" she said offhand to Amnandi.

"It's been my experience to fear only that which clearly intends me harm."

"Your brain will feel its voice. It'll hurt. It's teaching you to mimic it. Patterns, I was told. Stimulating the lightning in us. Won't hurt long, but you'll know you've been through it by the end. Most of my crew ain't ready."

Slap, then silence as it pulled.

Slap.

Warbles issued from belowdecks, first several songs, then haltingly merging into one, the mangiest choir a sea had yet heard.

"I know to whom my heart is bound..."

Amnandi and Maab waited.

Slap.

"You ready?"

Amnandi nodded.

The tip of the appendage affixed tightly to the rail, the second even more so, then, with quivering effort, the Mer slid its long body onto the deck, where it lay half-coiled for long moments, doing nothing but moving its head against the length of itself, applying mucus over jagged gill slits.

No one in Amnandi's family had ever seen a Mer. She'd know if they had.

Its worm-like head raised, followed by half its body, and even at this, it was taller than Amnandi. Its arm appendages hung limply. The odd-smelling body caught what little illumination there was and turned light into multi-colored bursts against a sky of glistening skin. The mucus gave hints of kelp and fruit to Amnandi, nearly a molasses. The Mer's body tapered to twin, flattened whips that looked long enough to wrap around Amnandi and perhaps (Amnandi noted how the whips stabilized the stiffening torso) even lift her.

"It prepares to speak," said Maab.

Amnandi drew a cleansing breath. Thoughts and expectations left her young mind. When the pain hit, she would know it as what it was: a possibility, a thing that was and then was not. A state of being, not a certainty.

It grew from an ache at the base of her spine, feeling as if the entirety of her was forcibly pulled outward via a pinprick and replaced by a scratchy stream of salt crystals chafing the bloodstream, accelerating her brain until her thoughts became so fleet, she thought of *everything,* but that particular thinking no longer hurt, not like thinking of everything used to when she was little. The initial discomfort became the base to an experience of more and more. In a matter of seconds—if even that long—she heard the world anew. Cacophony as symphony. Astoundingly intriguing. She made thorough mental note of it.

Maab held the light far away from the visitor.

Even standing upright, the Mer moved as though infused with differing musics played simultaneously: a balance adjustment undulated into a full-body vibration that ended with a slight swaying of appendages that looked like a beckoning. Moonlight smoothed its surface from tip to tail, glinting now and then off thick mucus pockets.

"Let me lash myself to you!" from the crew below.

"Friend?" said Maab.

No blood today.

"Name in fullness?"

Rukkai.

"Purpose in fullness?"

Amnandi kept close eye on the conversants, feeling the words as much as hearing them. Perhaps even feeling them sharper, funneled as they were through the Mer.

The sea dweller took a moment for the question, then: *I was given a sign. Follow the dry whale. You are the dry whale.*

"Well, I've been called worse. Speak your needs."

We wait. I was called; you were called. I watched.

"Might be a long night. What of tomorrow?"

Of no concern until it is here. We wait. It turned unceremoniously, dragged heavily to the railing, slid itself over, and dropped like a javelin into the darkglass sea.

The surface settled.

"And that, dear one," Maab said to the absolutely fascinated Amnandi, "is how you know you're on an adventure: you get company."

❋❋❋

Shortened night shifts and longer sleep periods made the crew agreeable the next day. A risen sun always lent outlandish events a sheen of dream, letting adrenaline settle until reality's jobs fell right in line with whatever uncertain horizon their dry whale traveled toward.

"Are there any wanting to leave?" Maab put to the crew. She herself had remained watchful most of the night, prodded awake now and again by Amnandi. Had the girl done some kind of wakefulness spell on herself, or was her stamina simply youth? Maab didn't know, but the young witch hadn't dozed a single instant.

The yawn Maab fought to avoid showing was gargantuan.

The night shift, asleep now, had already answered this question. The day answered as well: with silence. But Maab knew her crew and she knew people. There were always those who'd say nothing in public but whose hearts twisted over the loved ones they might not see again. She begrudged those hearts nothing.

She addressed the first mate standing with the crew before her. "Ms. Skye, would your kindness point us to Keer Island?"

"Would indeed, Captain. A detour!" Skye clomped a clear path through the crew as she gave orders. "Keer Island starboard, quick as you please!" Her navigator and helm were already consulting maps and calculating degrees. Trim teams raced for fabric.

Keer, being so frequently visited along this route, was a trusted and necessary waystation in all but taxable ways.

"We stop for special essentials first," Maab told the crew, "then on for the goddess's bidding." *Special essentials* was well-established Maab code for *Remain ashore if you wish; we'll return provided the* Bane *yet sails.* Passage elsewhere, in the meantime, could definitely be brokered with one of various ships docked for supplies, pleasure, or both.

No guarantee any one of those ships wouldn't be god-erranded itself. The crew knew this. The gears of the sea were practically primed with quests.

The captain's sister-in-law sidled up to her as bodies dispersed. "A word privately, Captain?"

Maab narrowed her eyes toward Amnandi's. Amnandi received the message and wobbled off to her berth.

Privacy and formality meant Leena wanted to speak as family, not crew. Maab led the way to her captain's quarters, cluttered with maps, trinkets, and more books than anyone needed to own.

Once inside, Maab said, "My attention's a waning, precious thing."

"I ask because you know it *must* be asked," Leena said. "Shall we heed every call of the gods? One so vague as this?"

"My ship had never turned from a quest."

Leena sat with a sharp sigh on a brocaded cushion.

"When have the gods ever made their intentions clear,

sister?" said Maab. "I submit that they *cannot*. They attempt to communicate with us as we do dogs!"

"By now, they should know our ways and our tongues," her kin said, eyes following Maab's wanderings about the quarters.

"They likely do." She shoved a bound map back into its tube. "But each time I've read to a dog, it only feigned interest. If I said 'treat,' it perked. Our *treats* have kept us afloat. Kept you in fine ingredients. Have you not come to trust me?"

"I do. But I worry," she said. "We all worry."

"Such compassion is the only reason I don't daily throw you off the ship." Maab accepted Leena's scowl as the russet-freckled woman's version of a smile.

"Can we not say no at least once? We are tired. Lovers wait. Home beckons."

I am tired, Maab thought. *I have no lover. The* Bane *is my home.*

"I've no interest in a stay on Keer Island," her sister-in-law continued. "I'm with you till we get home. I'd like to get home as swift as any fates decree."

"I promise you that decree, sister, and not a moment past. What else is on your mind?"

"With the witch aboard, you get foolhardy."

"That's a high charge. Evidence?"

The two stared at each other in mock seriousness, then burst out laughing at the plans made on a world such as Erah. There were fables of calmer places, but that was not this place.

Yet checks and balances were good things between honest souls.

"It's a quest but we're not fools. No rush. I'll have Amnandi sleep presently," Maab said.

"That plus give her extra portions when she awakes," said the cook.

That seemed wise.

✳✳✳

Amis didn't let Amnandi out of her sight. Peering over her mug at Amnandi: Amis. Sluicing the deck so Amnandi could swab it: Amis. Loitering suspiciously outside the loo as if their bodily functions had become synced: Amis.

It wasn't lost on Amis Emty Dotrig that Amnandi hadn't ported her all day. Nor had her friend said anything beyond necessary words. Amis knew fatigue for a witch was a worrisome thing indeed, and not solely for the witch. Amnandi's mother had definitely proven that.

The early portion of the day's sailing had been uneventful, but there was still a good bit before night. Amnandi had slept an hour or so, then woke up saying she needed to move. Amis had been there then. Maab's orders...although she'd have been there anyway. There were another three hours before they reached Keer.

Amis hadn't asked the obvious question, so she figured now—during a break tucked away in the galley—was the time.

"You all right?"

Amnandi, rarely inattentive, answered, but with little fire. Her "Yes" might as well have been the barest nod.

"Thinking?" Amis led.

"Thinking."

"About?"

"The Mer opened my hearing to unsettling things. I wonder what would have happened had it done so to the entire crew." Amnandi sketched in her small notebook. Barrels hid them from everyone.

Amis leaned in to peer. "It's like a human slug." She wrinkled her nose at Amnandi's excellent line work.

"I find it beautiful," said Amnandi. "It moves like it sculpts itself against the air."

"I'd like to know why it's following us."

"It's not. We were merely part of its path."

"You know, before you and your mother became part of my life, gods were just things greedy clerics and old sea folk went on about."

"Captain Maab's not ancient. I'm sure she's spoken of gods her entire life. The unusual is always more real than most will grant notice."

"That a witch saying?"

"It is," Amnandi said, then considered a moment. "Because I said it."

"Nobody in Waterfall ever thought much on the subject," Amis admitted, continuing to draw Amnandi out. Sometimes, the girl disappeared so fully into herself, she became a well. Granted, Nandi wasn't able to get away with it as much on a ship, but her scribbling and silences were tells.

"Clerics aren't interested in people knowing gods, only paying for access," Amnandi said, bending close to the pad to study the crosshatching she'd done on the Mer's prehensile fluke. The attempt to portray dark on dark in the dark was...difficult.

"Tell me about your eyes," said Amis.

Amnandi gradually smiled. Amis's soul lit up. "A trick I taught myself. It involves the body's lightning and my indomitable will."

"What's an indomitable, and what will it do?"

"Indomitable is the way you go after sausage and cheese. None can stop you."

"None can stop me," Amis agreed.

"I allow no amount of darkness to prevent my ability to see," said Amnandi.

"If magick were so easy," came the voice of the ship's cook from the other side of the barrels, "we'd all be flying. Take care, you two. You could have used your break to take a nap, you know." Leena rounded the barrier. "What is it you're drawing?"

Amnandi held the pad upward for the chef, who looked

nothing like Maab or Maab's sister except for the crinkles around her eyes, and who took good time studying it. "That what it really looks like, or you one of those weird new artists in love with squiggles?"

"Exactly like that," said Amnandi.

"Which of the two of you is chopping fish for tonight?" she asked, a task neither had known they were in line for, but, as it involved a large knife, Amis's hand flew forward. "Let's have it, then." Amis unspooled from her tightly packed position. The little friend gave Amnandi one good look-over, which meant *see you soon*, and nudged past the cook for the galley. She cast her eyes back, though, to hear Leena tell Amnandi, "I've known the captain to stay up a day or two without a yawn. Never known anyone of your age doing it. What made you stay by her side?"

"Need," Amnandi said.

"Need," Leena said. "Will you rest in kind now? I'll wake you."

Amis listened hard for Amnandi's answer, but patience wasn't Amis Dotrig's suit. She stood on tiptoes to peer over the barrels. She saw Amnandi tucking her gnarled pencil into the pad, the pad into the pocket universe in her sleeve, and then her lanky body into as comfortable a ball as she could make atop sacks of various grains.

GREETINGS

The first time Amnandi had gone to Waterfall she had been fascinated by the docks and main wharf. Not the vastness or diversity of it; she'd seen many docks and wharves along Afrela's coasts that made Waterfall's seem miniscule, but by the singular *intent* of it. Waterfall, as explained to her young eyes, existed *solely* for commerce.

Keer Island, on the other hand, boasted nothing but rags, tags, the smell of sun on skin, and such a mix of trades and goods, half of it had to be illegal. The one area that looked as though it was actually meant to be there was the repair docks, with a makeshift warehouse anchoring them.

Sarantain led two young assistants toward it.

Respect the repair dock was the only law of Keer patronage. Now and then a fight might break out, but on the whole there wasn't a better waystation toward bolstering a ship's morale than this small island, one of three in a chain, with the other two too tiny to be of any use besides punishment. Keer itself was walkable end to end before the sun could decently change position.

"Nothing but sailors needing rest," he said. "No constables, functionaries, or accessors. This could be paradise."

Two other ships were docked, Maab no doubt trading IOUs—Information of the Unusual—with her peer captains, giving any on board the *Bane* ample time and a non-watching eye (except, all knew, for Skye) to lose themselves along the beach or inner line of shacks, lean-tos, hammocks, and cooking pits that made up the community.

"Going to amend that," Sarantain said. "For an old man like me, this *is* paradise."

"You're not old," said Amis.

"I've seen you girls through calamity and acclaim," said the carpenter. "If that didn't age me a bit I wasn't properly involved. You managing with that cart, Ms. Dotrig?"

Sarantain's trading cart weighed at least three times as much as Amis. Half-full now with warped wood scraps, chipped pegs, slightly bent spikes long as two fingers, and several saws that were beyond quick mending, the cart fought every step of the way. The wheels caught every knot on the ramshackle pier.

Amis planted her foot on the bar that ran parallel to the rear axle and stomped. The cart's front canted upward, she hefted with all her might to raise the back wheels, and the entire thing obeyed to hop a particularly threatening cracked plank. "Aye," she grunted as answer, and hauled onward.

Amnandi, who had been given extra portions, extra rest, and extra attention, was also given nothing to carry. Her green robe with yellow sleeves was open to the wind over her protective hard-fabric wraps—protection ordered by Maab as standard for any and all on such forays; what paradise was true paradise that contained people? With her canvas breeches laced over her boots to deny the island's biting insects an easy meal, Amnandi seemed the very portrait of the Young Woman as Traveler burdened solely by sun and time.

Yet her mind was everywhere.

Sarantain knew her well enough to guess her efforts to contain it.

"The beach reminds me of one near my grandparents' vacation home," said Amnandi. "The same sun-bleaching and flecks of gold."

"You've got a grandda?" puffed Amis. "I just thought it was you and your mum. D'you have a sister?"

"No siblings."

"You two are sisters enough," said Sarantain. "Wee pale grub and coal-fired iron bar."

Amis used that small boost to maneuver the cart higher and surer over the next obstacle.

"Are you eager to get back to Grucca?" Amis asked, regarding Sarantain's husband.

"Very."

"But you're not staying here? Ride with another ship?"

"Eager doesn't override patience. Learn that. I'll sail with Pinyasama till she finds a dry ocean. Then I'll get out, point myself toward Waterfall, and walk."

"The captain would be right beside you," said Amnandi. "She might be more Mer than the Mer."

Sarantain pointed out the shack that would be their first stop. Amis grunted acknowledgment and pressed on. "Maab," he said, "will be an old woman retired on a chair on a raft."

"Current'll carry her around the world!" Amis said with a grinning snort.

"Very likely," said Sarantain.

When they reached the shack it was occupied by a bustling, almost elderly woman who used curses like musical notes. Her skin was a combination of sunburn and sawdust plastered to her by sweat. She tossed thick logs from one side of the shack to the other, yet was as bony as the moon casting night skeletons.

"How is it you always get to the rubbish shack before anyone else, Cedar?" Sarantain asked.

"I never leave," she said with a heave of a rowboat's splintered oar. "Even when I've shipped out, my stink remains."

"Peeing in corners has its advantages," Sarantain said.

"Territorial as all damnation." She twisted her neck left and right to crack it. "You bring honored guests."

"Amis Dotrig and Amnandi Khumalo."

"You're apprenticed to the only person I'm jealous of," Cedar told the young ladies.

"You're in love with Sarantain," said Amnandi before she could stop herself.

"Oh, this one sharpens dung, I see," said Cedar, smiling widely. "Speaks quick as a demon, too. A lot of mind in that one, huh, my love? And you, Miss Dotrig?"

"No mind in me," Amis blurted.

"Think on that and correct yourself, little one," said Cedar. "What's in the cart?"

"The *Bane*'s sloughed off some good bits," said Sarantain. "Most of this will be on the keep pile. Cooks will appreciate the kindling."

"Anything I can use on the *Dappled Whey*?"

"Lots for a skilled carpenter."

"That'd be everything then, you silky-nutted god." Cedar motioned Amis forward along the perfectly even planks of the shack. "Miss Amis, you taking note of these quality adjectives and whatnot?"

"I am."

"Good on you." The wiry woman inspected the cart. "How soon do you push off?" she asked Sarantain.

"Two hours."

"Barely enough time for foreplay. You two, get out."

"She's joking," Sarantain said.

"Not my fault the gods were shitty enough to let you fall in love before I got to you. Good eye, Miss Khumalo. Love is real."

"Love is real," Amnandi repeated.

"Nyim!" the woman then bellowed.

A boy of Amnandi's age zipped through the shack's open rear door.

"These people are shipping out in two hours. It's a good ship. You'll want to be on it."

"Why is that?" said Sarantain.

"Because otherwise, I'll kill him."

A BOY

Nyim Stone was seventeen, smelled perpetually of pickles as they were nearly all he ate, had a mind like a trap wherein ideas never crossed a certain line to disturb his brilliance, and had survived not yet being murdered—particularly by Cedar—by dint of being too proficient at basic carpentry to waste. Plus, he was attentive when need be.

Cedar shouting his name was one of those times.

He'd been put off his ship months ago, talked himself into passage on the *Dappled Whey*, was useful for several weeks, then insufferable unless there was a planer or wood chisel in his hand, which made him entirely Cedar Yau's problem.

Sarantain sent the youngsters out back to do whatever waiting youngsters did (stare at each other). Maab didn't mind taking people on. Crew-swapping was common enough amid seawide opportunities. Character, however, counted more than skill.

"One," said Cedar, "he's trying to get home. Says his parents are rich. Says they informed him their money was not necessarily his money. Tossed him out on both sides of his ass. Not without a skill, though. Woodcraft was his hobby. He does the work but, by fuck's unending lament, he is so full of himself his shats are descendants. My captain thinks time on island would do him good. I don't. I think this wad of young piss needs to get home before he's accidentally garroted."

"So, faux orphan hoping to mature into a dowry," said Sarantain. The shack's doors and shutters were open. The youths were right outside.

"They can hear you," said Cedar.

"I hope so. No time for someone incapable of not being glorified."

"Hush your seductive talk. Let him sail with you till your next port. We don't leave for several more days. There's no way I'd toss an absolutely useless prick your way."

"Nyim Stone," Sarantain called.

Nyim zipped in.

Sarantain knew a good sign when he saw one. "Take the cart. Wheel it toward the repair dock. Amnandi and Amis, attend. I'll be along shortly." He waited for the *thunk* of the cart moving along the uneven boardwalk, eyeing Cedar Yau the whole time. "There's a chance some of the *Bane* might stay here a bit," he finally said. "I expect you'll see to them."

She walked to him, tipped upward, and planted a brief kiss on his scraggly chin. "The girl's not wrong about me."

"The girl's not wrong about much."

✳✳✳

"So, you must be a bit of an ass," said Amis.

"I'm not an ass. You didn't call her an ass," Nyim said, jutting his hairless chin toward Amnandi. "I heard what she said about

Miss Yau being in love."

"That's because Nandi's not an ass. If you call her an ass, I'll kill you."

"Why are women always murdering me?" he said, automatically slowing his pace to keep them ahead of him.

"You must be extremely death-attracting," said Amis. She pointed to herself. "Amis, by the way." Walking backward, she hooked a thumb at Amnandi. "Amnandi. Nandi has no plans to kill you but she could. Easily."

Amnandi looked over her shoulder at Nyim. "True," she said.

Nyim's bronze deepened redder.

"Sarantain is family to us," said Amis. "Don't disappoint him."

"Stop threatening me. I'm older than you. Where's your respect?"

"Children can kill and get away with it. And you *might* be a year and a day older than me at best."

"You're short."

"Dear gods, you're insightful."

"Boy!" shouted Sarantain out the shack window. "Get that to Mingus double time, then gather your things even quicker."

"How will I know Mingus?"

"Walk in there and insult the *Lambchop*. Tell him the cart's owner will be there shortly."

Amis watched Nyim hustle the cart forward. He was a strange boy, quick to follow orders, slow to be respectful. It showed in his facial expressions and body language. She would have to interact with him if he was going to be Sarantain's apprentice. Likely not a lot, but annoying was annoying.

She checked the expression on Amnandi's face. Neutrally frowny.

Witches didn't tolerate annoying very well.

***

His introduction followed three of their crew's departure.

"You've been on the water long enough to keep your mouth shut when I speak," First Mate Skye said. "Fair marks for that. You a thief?"

"No, ma'am."

"Predator?"

His head shake was emphatic.

"Coward?"

"Very damn likely," said Amis.

Skye's dour glance eliminated any possibility of Amis adding further observation.

"Sarantain tells me you're to shadow Amnandi and Amis."

Amnandi's eyes widened. It was indeed possible to surprise a witch.

"You a minder of gods, young Mr. Nyim?" asked Skye.

"Mostly fable, superstition, and tools for powerful interests."

"Incorrect. On the *Bane*, you have two gods: the Captain and myself. Do we agree?"

He nodded.

"A pleasant journey for all, then. You bunk on a sickbed for now. Amnandi will make the introductions. In the mornings you help Chef, in the afternoon, Carpenter Sarantain, in the evening you check in with the captain, before bed you check in with me. What's your destination?"

"I...don't know yet."

"High marks again. Dismissed."

As the three teens walked away, Amis mumbled, "The entire hell is this?"

Skye's voice, softly and the more terrifying for it, stopped the young one as though it'd tapped her on the shoulder. "Miss Dotrig? A word."

* * *

"Where is this ship sailing?" Nyim asked Amnandi as she led him away.

"Don't know. We're on a mission from the goddess."

He said nothing else until she'd introduced him to several others. When they heard Skye bellow the order to cast off, he whispered, "Shit."

***

Amis hovered, a curious bee. She decided to be good at hovering. "What else don't you believe in?"

Nyim unpacked, which involved opening a sheet used as a carrier and rolling its contents under the cot provided.

"*Why* are you here?" he asked.

"This is my ship," she said.

"And you?" he said to Amnandi.

"Studying you," said Amnandi.

There was no getting away from whatever these two decided regarding him.

"Seems you're the only real thing in your wee world," said Amis. "Ever seen a wraith? A sea beast? You respect witches?"

"I respect those who respect me," he snapped. "Go away. Please."

She studied the frustrated upturn of his shapely lips, the fire in the eyes beneath what would have been a lovely unibrow had he had a unibrow. Amis loved unibrows. "We're trying to figure out when your inevitable betrayal will doom us," said Amis. "Stupid people bring doom."

"He's not stupid," said Amnandi.

"How do you know?" Amis said, having noticed nothing against.

Amnandi pointed under the cot. "That book. A volume of the writings of Bilo the Curious. An influence on Unina's and my travels."

Nyim's boot nudged the book deeper under the cot. "Unina someone else who would want to kill me?"

"Maybe," said Amis.

"No," said Amnandi, "she is my mother. Unina means mother."

Nyim narrowed his eyes at the accent and language. "Where are you from?"

"Insheree. Afrela."

"Khirt," he said of himself. "Southern Afrela. The high mountains."

"I know. Which languages do you speak?"

"Khirshem, Shefu, Toum, and Tak."

"Tak is Eurolan merchant standard," said Amis, the only tongue she knew.

"No one considers that a language," said Nyim.

"It's more a shorthand," Amnandi agreed. "Sorry," she told her friend. Even the very word for the world, *Erah*, had come from a long-ago Afrelan shore. The one word used everywhere.

Amis quieted.

"You're both unusual," said Nyim.

"You boarded a ship of unknown destination," Amnandi reminded. "Who's the more unusual?"

He turned his back in shame, pushing an item an extra inch from where it sat. "May I finish settling in peace?"

"Peace and be well, young Mr. Stone," Amnandi said, leaving and taking Amis with her.

JOURNALING

There's something odd about changing direction so smoothly, Unina. You and I do it, but that's the course of our life. Maab is captain of a ship with specific tasks and a crew with wages. Amis cultivates a clearly delineated path despite rebelling against it. And today a young man named Nyim joined us. An odd one. He's no traveler yet he drifts like flotsam. He studies the writings of Bilo yet doesn't apply them to the world at large. He's of no import to me, but isn't it fascinating how lives intersect? All these crisscrossing beings. A goddess touches us, we touch the Mer. Our ship touches a teeming island. One boy leaves with us. He's of money. Perhaps he will learn to grow out of that.

You're in my thoughts daily, Unina. These writings barely convey my love. Thank you. I'm not meditating as often as I should, which is tiring, but when I do, I think of you. Now on to Blue-tip Isle. The goddess has told us to seek the searavens there. Or, more accurately, perhaps she has already done so and waits for us there.

There is always a chance we're wrong. For now, know that I am safe, *curious, and learning. Three glorious, beautiful things.*

❊ ❊ ❊

The *Bane* approached the isle of ravens slowly, twenty metal scopes trained outward around the ship's perimeter. Noon sun and clear sky, yet the mood of approaching a storm persisted.

And in that perfect blue above, not a single searaven circling, not one streaking past a ship that even at its fastest would be an overladen scow to such water shrikes.

Maab dropped her yellow bonnet to hang by its straps at her back. Light hit her forehead full-on. At least this initial investigation wouldn't involve the Mer.

"Archers, rowers, and swords, if you please, Skye. Two skiffs down at fifty strokes out."

When the skiffs, built to be knives, hit the water, one moved immediately ahead of the other at double speed, making beach in minutes. In it: Maab, Amnandi, and four archers. Quills rose behind archers' shoulders, sword hilts above the other.

The second skiff remained at station twenty-five strokes out upon the water, with the *Bane* anchored another twenty-five strokes behind.

Maab suspected that the ship, to at least several pairs of eyes, seemed far away.

She stepped onto the dry sand.

Not a single mark of wing, claw, or feather on the shore. Nor footprint in human form. Searavens tended to be about the size of older children. They weren't known for making their presence scarce.

"Nor tide line," Maab said. She held position and studied the surf at their heels. The sea halted farther from shore than it should have. The captain directed Amnandi's attention to this fact. "Should we be wary?"

"Not yet."

Nevertheless, Maab nocked an arrow. "Forward," Maab ordered. The four archers fanned out beside and ahead.

Amnandi reached into her sleeve pocket and pulled out two half-staffs whose ends clicked to form a whole. The wood was so polished, it gave the appearance of honey.

Maab loved when the girl did things like that.

What the island lacked in visible population it made up for in smell. Searavens often used the centers of such small isles as shitteries. A wide array of tightly packed plant life took root, thriving toward the sun. The isles always had the entwined perfumes of warm spoiled fruit and salt-spiked ammonia. For the highly territorial searavens, communal spaces like these islands were exceedingly rare. Nearly holy, as evidenced by a complete lack of what they called "claiming stones" on the shore.

Island trees and tall sea grasses dotted the land away from the primary copse, but this was still a relatively new sanctuary for the ravens, one that could likely last a hundred years before it was too overgrown to serve avian purposes. Ravens had been known to fly a quarter of the way around the globe in a single day merely to gossip. It would be no surprise to find ravens from all around the world there.

The susurrating surf and beat of the sun tried their best convincing the cautious humans of the day's normalcy. The sand, even through the soles of their boots, remained warm and giving. Insects took nips at faces.

A sanctuary like this wouldn't normally let humans within a hundred strokes of its shores.

Six moved forward toward a thick forest whose giant fronds either beckoned or warned off. Interpretation depended entirely on the individual.

***

Sharp sun rays cut across bark shaped like fish scales. Wide oversized leaves clung to the very tip of the trees as though afraid to come down, a foolish thought but one Maab was certain felt honest. It wasn't supposed to be this quiet. Where were the roosted birds screaming curses at the humans for interrupting their chances at mating? Or the scuttle of things that tended to scuttle? No one had forgotten in the scant minutes they'd been walking that even the sea hadn't wanted to come ashore.

Niss, the archer on the left, kept watch high. Dedoura, at right, kept her eyes low. The gray that crept into each woman's hair hadn't dulled their senses a whit. The other archers, a brother and sister both so pale they approached froth, were as good with bows as humans could get.

If anything moved that didn't look like bird, searaven, or friend, it wouldn't find its next moments pleasant.

Maab, breeches tucked in high boots, knife holstered to each boot, ignored the sweat trailing from her pulled-back hair, giving her head a shake now and then to fling beads from her temples. Thick hair was a curse of the Pinyasamas. The moment they sailed for home, her plan was: a wash, expensive oils as it dried, and a bowl of grapes to eat while she read.

Minor distractions were good in jungles like this.

Maab evaluated Amnandi. The girl was alert on more planes of existence than Maab might experience in a year of dreaming. And although she *was* a young woman, she had only recently graduated from a child. A child of mischief and curiosity like any girl, but tempered by a thousand-year stare.

"Miss Khumalo?"

"Erasure. Violent absence."

"Turn back," Maab told her crew. "We come back with more people."

They departed as quietly as they came.

They returned. They searched and searched but found

nothing.

＊＊＊

By night, the island was ringed with torches and bonfires tended by the majority of Maab's crew. Weapons reassured souls that all would see morning. Hushed conversations under a sky overcrowded with stars kept weighty thoughts of solitude away. Amis recalled a poem: "*The universe had everything it needed but it still took lives each day.*"

"I don't like poetry," said Nyim without even looking down at Amis's upturned face.

His entire bearing formed the impression of the beautiful night farting directly up his nostrils, but Amis knew you couldn't serve on a ship without smelling worse. Did this gorgeous bastard have no genuine bone in his body?

"She brought us to a latrine," he said dourly, his third reference to the scent of bird poo in less than an hour.

Amis thought of staying, then decided better. She walked off.

"Wait," he called.

She ignored him. She didn't leave him standing sentry alone, but there was enough space between them to let him know he was an ass. The entire afternoon had been spent watching: watching the beach, watching the jungle copse, watching the sea and sky. Amis wished she knew where Amnandi was, but knowing she was off somewhere with the captain or First Mate kept her from worrying too much about her. Not so much about herself.

Young Ms. Dotrig didn't like the night anywhere near as much as she once had.

That poem was the only one, outside of dirty limericks, she kept in memory. She'd found it as a child in a book her da kept in a box, not hidden, just protected, which likely meant it had been her late ma's. And here she'd recited it to a handsome boy under heavy stars on a night surrounded by things unseen, who'd disregarded every bit of it.

She called back to him, "Standing beside a fool makes one a fool." She checked her sightlines. The torches cast enough light that anything coming behind Nyim would be seen, and same him fof her. Anything creeping between them could be arrowed or stabbed. "I am no one's fool." Watching the water was fairly pointless. The torches cast no light there. The crew aboard the *Bane* kept the ship's lights bright, but that only thickened the darkness beyond.

There could be any number of things rising from the sea.

Amis searched outward again.

Water as giving as stale bread.

She did not like this night much at all.

It was her next blink that shot intense pain through her, head to toes. She was on her knees, eyes flared open and brain in agony. Red, bleary vision showed that so was Nyim. And Hernando beyond him. And Rennie.

Blasting through their heads: not a word but the full and entire sense of the word *FLEE!*

And then, very faintly, from so far down the beach Amis's eyes saw nothing but torch flickers, a song. Maab's voice. Frantic, not even trying to sound like anything other than an order.

Amis, tears flowing, opened her mouth. The pain in her head consumed memory. She had no words.

So, she groaned out a rhythm.

Then saw the night running. A portion of it. Moving toward her with bright eyes.

Amnandi Khumalo.

Amnandi bellowing, "Sing!"

As Amnandi ran, a black curtain rose from the sea, but it was not made of the sea. The *Bane* remained steady.

Bodies, slick as ice and stretched to breaking, gripping one another in the oddest net Amis had ever seen, fanning upward, hundreds of them, dropping over the beached crew in fleshy domes.

Amis caught the pale blue flare of Amnandi throwing a portal before sand sprayed Amis's face from the impact of a moist dome.

Then nothing but darkness and fearful heartbeats, Amis's and the Mer's.

***

Through her screams she heard Amnandi outside the walls, saying, "You're fine, you're safe," but there was no way Amis could be sure she wasn't engulfed by a wraith, so she kept screaming. Pale blue light warmed her closed lids. Then hands touched her face. Gentle hands. Hands she knew. She opened her eyes. Amnandi's were doused.

"Nandi?"

"It's larger under here than I expected. Sing, sister."

"*I know to whom...*" Amis warbled.

"I'll be back for you." The skins of the joined Mer bounced blue back, then total darkness again.

"*My heart is bound,*" Amis sang, "*is bound for...*"

The pounding in her head was replaced with a sudden cottony emptiness. A quiet. Not even the beating of hearts.

She pulled herself into a ball.

Three breaths later, the sound of rain if rain weighed as much as bodies falling from the sky.

***

Amnandi silently apologized to each Mer cluster for the excessive light as she ported as many crewmates as she could to what she hoped was the safety of the *Bane* before fatigue stopped her. Dozens or more safe, with domes still dotting the shoreline.

Falling against those domes and all around: wraiths. These wraiths didn't attack. They were already dead.

The wraiths lay writhing from memories of dying, searavens by the scores, visible only as slightly luminescent tatters. Eyes, however, weren't the only means of knowing.

Amnandi felt them. They lodged in her throat and stomach like swallowed rocks, jangles of shock and fear. What must the Mer have felt?

"Khumalo!" A distant voice. Searching for her.

Amnandi knew the Mer didn't sense light with eyes, but she had to risk it. She blazed her eyes brightly, becoming a sudden beacon on the sand.

By all appearances the rain had stopped, the dead literally come to roost.

And it was a lie that the dead were somehow immaterial. Amnandi swung her view. The beach was pocked with craters. Twisted, bent, crumbled, melting ravens littered the human-trampled sand, some near the surf where the sea still refused to advance.

Maab reached Amnandi—albeit haltingly, having to train her torch more to the ground than ahead. "You unharmed?"

"I wasn't successful," said Amnandi.

"How many rescued?"

"Seventeen."

"You were successful."

"I told crews to row ashore for any injured," Amnandi said. Lights aboard rowboats were only now approaching the island.

The Mer silently disentangled. Of Maab's crew, there were the standing, the kneeling, the praying, the crying, and the confused. But none dead. Maab went to as many as she could, Amnandi following. The captain studied pupils by lamplight.

A quarter of the way along the beach's perimeter, a Mer sidled toward them. They knew its undulations even by lamplight, which Maab held away when it reached her.

"It hurts when you speak to us. Only at first," said Maab, sensing the Mer's confusion.

We were not aware. We thought you were inherently fragile.

"We are. I will teach them to hear you."

"What if we had been touched by them?" asked Amnandi, studying the smoking tatter of a raven.

Madness. We have seen this when one or two die who did not wish to die. We felt the one or two in the sky, then it quickly became thousands.

"What could kill thousands of searavens in one swoop?" Maab wondered.

A god.

"That," said Maab. She swiped a tear away. "Or themselves."

✳✳✳

With the last of the shore contingent safely aboard the *Bane*, Skye asked the captain, "Captain, do we stay?"

"There's always a decision in these, but I think ours was foreknown. We know this island is somehow damned. We found it; it's ours to fix. No duties beyond watch tonight or tomorrow, and I'll wind up doing most of that myself. You're better at helping the doc and Leena than I am. Dedoura and Niss can assist. Goddess knows they've stitched each other often enough. Have the new boy provide any comforts he sees someone needs. Keep Amnandi and Amis together. Have them do nothing and see that they do it without complaint."

"When should I relieve you at watch?"

"When I slump over, which I know you'll be watching for. We stay at least another day."

"It's going to be a long night, isn't it?"

Maab didn't answer. She turned her attention to the water

directly under the moon, the crescent wavering slightly on the waves, and sighed.

"Aye," Skye agreed, and set about seeing to the crew.

Fewer headaches than expected came with the following morning. Maab surveyed the beachhead through her scope. It was another bright, nearly cloudless day. Hot. Humid enough to feel sweaty just thinking, the type of morning that might lead to taking shortcuts with important decisions. Made a body doubt what it needed to do. There wasn't a single raven on the beach, nor a feather. Chaos? The circle of her scope showed plenty. Spent torches dotted the sand like castaways, buckets used for latrines sat abandoned, and the crisscrossing tracks of the Mer dragging themselves back to the sea mimicked massive welts.

A pang of gratitude at those tracks took Maab's heart, squeezing water from her eyes.

The *Bane* did not travel alone.

Today she wore her feather sarong over her breeches. Her intention was to go ashore again to find what they'd missed, because nothing trivial could anguish so many dead. Or cause the wind—under her very eyes—to erase any trace of evidence as it now did, a wind that moved with such intent, it had to have been directed. As though Maab Pinyasama had no auspice whatsoever on the scene, Blue-tip Isle smoothed itself over so unhurriedly, the sight terrified her a moment.

"There are magicks too deep for you to swim with, Maab Pinyasama," she muttered to herself. "Heed."

To which her brain tutted, *I'll heed when I need to heed.*

Skye came beside her and took the scope from her, training the sight on the same section of beach that had held the captain so studious. After several seconds, with Maab saying nothing, the mate announced, "I'll be going ashore with you."

"Get a round of volunteers. Let the entire crew know there's no shame in staying aboard. We leave as soon as fifteen people stand before me on deck. No sooner, no less. Kitted for battle, every one of them, shields included. My guess is the spirits of the dead crash their way through the thinner veils at night."

"You sound more like a witch every day," said Skye.

"I hope so. If I'm correct, we've got all day to continue learning. We've got an ocean's contingent of Mer working alongside us, Patrice. When's that ever happened?"

"I won't lie and say that it ever has."

"So, it stands that important things are afoot." Maab ran a hand across several sarong feathers. "If these are to be lucky, now's a good time to entreat them."

"You use my first name when you're nervous. And if we find no magicks or ruination?"

"Then we've all day to find some bodies and see to them properly."

✻✻✻

Fifteen stood on the deck of the *Bane*, led, de facto, by Niss, Dedoura, and Sarantain. Maab was pleased to see Amnandi and Amis not among them, despite sorely wishing for Amnandi's insights. The captain had, however, learned Mer-speak, garnered raven favor, and kept the lizard folk's existence a secret, all without the aid of a witch.

"None of us stays on that island after nightfall," said Pinyasama, holding each's gaze to confirm. "Whether their intrepid ass wants to or not!" she quickly boomed, which drew laughter and sobriety. "We know what happens at night. Something supremely evil happened here and the world shouldn't have to abide that. May the goddess lead us to the source of this pain. To your boats."

Four rowboats lowered, crewed by warriors, Maab making person sixteen. Weapons, shields, scopes, picks, and shovels had the four sturdy boats kissing the water deeply, but that kiss was just proof the sea loved them that much more. Droplets hitting their skin, salt tasting their lips: signs that each person was seen and felt. Each strong stroke sealed a covenant.

The *Bane*, for its part, kept watchful eye on them all.

The four crews crossed the early shallows and pulled their craft ashore, immediately splitting into assigned teams, each person with a horn around their neck, shield on a forearm, and weapon of choice in a favored weapon hand. Rolls containing shovels, picks, and rope nestled across backs.

Each team already knew which direction it was to take.

Maab led two teams center. As before, the day was the day. Beautiful sun, swaying fronds, the sticky pungency of land and salt. All in perfect mirror of the day before.

But now they knew the mirror for the lie it was. This island died every night and scrubbed its stains away. This wasn't a search for what was unusual but for things that were too normal. Where tracks should have been, where limbs, fronds, or twigs ought to have fallen.

The only things that didn't care to hide were the insects. After slapping her neck, Maab smeared a speck of blood on her feathers. "They got a taste of us yesterday; now they're greedy."

"Skye's sourness would keep them at bay," said Niss.

"I'll tell her next time," said Maab.

There would always be a next time.

Every half hour, each team used the horns to proclaim their status.

"Maab is well!" with the other team of four well in sight.

"Skye is well!"

"Sarantain is well!"

By the third hour of nothing, Maab's voice bellowed across the island for all to reconvene.

At the beach, waiting for the final crew to return, the captain rested her butt against the rowboat and studied the water. There was nothing on this island to be found, and she didn't plan to have her crew dig straight through to claim otherwise. The goddess needed to give a clue, something clear, something solid.

Two tide lines. An experienced eye could tell the difference. Sand density and discoloration.

The experienced eye.

She damned herself for a fool. She shot away from the rowboat as if propelled.

Niss watched her captain take her boots off en route and slap feet on moist sand toward the water's edge. Maab continued into the water. Far down the beach, the last party approached. "Captain?" called Niss.

Pinyasama went only so far as to float the very bottom of her long skirt, feathers spreading around her calves in a circular fluke. She stood with hands on hips, eyes downcast. She turned to Niss. "It ain't the dirt," she said. "It ain't the dirt." Sarantain's party would be with them momentarily. "Mate Skye," said Pinyasama, "new volunteers when we're one. Divers."

✳ ✳ ✳

Fifteen pairs of eyes repeatedly glanced at the water while Pinyasama spoke. "The truth's got to be underwater. We've seen enough wet graveyards to know. I think we should poke about."

"Shouldn't the Mer have said something yesterday?" said Skye. "I mean, they're out there right now."

"The Mer don't come above a certain point during daylight."

"How's it you come to know so much about the Mer, Captain?" said Sarantain. "Asking only as there's a lot to rely on them with little time for conferring."

"Sometimes leaning too far out for a moonlight kiss lands a body in the sea," said Maab.

Nods all around.

"I need two strong swimmers." She knew her crew. That would be Niss and Jackson.

The two stepped forward, Niss already doffing shield and tools.

"Straight away, Captain?" asked Skye.

"Straight away rather than wait." Maab unfastened her lucky feather sarong, stepped out of her breeches, and laid her tunic atop, keeping only the protective wraps chest to toe and a dagger. The other two matched her.

"And you're sure the Mer won't see and help?" said Skye.

Maab shrugged. "No Mer I've spoken to has ever mentioned the sun kindly."

"How many would that be, ma'am?"

"Twelve. I'm somewhat celebrated." Maab started her breathing exercises and stretches. Young Jackson did not. And it seemed Niss barely breathed anyway.

"Flare for Amnandi when you think we've been down too long," Maab said, accepting Skye's nod as permission to leave. She, Niss, and Jackson made for the water. It received them without incident: shins, knees, waists, shoulders. Then each sliced into the sea. With strong kicks, they were gone.

✳✳✳

They'd all been underwater so often, the ocean was just water on their faces. Visibility in those salty shallows dimmed, but they knew the shapes and feels of things. Deeper down, corals. The stacked shale of the island's pillar performed slopes and odd geometries. Fish chased fish. Sharks watched everything.

They searched until the first of them felt their lungs burning and signaled with a thumb they were going up. The others followed. Breaking the surface, they saw they were farther down the beach but still within the quick jog of the watchful eyes on shore. A brief tread, a deep breath, and under once more.

Niss went hand by hand along a sharp incline of shale overgrown by lichen. Maab caught skulking movement ahead of the old warrior and swam at her periphery to get her to stop. The shark wasn't large enough to be a danger, but it had come from the rock, perhaps fifteen strokes ahead, rather than from behind it. Niss nodded and waved Jackson to her side. All three pulled daggers. Pockets called for caution.

The cave could have been large enough to call a grotto, except it was filled with water and tattered wings. And tattered bodies.

Blue raven faces moved with the current against black raven backs, some of them the same body, twisted. Legs crossed necks. Mouths hung open to invite the entirety of the sea, but only so much could enter. Maab's mind automatically calculated how many ravens were there by how many children could get crammed in that space, causing gorge to burn so hot and fast, she immediately pulled herself upward against the stone and kicked hard for the surface.

By the time she and the other frantic swimmers stood wringing water backward from their hair, thirteen people held weapons at the ready.

A flask of fresh water from the mate was passed between the swimmers, who poured it in their eyes and blinked furiously.

"Dead. At least a thousand of them," said Niss.

"More than dead," said Maab. "Shattered. Broken."

"Damned," said Jackson. "You can't die like that and not be damned." He took a hard drink to quell the shakes. "Not like any shipwreck I've seen."

"These souls were pulled by their teeth screaming," said Maab. "My *skin* hears it now that I've seen them. We don't go home until we've seen this through."

Maab moved up the beach for her clothes.

✳✳✳

The silence on a ship waiting for night to come carried weight.

In the dark, Maab lowered herself in a rowboat and waited. She listened to the crew's song as she did so, and tried clearing her mind of thoughts.

The soft *plip* of a Mer surfacing brought her back.

And then another *plip*. And others. Four in total, ringing the rowboat as it gently rocked.

Astoundingly unprecedented.

She doused her lantern.

Clouds blocked everything but a patch of sparse stars. There, in the lee of the *Bane*, it was nearly pitch black. Maab closed weary eyes.

The Mer's minds joined hers.

You describe, please. I am sorry. Pirielle. Dashred. Von. You describe, please.

"If there's a greater sufferance," Maab said, "than knowing someone enjoyed killing someone, I don't know what it is. That's what I saw. Where do we go? I haven't gotten another sign." Maab opened her eyes but the darkness was still total.

We have received sign. This from Rukkai, the thoughts and impressions coming from the assembly more ordered now.

We are the way. From Dashred.

Do you accede? Pirielle.

Von's message vibrated through its body so fully, the water rippled. *This is counsel. Follow.*

"Tell me the sign."

A Raven King.

"Most Raven Kings are insane," Maab said to the night. To her unseen counselors: "When we need contact, we'll lower a metal pole and strike it. We'll follow."

No. We carry.

From behind her and all around the *Bane*, many *plip*s. Wet slaps resounded against the bobbing hull. The great ship lurched. Maab's drop line tightened. She immediately gave herself more slack. The rowboat jerked hard enough that her teeth rattled. "Mates, slowly upward," she called. The rowboat gingerly made it to its mother's side, then a slow ascent.

There'd been no need to thank the Mer for yesterday. The Mer did what they needed to do.

*****

"We're not going to bury them?" asked Amis.

Amnandi didn't answer. She was fascinated at the Mer spectacle below, whip flukes working in perfect unison. Maab had forbidden torches or lanterns held out for a view. Amnandi kept her eyes dimmed to the merest whisper. She couldn't make out individual bodies, but if someone had asserted the ocean had grown a skin, she would have readily agreed. The glint from her eyes undulated from back to tail. She had read stories of magick carpets soaring as expertly as kestrels. None had mentioned the effect such soaring would have on the sea, in the dark, during what was now clearly a mission.

It was intoxicating.

"The captain could have had the Mer wait," Amis went on, "or turn back." Not caring for the dead didn't sit well on her.

"The sea's an efficient mortician," said Amnandi. "Respectful, too."

"Promise me two things," said Amis, putting a hand on her friend's shoulder for full attention. Amnandi glanced at Amis with her slightly glowing eyes. The effect was still unsettling. "Promise me you won't be foolish or too caring."

"Too caring?" Amnandi normalized her eyes. The two friends were lit by Amis's lantern held low between them. "That's odd."

"None of us can do everything. Not you, not Captain, not Mate, not me. Not even your mother."

"I don't think they've ever tried."

"But they would if necessary. Promise me you'll only do what you can do."

Amnandi was genuinely confused. "Amis...that's a given."

"You won't promise?"

"No."

They both quieted. The natural noises of the night bloomed.

Amnandi reset things. "You boarded this ship in Waterfall months ago, hoping for adventure. Every person aboard has the same wish, whether they voice it or not. This is that adventure."

"Come what may?"

"Come what may, provided we are careful, intelligent, and caring."

"Adventure shouldn't involve death."

Amnandi shrugged.

"You're not bothered we're pulled along by our short hairs?"

"Not pulled along. Temporarily guided. This is no different than accompanying Madam Tourmaline to the market."

"Not as many deaths in the market."

Nyim approached. He always approached too quickly. Perhaps he thought to snare people before they could get away? Amnandi and Amis halted their conversation before he came into the light, his own lantern burning so low it nearly sputtered.

He said nothing. Instead, he pretended to study the void over the railing as if he could actually see things.

Yet he had certainly seen all of Amnandi's magicks.

He tried to sound older than he was. "Will no one speak on the wonders we've witnessed?"

"Not if you won't," said Amis.

"My grandfather used to tell me stories in the pitch dark," said Amnandi. "Said sometimes eyes interfere. What would you like to know about today?"

"Does the captain keep you because you're a witch?"

"No."

He indicated Amis. "Are both of you witches?"

"I know a few surprises," said Amis, leaving it at that.

"Did either of you see the goddess?"

"Did you hear nothing of what I said about my grandfather? Seeing does not automatically impart truth."

"But it's a damn good start," Nyim said. "You heard what the captain said at assembly. We're taken to a Raven King. I don't even know what that is."

"We do," said Amnandi.

"I've been on this ship less than two full days and my soul feels half-dead, with the other half fearful of joining it. I'm not here for that."

Both ladies shrugged.

Nyim changed tactics. "You dislike me for false reasons."

"We don't dislike you," said Amnandi.

"Don't like you, either," Amis added. "Neutral till otherwise."

"I've no plans to prove myself to you," said Nyim.

"Edging more toward one side than the other, you are," said Amis. "Why'd you come bothering us?"

"Let him stay," said Amnandi.

No one was going to sleep tonight. The crew was edgy and afraid. What point being edgy and afraid alone?

"That song," he said. "The one about going home."

"Mate says to sing it when they speak," said Amis.

"I've never heard it before," he said.

Amis reached up and clapped him on the shoulder. "Expect to get sick of it."

***

We were taken that night to another isle, one not even Maab knew of, which is not the most astounding thing. The most astounding thing is that the Mer did not depart. Not entirely. Now and then, a burst of bubbles would ring the ship. Amis opined on orifice source. I believe she missed the fact that the Mer had not submerged to their usual depth. They kept watch, advising us to wait for sunrise for our encounter with the Raven King.

I've felt no danger at all. Does that mean I'm not challenged? I've done as a witch does. Amis tells me not to be foolish or too brave—foolish, as though a witch even contemplates such a thing; brave, as if bravery is a controlled benefit.

The new boy, Nyim, thinks bravery is valuable. This may get him killed. I will try to prevent that when the situation arises. I am fairly certain it will.

Perhaps that's a large measure of the crew's discomfort. They know they have Maab's respect, but I suspect some wonder if they have that of the gods. Is bravery sufficient? I feel as if I should know.

Perhaps I am foolish.

Amnandi placed her pad in its pocket, stood to stretch her legs and back, then prodded Nyim and Amis awake. There was an hour till dawn.

A few minutes before the sun rose, those escorting the *Bane* disappeared, but the archipelago the ship's momentum drew them near stood clear and stark, with the distinct impression that it watched their approach.

THE RAVEN KING

He watched them and immediately hated them.

He watched them as day's dawning peeled dreams. Peeled like leeches.

But weren't humans themselves leeches? Stuck to every rock and shore, and constantly smelling of meat not their own.

He thought to fly out and kill them, but they had found his island, which meant they'd had help. Humans were stupid when it came to piercing magicks. He had shrouded this hiding place well. Killing would start once he knew their allies. That was the way of kings.

He watched from the top of a high tree. He spotted out the captain, a woman with the audacity to wear feathers. He'd kill her.

He spotted out the second-in-command, a muscled woman who might do him harm if he fought fair. He would drive his talons into her back and wage all attack from the rear.

Then all the random humans. Meat-smelling nobodies would

be picked off at whim. Slash them and drop them far enough in the ocean for the hungry to notice.

The allies remained a question.

That is, until he spotted the witch. The wavering air around her head was unmistakable. And not just any witch but the daughter of Ayanda Khumalo—whom the searavens had made it their business to know after a thrilling affair some years past—and friend of Bog the Unsmiling, whom the ravens had made special business to know after the brute had murdered a good and just Raven King on his own.

The death of the young witch to erase a shameful link in Raven history.

A good plan.

A rowboat left the ship.

Eventually, it touched the shore.

The Raven King fluffed his feathers.

He made a grand show of flying upward, then arrowing downward to greet them.

* * *

The instant his bird feet hit the ground, his human form flowed upward.

He spoke in clipped, bothered bursts.

"My island. My claimant stones. Your names? Your names to ward trespass."

"Captain Maab Pinyasama of all Erah's seas."

"We have heard the name." He looked pointedly at her clothing. "Wearing feathers?"

"Gifts of the goddess."

He cocked his head toward the one he would have to attack from the back.

"Patrice Skye, Majesty, First Mate of the *Bane*."

"Majesty? Who gives you such knowledge?" Unfocused yellow eyes bounced from Skye to Maab.

"It is evident," Maab interjected.

The King smiled. He stood barely taller than Amis, so had to look upward to continue his appraisal of Skye. "No weapons?"

The Mate opened her arms. "Only ourselves before you."

"If you seek me, the news is dire. Speak it."

"We cannot, Majesty," said Maab. "Not until the moon is upon the water."

"Magicks," he said, nodding sagely.

"Magicks," Maab confirmed.

"Witchery?"

Maab wanted to say no but decided instead to be as cagey as the king. "Not as yet."

The King regarded Maab, Skye, and one other interloper who had remained sitting in the rowboat. She was old but sharp. Their larger ship was watchful too. Killing would wait. "You have a question," said the Raven King. "Speak it."

The captain bent with hands on her knees to stand eye-to-eye with him. "Are you well, bird?"

In a flash, he was a four-foot-tall raven with coal-black yellow-ringed eyes, small red feathers along each brow, talons that gouged the sand as if wanting to seize struggling prey, and the opened wingspan to show he could do it.

He was pleased to see that the two meat-smelling humans immediately backed away from his answer. He folded his wings and watched them a long moment. Implacably.

He counted in his head: a moment more.

A moment more.

And...*change back...*

...into a small, naked, slightly iridescent man again standing before them. "What a splendid display of superiority," he said aloud, not realizing he'd said it aloud. "Mark this spot," he advised them. "I will meet you here at moontime."

The King whipped away from them in a fluid hop, took to wing, and was away after three impressive flaps.

ALL HANDS

"**A** Raven King rules nothing," said Amnandi. Her friends, expressions agreeing with this, were conflicted about tying her up. "I think that is what drives them mad."

Maab checked their knot work. Two ropes, one at torso, one at thighs, each coiling around Amnandi's lanky form and the center mast twice. The knots were well done. "He gleaned far too much about magick," said Maab. "Our girl here is no one's target. If he comes near, swing those swords as though dancing. If Amnandi asks you to cut her loose, do so immediately whether the King is here or not."

"If he does something that makes her mad enough to spit," Amis said to her knot mate Nyim, "run."

"Heed Ms. Dotrig," Maab said, her tone serious. "There's a game afoot by someone who thinks himself clever, meaning he'll rely on violence."

"What if this King is true?" said Nyim.

"I've been in guilt's presence enough to know the sign and scent," said Maab. "Be ready for an attack, be ready to defend Nandi, and, above all, should you sense the Mer, sing. Sing even if droplets of blood rain on you. Do you understand?"

Everyone nodded.

The sun set.

An hour later, darkness was total. A sliver of moon rested on the water.

Maab, Skye, and Niss returned to shore, their lanterns blazing, each sailor careful not to look directly at their glow. Behind them, the *Bane* also blazed with light.

Just as they alighted on the beach, the dark shape glided whisper-quiet from a high perch, heaving a strong, stealthy flap over water, which sent it zipping toward the *Bane*.

It circled the ship at a distance, its eyes better in the dark than a shipful of pitiful humans, but eyes also overburdened by all the light the ship cast. He tightened his circle downward until the King's great span nearly touched the edge of the light and his eyes adjusted.

The one he sought, their ally, shone blue. He prepared to dive.

He hesitated.

They had her bound. Not that it mattered to him. An unwilling ally against him was merely *enemy* misspelled. But those guarding her might not fight so hard to keep her as they would a true ally, which might make his taking her and dashing her against a large rock feasible as both breakfast and lunch. Let her be meat.

So first: sow panic. He dipped arrow-fast to ram a man hard enough to send him overboard. Nothing panicked a sailor more than suddenly being in water. As others ran toward the commotion, he climbed, invisible as ash on tar, picked a new victim at the other end of the ship, and descended, this time deciding to announce himself with a shriek. His talons sank into the tunic of someone who smelled of sawdust. The point of the King's beak went for the neck. His piercing killing move was a thing of perfection. The beak would tear the flesh, becoming a spike; the king's large black wings would enfold the doomed, becoming both casket and moment of intimacy. Death as exhibition was for the gaudy. The attention-seekers. He was an artist.

His hard beak glanced off the neck. Thrashing light revealed the culprit: wrappings. One peck wouldn't do it. Three or four might.

The King's head reared and he rammed the neck again, doubly hard. The sawdust man gagged but didn't fall. In fact, he had the presence of mind to set his lantern down, leaving two large hands free to take parts of the king in them, twisting so painfully the king struggled free and flew away.

He picked the next fool. Discord and disarray *would* yield a death. It was his due. Ten thousand ravens around the world had died to suit his needs. He knew because that was the number he requested. To deny him three or four paltry sailors would insult him as a king.

And then the witch. Any magick he could consume from her would only elevate him. The blue aura his heightened eyes detected around her was a powerful thing, nearly a direct connection to Erah's gods. A shame the child wasn't her mother; consuming a bit of the blue of that particular meddling witch might turn the King into God Emperor of Ravens. What a title that would be! Just feeling its sheer destiny spurred lightning-fast twists and dips in flight.

Meat-sack humans. If they decided to protect their bodies, he would simply go for faces, eyes being ridiculous yolk sacs anyway. Humans would live better in darkness.

He attacked three. None of them saw him until he was upon them. The first he raked across the cheek in a single deft swoop, the next an overflowing gash across the forehead, and the third talon marks at the back of the head, all three painful enough to elicit screams, but no eyes yet.

As he angled upward away from the light again to swim the night, he caught a glimpse of the eyes of the witch. Glowing. Glowing very brightly. And following him. "Cut me loose," he heard her say, which seemed odd but not of immediate consequence. The air whistling across his feathers told him he was the master—not merely of tonight but *every* night. Every heartbeat of the witch's life would soon belong to him to either count or nip off. What did it matter if she moved around on this filthy boat in the middle of the water? There was no escape. The King could soar a league-wide circle around the ship before anyone raised a sail.

It was perhaps a trick of his eyes against the bright lanterns and the solid night that the hue of energies around her quickly grew deep as topaz blue.

Her hands darted outward, as though the girl could see where he merged with the dark, as though she anticipated where he would be.

Had he gotten careless, seeing her tied up? Had that compromised his flight?

No, he—

Entered a portal ringed by lightning blue. The instant he was inside it, he felt his body and spirit being directed elsewhere.

Down.

Down toward the inky water, which unexpectedly parted before he hit it and, if the King were to be asked, closed in very decisively.

Gripped from all sides and held under, the King soon felt the vibrations of oars pushing water. Strong appendages raised him upward. Only his large bird head showed above the mass of thick bodies. He didn't even attempt to snap or peck.

He felt an inrush of water as a way parted for the boat. Its rower stopped a stroke away.

"Now," said the feathered woman, "we talk." Lanterns, hers, that of the others with her, and those aboard the ship, bright, luscious points of light, dimmed till there was nothing but dark.

And staring down from the railing of the ship above, the eyes of a very silent, huge cat.

✸✸✸

"That one," said Maab, "with the eyes? She can see you and is very good with a bow. Shall we have a word or two or a funeral? I prefer you unable to fly."

The Mer released him briefly, then resumed hold of his now-bobbing human-like form.

"The goddess spoke to the Mer of you," said Mab. "The Mer spoke of you to me. What makes you so interesting, King of None?"

"I am King by right," the shapeshifter spat.

"True, certain males of your kind are acknowledged as kings, and might even do a thing or two, but most claim the title via pretense alone. It's been said your diet causes insanity."

"Kings receive only the best into their bodies."

"The best hallucinogens. The best intoxicants. The red in your brow comes from wort mold. You mark yourself a mad king." Maab was glad for the darkness, the silence of the Mer, and the conversation of nothing but voice. It allowed for a distancing from worry or consequences, two things she felt the King's very presence might dramatically increase. "The Mer were given notice of you as a poison. Tell me, King: where's the pleasure in the death of your own? And know this: for every lie, the Mer find you that much heavier to hold up. Do you know what's been done?" She said every word gently in case there was even the slimmest chance what she suspected was not so. She remained calm. The world of Erah was random and chaotic but rarely outright evil.

And yet, hadn't she seen evil several times over her forty

years?

She allowed the moment to stretch to let the king know she was waiting on him. She had all night. The Mer, not so. He wouldn't want to be in their embrace when they left.

"The gods misunderstand a raven's heart," he said as softly as she had into the dark. "I asked for ten thousand when I wanted ten times more. I asked for poison, and she tapped a vein so pure, it encircled the world. I asked to be known and she answered."

Maab's unbidden thought was *You are not known.* "Why would she answer?"

"Do any ever know? Perhaps, human thing, perhaps I am my *own god* bequeathing my own dreams. I may get my ten times more. I will be known."

"Name your god."

"Chiave."

"What is her aspect?"

"The deep earth, the sludge."

"Speak to her now," Maab said, knowing the watchful cat eyes above stayed fixed on them.

The raven disturbed the water with a pointless thrash. "There is nothing to say to a god who has granted something. They are lesser at that point. I stand apart."

"You float at the Mer's discretion. It'd do you well to speak."

A prayer, the raven told them, was a waking dream. A dream was a link to the ether. The gods were nothing but ether dreaming, rumored to be tangible at times.

The raven's prayer seeped invisibly from its entire body, seeped through the molecules of the sea, seeped deeper, heavier, faster through the dimensional barrier that kept the living sane, traveled simultaneously through the past, present, and future of the world, and, in exactly six breaths, settled upon the surface of something bleeding, whereupon that thing's pores opened automatically and drew each drifting bit of a king's intention into itself.

As the Mad King had reached downward, Chiave—the Ancient Devourer—had reached up.

The rowboat shook. Amnandi's bright eyes briefly flared out of control. Maab's heart raced as she watched the girl's light reassert discipline. The rowboat settled. The sea had shaken in a great Mer shudder, having felt this god's soul recalling unending decay as a goal, each being and recoiling from its locus, the King.

The King was too enrapt in his dream fever to take advantage of this lapse. He completed his tale and waited upon the dim comprehension of the humans and Mer. Witches had the dirt, Mer had the sea, but ravens had mastery of all, solid enough to be grounded, fluid enough for powerful change. Stubborn enough to bend reality. A searaven knew what belonged to it: everything.

A searaven—a Raven King, no less—knew a god was but a tool, even—or especially—for the deaths of other ravens. Fiefdom was all.

Even upon an uninhabited island housing a tall tree.

The King let a small sentence drift into the night. "This world is poisoned with gods."

* * *

A poisoned part of Chiave seeped ever deeper into the waters, having already circled the globe. Called only to attack ravens initially, it learned by touch and inhabitation to become the antithesis of things. It was a chain, one whose links stretched unending in any direction of its choosing. More than sentience, it was existence.

It was a poison meant to allow no other gods before it.

The goddess Maab knew would not permit this.

Maab realized that she had somehow been drawn into a war.

* * *

The Mer closed upon the King until only his hairless head shone. Maab's relit lantern was at its lowest, but she wanted him to see her eyes, which might be the last thing he'd ever see upon her leaving.

"Why," she asked, "would you kill your kin?"

"If they do not fear me, they forget to respect me," said this King. He wanted to burst free and display his feathers, but he was small, pale, and in the dark. Flightless in human form. Barely a glimmer under the wan light.

Freedom was far away.

Maab withdrew. "We have what we need," she said to the silent Mer. She set the lantern between her feet, casting even less light outward. "Apologies for the pains you've endured, friends. Gratitude for continuing your travels beside us." She motioned for Niss to row outward, then raised her lantern and swung it twice. The lights aboard the *Bane* dimmed in quick succession, Amnandi's as well.

The witch dimmed...but didn't go out. Nor did her eyes waver from sight of the raven, with barely the interruption of a blink.

Maab wondered if this situation constituted a challenge the girl's mother should be aware of, but when hadn't Ayanda Khumalo, either with daughter on her hip, crawling as a babe, or standing right beside her, dealt with Erah's nameless powers despite the names humans, ravens, or even Mer tried to give them?

But if, as many believed, everything was truly connected, all gods might slowly turn into poison, leaving Erah a waste. Why bother a witch with something so simple as saving the world? Or more likely with Mother Khumalo, why disturb a witch—even if they could—saving her part of it?

The ship knew what had happened. They now knew why the goddess had voiced her wordless scream. There were myths about conflicts between gods. Stories of continents splitting, oceans lifted over mountaintops, or rain turned to life-killing bile.

Very little to do, as the saying went in Waterfall, with the price of good bread.

This, then, would be an errand of mercy. The *Bane* would fly the orange flag of rescue, granting it assistance from any ship with healing in its heart, no different from delivering medicines to a settlement ravaged by disease or aiding a ship too tossed by storms to swim on its own. They would deliver medicine to the goddess.

And should no one see that flag, the *Bane* would sail alone.

***

The crew diminished by eight during a hello with a passenger ship offering assistance to the orange.

The two ships went their ways, one with no mind toward gods beneath the waves.

The teardrop-shaped one with intricate gossamer sails that danced a ballet with the wind, well known for its beauty and technical wizardry, trailed a sure wake toward Fabbin Keep, a coastal zone known worldwide first for its magicks and second its stringent desire to be left primarily alone. It was a journey of four days with the right wind.

Fabbin would know about direct connections with gods.

Rukkai traveled with them, speaking gently each night but no longer needing to struggle its way aboard. A rope trailed; if Rukkai tugged, a bell rang, a boat was dropped, and the Mer was hoisted. The crew was getting used to the "sound" of its voice. Fewer headaches, softer singing, some not singing at all.

Maab thanked the goddess for these long, uneventful four days. A quest was good but best done in sprints rather than a marathon.

During those days, Maab had a chance to assess her loved ones. Skye worried but would put the ship on her back and swim if necessary. Skye was fine.

The *Bane* hadn't been due into Waterfall's ports for another two weeks, Amnandi not at Insheree for a month afterward. Amis and crew would feel their loved ones' arms soon enough. Besides which, young Amis found distraction in harrying young Mr. Nyim.

Amnandi Khumalo, however, had grown quieter, which for an already quiet spirit was a feat. She didn't brood or worry. Contemplation, it was, witchy contemplation down to the very grain of the *Bane*'s wood, the crew, how the people, the ship, the sea, and the sky intertwined. She was learning connections, Maab realized one day, stumbling upon Amnandi literally studying a knot. The main sail bowline knot.

Maab left Amnandi undisturbed.

Everyone would be fine, herself, her crew, the goddess, the sea, the Mer, and the bedamned, always-frustrating ravens who had no use for the kings they had but mourned the kings they were without. Maab's birthday had passed a day ago, unremarked upon by all save Skye and Amnandi. The world had grown another year older under her feet. Connections, that's how she knew things would be fine. Erah moved within her and outside her. Everything being a part of something, she, the sea, and the dirt saw each other year after year. She now counted herself accidental ambassador to the Mer.

By all gods, hadn't she been the one to find the desert cave that led to the even-deeper cave that opened into a much larger belly of Erah itself that housed the lizard people—and this she had done alone during time away from sailing while craftspeople refurbished half of the ship? She'd felt the goddess's approval of her in dreams and been led to collect feathers from that same being's watery belly, thighs, comforting bosom and strong back.

Why, just last year, she had been accepted by a council of witches as kin at Ayanda's recommendation.

Healing a god was simply a matter of dreams and knowledge.

The world was a ship. Existence, a sea. Everyone sailed connected. It was the way of things. If anyone at hand had the means of seeing those silver connections to lay hands on kinks in a line, it would be someone at Fabbin.

Inwardly, the captain sighd. She had no contacts at Fabbin. No one owed her favors there. But if they were weavers of the deeper things, Maab Pinyasama would definitely tempt them to sew.

She exited her reverie among the spray at the prow of the ship. She gave a look around. The crew didn't waver in a single duty. She caught Skye's eye looking her way. Maab nodded. Skye nodded. She caught Amnandi looking away.

GREEN HILLS

As Leena prepared spice pouches, Sarantain a box of useful tools, and Skye composed as lovely a poem as any peered at by romantic scholars, Maab had supper with the witch. It seemed intense bursts of cleaning and rearranging had occurred in the captain's quarters over the four days. Not a single scroll was out of place. "Only you and I will be seeking the mystics' counsel. Has your mother ever spoken of Fabbin?"

Amnandi answered around a cheekful of sweetbread and savory rice. "No, but I heard Bog mention it to traders once. As a joke." Her suddenly toothy smile caught the light from Maab's lantern that spread over her dark skin. "If you can sell wares to Fabbin, you can interest fish in water."

"No one sells wares to Fabbin; they give and hope for good fortune."

"Minor gods," Amnandi noted.

"Even when not dealing with gods, folks are dealing with gods.

Fabbin's supposedly been the source of most knowledge since the ancient disappearance of Bilo the Wanderer. Or is that Bilo the Curious?"

"All Bilo are Bilo. Perhaps Bilo established Fabbin."

"We can hope." Maab raised a mug to Amnandi. "Here's to Afrelans forever wandering." She speared fruit and stuffed her mouth. "So...have you thought of porting yourself home yet, luv?"

"No, it would exhaust— Oh. I should say instead, Unina would want me to see this through."

Good girl, Maab thought. "And you, my daughter, what do you want?"

"A world of peace and health."

"Then, by gods, that's what we'll have. Truth be told, it's what we've got. Erah's a good place."

The younger Khumalo smiled again. "Said like you've been elsewhere."

"Oh, I'm sure there are other worlds. There's Sharda moon. We can practically tickle her. Maybe I've been off-world and you're not privy to hear about that." She speared another fruit cube, then pushed backward in her chair, effortlessly balancing on the two rear legs. She sighed, loving this young witch making her way in a big world. "I have never regretted anything I've done, luv. You feeling obligated toward any of this would be the first. Speak on it."

"You've called me 'luv' twice. You do that when you're worried. I wish Amis had gone home and most of those still on board had remained at Keer Island, but I don't think I would be anywhere but here."

"Even if I told you to go home?"

"Even then. I'd simply keep popping up in unexpected places."

"Outside the loo while I'm singing."

Amnandi's face screwed up. "Gods, no."

"When we get to Fabbin, when our feet are actually on the dirt and its towers are telling us to go the hushed gods away, should you sense anything more dangerous than a stubbed toe, we leave."

"But I didn't sense the Mer. Or what happened to the ravens. Not even the sick god. I've been lax in meditation."

"No one's aware of everything when everything happens all at once. There's not a brain on Erah equipped for that. I trust your senses more than my own experience; know that."

Amnandi gave a respectful nod.

"No weapons. No staffs. Not even in your magickal sleeves. We carry only what might benefit them. They'll know."

"Will they?"

"I assume they will. Mystics."

"Aye." Amnandi considered for a moment. "What if they want to keep us?"

"You port away. The *Bane* leaves. I stay, read a lot, and become Erah's Witch Supreme."

"There's no such."

Maab beamed. "I've a thing for firsts, or had you not noticed? And I'm entirely serious in what I said. Skye knows to take the ship at all speed and let the crew live good lives. If I'm to learn to heal Erah's latest wound, I can be patient about it. We've no worries, luv. There's nothing that says Fabbin is untoward, just emphatic about privacy. Once they see us—"

"They'd better respect our mission."

Maab saluted with her cube of cantaloupe. "That's my girl."

✳ ✳ ✳

Fabbin Keep's green hills were a decent ride by wagon inland from the coast of Dallock. Dallock itself was an emerald space, barely forested but a paradise to grazers. Roads leading up to and all around the Keep were well maintained without a hint of rut to their hardpacked dirt. If there were a cure, Fabbin might know it.

If there were additional counsel, Fabbin might illuminate.

The horses pulling the small wagon didn't care. Amnandi had asked them. Both strong horses were excellent runners, attentive, and glad to be out of the livestock hold of the ship, ships being boring. Her horse back home, Natuun, could have gotten them there and back in half the time. Slate-speckled Rock was the horse to Amnandi's left, and dotted-wheat Paper to her right.

She would have to come up with games or puzzles for them aboard ship.

Maab interrupted her silence. "What's on your mind?" she asked.

For someone whose mind somehow existed in several dimensions at once, this question used to flummox Amnandi. Now, though, she'd learned how to answer it. "Nothing."

"A horse's rear isn't as fascinating as some might hope."

Amnandi opened her mouth to speak, closed it when the words quickly reformulated themselves, frowned to consider the new shape, frowned deeper to agree with it, and said, "*Why* do we do what we do? What differentiates us from those on Keer, if we are indeed different? I've wondered if we are."

"We are not," said Maab, "and we do nothing that isn't being done in every corner of Erah this precise moment. Ask Sarantain why he builds or Skye why she writes. People find the best parts of life and they proceed with it. Yours and mine is the inability to see a mystery go to waste."

"This isn't a mystery."

"Isn't it? An injustice occurred. That's always a mystery no matter who commits it. A tragedy."

"Unina says the most disheartening of thoughts is knowing tragedy is time simply delayed."

"That one of her bedtime stories to you?"

"No, I was twelve."

"I suspect, as your unina's not a fatalist, that she told you that to set your path focused on compassion. Are you focused on compassion, Miss Khumalo?"

"I am."

Amnandi had noted long ago that Maab's ear was trained to catch hesitance as slight as a gnat's passage, and was glad that the captain elected not to speak on Amnandi's now. Sometimes, the world was too...*confusing* for compassion. "We're not the only ones who've ever headed to Fabbin Keep for knowledge of the fantastic," said the captain. "Likely not even the only ones this month. We"—Maab tapped Amnandi's shoulder then her own chest—"tend to heal, which is the most natural thing in existence, yes? An earthquake seals itself, a volcano cools its lava, a flood recedes to allow new shoots." She swept a hand outward. The horses moved steadily. "Green things such as this. Everyone won't undertake a journey," she said with a shrug, "but more heal than not. That's the one guarantee as your adopted mother I can give you."

"Your other guarantees being guesses and lies," said Amnandi, the grin so unfettered, Maab's laugh came out as a snort.

"Suppositions, not lies," Maab said. "Do you take me for a functionary?"

"Madam Tourmaline might not like that," Amnandi said, Amis's aunt being the best functionary Waterfall had ever seen.

"Madam Tourmaline doesn't hunt gods, monsters, or poisoned beaches, so there's no harm here, is there?"

"But at some point, our lives will become merely stories, yes?"

"Luv, the storyteller's is the hardest lot. She's got to make all this"— Maab circled a hand in the air to encompass life—"make sense."

"I hope to do that."

"You succeed more often than not."

The soft *clop* of the horses carried the day for several seconds. Rock and Paper, who had traveled the world as a team under

Maab Pinyasama's care, had never given a thought to alternatives, destinies, or the diverse lots of life. They felt the magickal mystical energies around them on this excellent path, but it was as common an occurrence as swatting flies from their butts.

It did smell good here, though. A pervasive savory dampness rode the coastal wind.

"I'd worry more," Maab inserted over the unhurried clops, "if this was all we did. Can you imagine our friend Bog on holiday?"

"I haven't seen him for years."

"Not likely he's hammocked on a beach. Probably dangling from a demon's teste this moment. Saving an orphanage made of glass. Atop a talking mountain. Are there talking mountains?"

After a bit, the road forked. Straight ahead, the barest of the Keep's stone structures. To the right, the way to farmland and settlements, no doubt. The wagon kept straight. The increase in volume and excitement of nested birds was substantial.

"Announcing us?" said Maab.

"Yes."

"You still feel clear?"

"Very." Amnandi thought further. "Actually, oddly so. There are no protection spells."

"That unusual among all you magick types?"

"We tend to be protective of our homes with good cause."

"Aye. Surprised you and your mother never visited here."

"Likely no cause to," said Amnandi. Fabbin so far was gentle hills, steady humid breezes, and a sense of openness. Even the way leading toward settlements was free of danger signs.

Perhaps Unina had not visited because she wanted her daughter to enjoy it for herself?

The slow, even ride wasn't interrupted by so much as a decent-sized stone in the path. The birds, having warned the Keep in both voice and flight, had settled to watch, under the hope that travelers coming from the direction of the sea tended to be interesting.

The stones of the Keep were as weathered and moss-covered as a sunken ship's attraction to barnacles. From the wagon's distance, the structure and its surrounding wall appeared a single edifice given rivulets, embankments, and a single off-center silo taller than anything Amnandi had seen of Eurolan construction yet. The design was definitely influenced by Bilo and the Dogt of Afrela. Their penchant for sculpting—rather than merely constructing— left towers blended seamlessly with the ground, homes with the grass, windows with every temperament of weather. Fabbin had square and round-cut openings all over it, spaces which caused the Keep to whistle. At a distance, nearly subsonic, but eventually even Maab heard it and turned to Amnandi for confirmation. "There's a melody to it!" said Maab.

"Perhaps the goddess hums like this."

"A good sign if so. Damned good sign."

Rock and Paper stopped within clear sight of the Keep's encircling wall. Maab had not stopped them.

"What are your concerns?" Amnandi said to the team, bringing head shakes, ear twitches, and soft snorts.

"They said the land directs them to wait," said Amnandi.

Maab searched the façade for any glint of a spyglass in a window.

"Should we make an appeal?" said Maab.

The horses' ears drew Amnandi's eyes. They were relaxed and to the sides against the team's heads, content and attentive. "No."

"Then we wait." Maab hopped down. "We eat. We rest."

They did so. Even allowed Rock and Paper to roam loose, where the horses gamboled to work out kinks or sampled new-to-them grass here and there.

During Amnandi's and Maab's third game of Intrist, it became clear the wait was to be a long one. Amnandi showed the Intrist goal, dealt the cards, and the players went about mathematically deconstructing that goal until one player was left with one card in their hand.

"What do you think they're looking for in us?" Maab said, laying down on her first turn—and to Amnandi's surprise—a suit that equaled the total of the Intrist hand. Maab was no neophyte. An adventurer never traveled without a means to pass the time.

"Humility from us?" said Amnandi.

Which was as good as any. "That," said Maab, "coupled with the patience we've shown, should put us in good standing." The sun had visibly tracked from one part of the sky to another. "I'll give them until dusk, then try again in the morning."

She was about to win her fourth hand when Rock and Paper ambled back. They waited precisely by the bridle.

Amnandi and Maab gathered their cards and rose from the warm grass to attach the horses.

With a flick of leather reins, they were off.

❋❋❋

Much of that final leg was uphill. A gently winding hill. The horses corkscrewed their way without complaint but were clearly winded when Maab and Amnandi dismounted. The sun's drag downward made the land seem tired. There was no sign of anyone to greet them.

The Keep's massive arched gate was open. The horses would not enter.

Amnandi tossed Maab two fat apples from their sack. Maab caught them in both hands and removed Paper's bridle. Amnandi did the same, standing beside Rock. The crunching from both horses provided the only sound around.

There was no magick at the gate, no invisibility spell wiping bustling mystics from view. The Keep's denizens simply weren't there.

After each horse finished two apples each, the witch and the sailor snacked on dried meats and various well-traveling fruits. Then long pulls from their water sacks. The horses took strong slops from uncasked buckets.

If Fabbin wanted them to wait, there'd be championship waiting.

The setting sun gave up the high umber from its heart. Soon it would splash purple and grays, then erase everything as it went to bed.

Maab lit a lantern. Wide-spaced footfalls, loud as a grave danced on after a day of quiet, approached from the wall's interior, as though someone had suddenly appeared near it, then simply decided to walk. Maab glanced at Amnandi to see if the girl had sensed anything, but young Khumalo was just as struck as she.

Then, at the gate, finally someone from Fabbin, except he was a giant.

Not like giants of the old stories, the ones full of beards and furs and grinding teeth, but someone tall enough to have been born a stout tree.

Massive enough to leave dents when he walked.

Yet quiet enough to have registered no presence until now.

If his voice were not that of a mountain's, Maab would be disappointed.

It was.

"What knowledge have you brought?" The tones rumbled down their heads into their throats, then filled their chests.

"Important knowledge," said Maab, "in the form of questions."

The giant bent to appraise Amnandi. "A witch."

Amnandi touched her hand to her forehead respectfully.

"I was not aware a human could grow so tall," Amnandi said.

"My first question," said Maab. "Are you human?"

"I am." As the giant said this, he gave a smile.

"Second question," she said to his basso profundo. "Will you sing with me?"

"I don't sing."

"That'll change." She pulled herself to her full height. "I present myself to you as Captain Maab Pinyasama. My companion, Amnandi Khumalo, presented as my child."

The giant grunted acknowledgment. "I take you at your word, ship's captain."

"And why a ship?" asked Maab.

"You smell of the sea, not of military bearing, nor industry."

"Plus, you watched my boat."

His warm smile was all the acquiescence Maab needed.

"Are you..." Maab prompted, hoping for information. A name or title.

The giant ignored the prompt. "I am." He stood, casting a shadow against the wider gloom.

"We're here at the behest of the goddess," said Maab upward. He actually seemed even taller now, which had to be a trick of the waning light. Then she noticed Amnandi's furrowed brow. By the goddess, he *was* getting bigger. His loose clothing didn't hang as loose; those gray eyes seemed even larger pools. He stood at least twenty feet.

"Which this time?" he said.

"We know her by 'the goddess' and know of whom we speak in the moment."

"Are you erranded to find love?"

"No."

"Bypass death?"

"Not given to foolishness outside of trying to hit certain high notes."

"We welcome death," Amnandi said. "Preferably a long way off."

"This one," he said to her, "claims you as mother. Name your birth mother if possible."

"Ayanda Khumalo. Have you heard of her?"

"No. It is not ours to keep track of witches. They are windblown seeds and fish."

"You've not blessed us with your name," said Maab.

The giant stood aside from the gateway. "You may sleep in any building that greets you with a light."

"And we're to find this by?" said Maab.

"Wandering." To the horses he said, "The stables are that way," and pointed. Rock and Paper trotted off with the wagon.

"Who'll relieve them of their burden?" asked Maab.

"They will receive care." He bent under the arch and came to their side. Amnandi and Maab entered the Keep. "Don't wander out here," he advised under increasing moonlight and a bounty of stars, and left along the road they'd taken, each stride growing his prodigious height a little more.

Fabbin Keep's new guests left him to his privacy.

The inner circle of buildings were also of Dogt design, although considerably smaller than the silos that formed the outer layer. They were all spread a good distance from each other, all multi-windowed, and all dark, not a flicker to indicate living souls.

Amnandi threw a soft glow ahead of them.

Nothing stirred except a fractured breeze that came from multiple directions. Here warm, there cool, one meadow-scented, the next dryer than kindling, yet perturbing when it was gone altogether, as though the Keep had swallowed everything.

Maab decided perhaps the lights would appear if they approached a door rather than searched from the hardpack. Cobblestone whorls served as welcome mats. She marched up to one. The structure remained dark. Crossed to another. Nothing.

She abandoned the theory when she saw Amnandi received the same result. "We can bed in the wagon," Maab said, although her feet kept walking forward. There was something eerily attractive about this place, its standoffishness being highly inviting. The silos were built in compounds of six on either side of the hardpack lane, each grouping separated by a midsized farming plot. She and Amnandi had passed two sets.

A light settled into a window as they wandered the third set.

When they were within two steps of the door, Maab caught a smile crossing Amnandi's face. Maab took hold of the coiled vine that served as a door handle and pulled.

A desert lay before them. They stepped through. The moon was almost in the same position from where they'd left. A large cot with netting tied to posts beside a sealed water urn wasn't far from the door. The urn sat atop a crate, the crate atop another whirling of cobblestones.

A lantern, an inkwell, and a writing pad shared the crate.

"Every door a portal," Amnandi said. She closed her eyes to attune herself and turned a circle, searching for the return portal while Maab watched. The portal was two sickly cacti away.

The grit underfoot had an especially arid feel. There'd been no moisture in this place for some time. Amnandi kept her illuminating eyes on the crate long enough for Maab to find a match to light the lantern.

Maab, after inspecting the bed and their surroundings, lay on the cot with her dirty boots hanging over. Amnandi squeezed beside her and did the same. Maab gazed upward. She wondered what part of Erah they were on, then said, "No more thinking for the night." Would anyone ever sail the spaces between the stars? Potent dreams were likely hidden up there.

That was more than enough to drift off to.

***

In the morning, all manner of mystics buzzed about.

Shimmerers. Levitators. Poet magicians and long-form spell

writers. Mumblers. People staring at things. People staring at Amnandi and Maab.

But everyone made way for the deep voice calling out, "Strangers!"

Maab made for the giant who, though still excessively tall, wasn't as giant as he'd been before.

"So, you're real and not just a trick of the light," Maab said.

"Light does nothing but trick."

Skin the same sandstone as Nyim's stole every bit of the day's brightness. Tattoos down his biceps, both sides of the neck, and upper chest caught her eye. She wasn't a mathematician, but they seemed to be equations. Maab swore the longer she looked at him, he seemed to glow just perceptibly enough that it could be dismissed as a play of the eye.

"Your horses are brushed, fed, and watered. Offerings: appreciated by many hands."

"You're early risers here."

"A few never sleep." Emerald rings dangling from his ears wobbled when he turned to Amnandi. "The thousand questions will have to wait," he told her. "Your mother wouldn't be here if not for important, possibly dire things."

A small man with pointed ears crossed their path. "When aren't they important and dire?" he interjected without waiting for answer as he hurried after an inquisitive shade of blue that hadn't paused with him.

"Jud listens to everyone's conversations for hidden patterns," said the giant.

"Then might he know why I'm here?" said Maab.

"Perhaps a piece of it within a million."

"Who will counsel us on important matters?" Maab asked. "Is there a time or place? An elder?"

"I be two hundred twenty-two years old."

"No disrespect meant."

"You gained entry by me," he said. "You will speak to me."

"We are erranded to correct an illness."

"I would not imagine an adventurer and a witch traveling here for herbs and palliatives."

"The gods themselves are ill. A god, at least."

No pithy comeback to this. The giant used three of five seconds to stare into Maab's eyes, with the final two focused on Amnandi.

"Has no one here sensed this?" Maab demanded. It seemed Fabbin was aflutter with knowledge.

"Those who sense things deal in dreams that confuse even themselves," said the giant.

"*We* were awake. We saw the poisoning sign. We know the source. We *hoped* for a cure," said Maab.

The giant's gentle eye went back to Amnandi. "Young quiet witch, speak on this."

"I believe the goddess reached out in desperation. The Mer were touched as well," said Amnandi.

The steady bustle of Fabbin Keep moved around them. "Is this the place to speak of this?" said Maab.

Various ears had directed themselves their way at the mention of the goddess. "Eat while I gather an assembly." He pointed out what looked to be a door set into a hillock. "Food from every point on Erah."

"Free?" said Maab.

"Free."

"Then you mystics have at least learned that. Come, daughter. Where, sir, should we see you next?"

"Continue walking north. The last of the circles you come to. The building in the center of it. Eat your fill and be leisurely about it. We are dealing with gods; no amount of time we take will be significant." With that, he left.

Amnandi, watching his long strides, asked, "Do you believe that about time?"

"Not in the least. We'll be significant, luv. Believe it."

THE MEETING HALL

An ancient woman was guided in because her eyes saw everything, meaning she was never sure of her surroundings.

A child with the saddest resting face the world had ever seen took a seat directly in front of Maab and Amnandi, and silently, patiently stared at them.

Identical twin women who constantly morphed into one another but few could ever tell, swung folding stools from their backs, shook them out, and sat.

The giant, whom Maab kept watch on from the moment he entered and through his brief introductions, gave the captain leave to speak.

Or so she thought. When she opened her mouth, the giant held up a long finger. "There is one more."

Practically on cue, a bald man smiling so much he had to have told a joke mere steps away entered, beaming his eyes at everyone as though all were in on the joke and—though he said not a word—raucously found a preferred spot on the floor and dropped down easily into a cross-legged position. He was identically tattooed to the giant, muscled but in a soft way excellent for hugging, and smelled of ginger.

"Daoud Dj'ntree, physician," said the giant.

Daoud bowed a skull that featured more math toward the guests at the front of the room.

The giant ceded the floor.

Maab immediately said, "I am troubled that none here is aware of what's happening to the world. It'd do me no good to speak without saying so. Sicknesses are spreading. I know there's no fuller source of wisdom or information anywhere on Erah than what goes on within these walls. A mad Raven King became an infection, one reaching as deeply as Erah's soul."

The physician interrupted. "His thoughts were that potent?"

"Potent, virulent, or lucky enough to land where they needn't have. We were given a vision of death. Ravens. Scores and scores. The Mer were shown the King. Together, we found him."

"And?"

"And?" Maab mirrored the giant, incredulous. "We need your help. There is no *and*. My words and our need—all our needs—are one and the same."

"Is it?" the giant asked.

"We found actual death. Mangled bodies as though squeezed by will alone."

The Ancient Woman spoke. "Searchers always reach a point where all ground slips beneath them. Where naught surrounds them but exhaustion. Exhaustion becomes disillusion. Disillusioned people retreat toward certainty."

"A fancy way of saying water will wet," said Maab. "We do not give up."

"Every questor says such," said the old woman. "Erah handles more than you know."

"Blessings to you, elder, but what I don't know could rope Sharda and pull her to us. That won't change the suffering of a single raven, child, fool, or mystic. My mother would forgive me for being impolite in this instance, and perhaps in your eyes there is no urgency here, but I see Erah with *my* eyes. I see what is happening."

"We were unable," said Amnandi, "to administer."

"Not to him, ravenkind, or Erah," Maab pointed out. "We've not the knowledge."

"You are incorrect in three things," said the ancient. "That all here are unaware, that none here stand to care, and that you have wasted precious time in coming."

"I beseech, then: teach!"

The physician, Daoud, spoke. "Consider this fourth assumption equally incorrect: that we will not help. Your mind moves quickly, gracious Pinyasama, but not so quickly it can't be seen. We *will* help, but there's only so much we can do from here."

"But you retire everywhere."

"Which is a big place. We need a fine-tip." The physician and the giant exchanged silent views, ending with the giant nodding once. "The elder never leaves," said Daoud. "The child shouldn't leave. The twins cannot function outside these walls. My younger brother there is in his growing season. Leaving for him would be problematic. I'll go with you to ascertain damages, perhaps glean a physic."

"Are you a giant as well?" said Maab.

"Should it be required."

Riddles. Riddles and mystics and learned obfuscations, when what was needed was a magick, or lightning bolts, or a healing song, something someone named Maab Pinyasama could sail with, hold aloft, and seal.

Was impatience a symptom of the King's poison? Who could say how fast the disease could spread from god to every aspect of Erah, its peoples included? She was certain this explained so much.

"Do we accept his expertise?" Amnandi said to break her seafaring godmother's brief spell of distaste.

"We do. Graciously. How soon can you leave?"

"The moment you gather your cart."

"Then we three are on our way to rendezvous with the Mer."

❋ ❋ ❋

What most noticed about the physician, or *mystic* as he preferred, was that he spent a great deal of time on the *Bane* meditating behind a partition. No food, no water, no movement, no sound. Amnandi and Amis were assigned to peer in on him at set times. He had been given good cushions to stretch upon, so he was comfortable at least. But a week's journey stretched on one's back leeched comfort from even the most ardent.

"He'll be sore as tired goats when he gets up," said Amis, pushing the partition tarp back into place from their midday checkup. "Maybe mystics like pain?"

"Very unlike witches in that regard, then." Amnandi had been trying to memorize his markings in case there was a hidden philosophy or spell there. They were definitely mathematical symbols but paired in ways she had never encountered. So far, nothing. All she knew was that he was a mystic, someone who had devoted his life to learning.

So was her mother.

Which meant so was she, unless mystics were solely interested in acquiring, not applying.

Amnandi hoped not.

As they emerged into the light of the main deck, Nyim crossed their path. Amis nodded at him; Nyim nodded at Amis. He continued on.

"A truce has been called," Amnandi noted. "A lasting one. Intriguing."

"Skye pulled me aside and told me there are no enemies aboard a ship."

"He wasn't your enemy in the first place."

"No, but it was fun to poke him." She took Amnandi's hand and held it as they walked. "I'm your sister and I love you, but you're pretty much unpokeable."

"Very much so."

The captain spotted them. "Ah! You two!"

They trotted to meet her.

"No change?" Maab asked.

"Mysticism looks a lot like napping," said Amis.

"Perhaps his dreams carry him elsewhere," said Maab. "He might be fighting battles of which we have no ken. By the gods, he might wake with an immediate solution."

"Maybe he could teach the crew another song to sing," said Nyim, who had doubled back, hefting the thick coil of rope he'd been erranded for.

"We need but one song in our hearts, young sir, provided that song be true. Mark that," said Maab.

"Aye, ma'am. Apologies for being indelicate, ma'am."

"That coil at the mate's behest?"

"Aye."

"Away, then."

They watched him hurry off.

"Has he been any trouble, Ms. Dotrig?" asked Maab.

"Full of himself enough to skip meals."

"I trust your eye will train on him as needs be. All right, away with you both. I don't yet have a ship that'll run itself. That'd be delightful, though. Give everybody on board a pleasure cruise. Books, music, and fruit juice for everyone." Maab barely noticed the little sigh that came out of herself at this. "Carry on."

Above them, bright sky. Below them, the sea. Deep below that, an arrow of Mer to pinpoint the spot of the goddess's first lament.

And then...

"And then," Maab said within earshot of Amis and Amnandi but to the wind, "a mystic."

AMNANDI AND THE MYSTIC

Amnandi hit the water first but Daoud's bare *plip* practically merged with her wake. The inky darkness was so absolute that her glow vision over the Mer's skin barely affected them. That, plus they had been taking endurance-building forays closer and closer to daylit waters.

The mystic expertly affixed a loose rope around Amnandi's waist, anchored to his own. Then they clasped hands and she led.

Fish darted away.

Four Mer surrounded them, guiding them with bioluminescent flashes of speckles.

The mystic had said he could hold his breath for as long as was necessary. Amnandi could go for fifteen minutes at least.

The Mer would take them deep but not too deep. The source radiated outward so powerfully that even the humans would feel it reaching toward them, a jagged, prickly scratch of malicious intent.

The moment it nicked Daoud's leg, his grip tightened on Amnandi's hand to stop. A finger tap told her to go dark. She did so. They spun in the absence of light. Neither pair of eyes comprehended the sudden lack of *everything*. Amnandi had been in total darkness before, many times even, and she was confident Daoud had too, yet something disturbed her here, something more than feeling weightless while still having to fight gravity, subtly more physical than currents swirling at her legs. It was an unease that was cunning.

Rukkai flickered blue in front of her. She felt the Mer attempting to speak and let its voice swell.

Are you well?

Two quick blinks of her eyes meant yes.

The mystic, having spoken to many Mer, heard as well.

Rukkai swam closer, remaining lit, enveloping them in a glow of blue.

I will touch.

Having been previously told what to expect, they readied themselves.

Rukkai slid an appendage along each's shoulder.

Reality rebelled and became an undersea flood of anguish, a regret so pronounced, existence was both crime and punishment.

Rukkai withdrew the touch.

Had sadness been made of stone, the mystic suddenly carried his weight in it. He went slack and slowly dropped away from Amnandi. She jerked the rope sharply, bringing him back to himself. His feet resumed their slow, station-keeping tread.

What he sensed was not merely death but the total awareness from the ravens that they were dying an absolutely unnecessary death though they knew not its source.

Every possibility they might have known was as useless as

dross.

Each raven had spread its mind in a communal shock from throats caught between humanlike and bird, in screech from birdlike to human.

The mystic opened his inner eye to the pain that must have hit the Mer when they initially felt this, the sea become an inescapable, diseased cauldron. He reached to touch Rukkai but stopped, knowing contact again would likely return his body to feeling like a sinking stone.

It was Daoud who jerked the rope this time. Jerked it upward. Amnandi increased her glow. Daoud's eyes, so clear to Amnandi's, said to her, *Take me away from this place.* Had she not obliged, he might have begged. She kicked hard upward, and swept the rope and him with her, until their feet and arms matched stroke for stroke while the Mer circled them.

Their two heads broke the surface of the black sea, neither person able to speak and glad of it.

"Are you injured?" Amnandi eventually asked.

The mystic's shuddering agitated the water. "Get—get us back to the ship," he chittered.

Amnandi flared her eyes their brightest and spun herself. An answering burst of light appeared a distance away. It hadn't seemed to her they'd swum that far, but water did what it would.

The mystic continued to shiver.

❉ ❉ ❉

The mystic, still wrapped in the blanket from the skiff, barely laid sole to the *Bane's* planks before telling the captain, "We can't fight this."

"I'm not one to give up. Have you forgotten I spoke on that already?"

"You misunderstand," he said impatiently. "*We* cannot fight it.

Nor can we heal it."

"That's why you're here," said Maab. Her face took on the edge of metal. "I will not give up, sir."

"I hardly expect that, madam!" Daoud snapped. He pulled the blanket tighter and collected his thoughts. He spoke with care so as to calm himself as well as the captain. "What's been done here has rarely been done before. The false king has turned his failings into a javelin and thrown it with force, force which his own mind could not possibly have survived whole. We don't have the means to dislodge it from his target's chest, and if we wait for it to fall away of its own accord, there could be too little of Erah left."

"Yet you speak with hope in your voice," said Maab. "What must we do?"

"This ship, you, your crew. Are you prepared to follow me toward the end of all things?"

"Unnecessarily foreboding," said Maab.

"Confidence will not help where we are going."

"Speak plainly on it. Be clear."

"We seek the dragoon," said Daoud the Mystic.

Very clearly.

***

The mystic had thought his pronouncement sharp, the meaning plain. He was prepared for no greater exertion this night, mental or otherwise, than a hot sluice, dry blankets, and his own burrowing under rough, musty warmth. Questions could wait till morning's light.

Except they didn't.

"If you're speaking of hardened footprints the size of islands or a bone here and there that might span a lake," said Maab, "you're about as helpful as my arthritic grandmother in a fight."

"They haven't walked Erah's skin, true, but walk they do," said the mystic.

"Damn it, man, no riddles!"

For a moment, two small tattoos on the sides of his neck flared red. Maab instinctively touched ready fingers to the hilt of the knife at the small of her back, a motion the darkness kept between her and her sense of caution.

"I speak," Daoud said tersely, "as...clear...as may be understood. The dragoon live within Erah's shell."

"Dragoon," Maab said. She was not impressed.

"Dragoon. Dragon. Endra'hoonj. They are called many things but they are one. They are the very lightning inside us. Inside Erah."

"And they're real?"

"Yes."

Maab's hands—knife free—flew upward. "How painful was that to say?" She needed a direction. "Where?"

"You do not approach a cosmic entity without respect," said Daoud.

"This is true," said Amnandi. No one currently breathing Erah's air had ever encountered a dragoon, but Unina had taught her the legends.

Amnandi's voice reminded everyone that there were two cold, wet people on deck, one visibly shivering, the other breathing deeply and evenly to draw warmth from the air.

"On the morrow," Maab said.

"On the morrow," Daoud agreed.

***

Warm, dry, and rested, the mystic spoke to Amnandi. Amis snored softly nearby. During the conversation, he'd shed blankets until down to one.

"Your chill was not of temperature," Amnandi noted.

"I am attuned to the feelings of others. Any ebullience I exhibit is a shield. The tattoos channel sudden extremes outward."

"My mother and I have seen such marking magick successfully done solely in Tyn."

"It is where I had it successfully scribed for me. In the water... I haven't been so overwhelmed in a long time."

"You didn't channel it outward."

"I needed to feel everything. To know each death's name. To know the king's madness and this disease in fullness. The last time this occurred, a queen was responsible. A thousand years ago. Piet, the elder at the convening, wrote an account of it. Piet was barely older than you at the time. She exists differently in time, walking in and out of it. She says she witnessed a dragoon walking our lands and feared the planet would crack with each step. Oh, the things she has seen."

"She can't see our path for us?"

"She can't see paths at all anymore. Those days are over for her. Time collects its due."

"Fabbin is a refuge for the tortured."

"The queen I spoke of? She was of your lands, one of the first great queens of Afrela."

"There is no record of this."

"Piet made sure of that."

"Was it greed that poisoned her?"

"It was love. Love becomes its own type of sickness if never questioned. She loved that people loved her, and in her deepest heart decreed that, as she was a good queen, all the world should."

"That," said Amnandi, "is called narcissism."

"You'd be amazed how often the gods are merely passageways for our foolishness."

"If I know what happened a thousand years ago, will it help me with today?"

"Not necessarily."

"And the dragoon?"

"Dragoon burn away foolishness. Literally, figuratively, however is needed, however they wish."

"And the dragoon were here before the gods?"

"They were here with. Simultaneously. The gods merged with Erah; the dragoon remained beside it." He blew out the candle between them. "Rest yourself, young Khumalo. In the morning, prepare word for your loved ones that you may not be home for a very long time, should you wish to see this through."

"I do."

"Go and dream well, Amnandi Khumalo."

NECESSITIES

The mystic advised the same for all aboard the ship, who knew that by the time a message reached their loved ones, the senders could well be spirits observing them.

Another handful of people asked to be put off the ship. Maab returned to Keer Island for them. Five departed. One meant to come on board. A wiry, spry woman.

Sarantain introduced her to Mate Skye. "Ms. Cedar Yau."

"Captain's not taking on passengers," said Skye.

"Not a passenger, your grace. Crew," said Cedar.

"Captain's not taking on crew."

"She's a better carpenter than I am," said Sarantain. "We may very well need her."

The mate looked Cedar dead in the eyes. "You don't know where we sail."

"You unload here twice, you're bound for more glory than I'm likely to see in years. I define glory quite damn loosely, by the way."

"Mr. Sarantain," said Skye, "is she set to repair a ship smashed to splinters?"

"I point to the *Dappled Whey*," said the woman, "whose captain and I no longer favor each other." The *Dappled Whey* was less a ship and more a masterwork of repairs.

Skye shouted toward the pilot station, sidestepping to allow Cedar and Sarantain to board, "Captain! We sail!"

That bellow was all those at the ropes needed to clear the *Bane's* moorings and retract the plank after Skye led Sarantain and party to the deck.

The captain's voice boomed back, "Sail away, Ms. Skye!"

Onward, then, the *Bane*.

✳✳✳

Unina, if you were here, you would ask the mystic, "Have you ever spoken to a dragoon?" Following that, you would ask, "Has anyone here ever beseeched the goddess to approach a dragoon?" Both answers would be no, but I don't think you'd advise us to stop or turn back. I'll send this message by the first reliable means I come across.

Please know there is no sense of fear on this boat. We approach cautiously, mindfully, and necessarily. Does that constitute duty? The efforts you made to get physicians worldwide to do no harm feels like this. Maab will not allow Erah to be poisoned by false medicines.

Daoud of Fabbin Keep says he knows where a dragoon sleeps.

The remaining crew seem intent on making sure this is just another voyage; otherwise, they would go mad. I understand that. Hatred is a silly, lazy weapon, yet it will cut like any blade. A journey undertaken because of one being's failings is a terrible thing.

Our first stop, per the mystic, is to once again see this sad, hateful king.

✳✳✳

When the mystic returned from the mad king, his tattoos were blurred as if vibrating. He had insisted on going alone, and stood on our deck tight-lipped despite Maab's many questions. His short answers: the king himself was no longer a problem; the island was dead; he would speak on it no further. He retired to his bed for two days without telling us where to go.

On the third day, he provided our course.

THE ISLE OF LIGHT

"I've not known anything to lay along these lines," Maab had initially said, and had been reluctant to commit the *Bane* toward what might be folly, mystic or no. Yes, the world was the world, meaning packed with mysteries, but she had sailed near that course twice and had noted nothing more remarkable than small ice floes and animals confused enough to play in the cold.

She also considered whether or not to enlist others. She knew several ships that sailed the wide gap between where she was and where she was going. The *Xela*, *Cornell*, *Obeisance*, and *Collin's Consort* were fine ships, their captains caring more for freedom and sea spray than riches. She contented herself with the fact that the *Bane* already flew the orange flag of rescue; if they saw it, they would come.

Provided they weren't already on their *own* quests. Was there ever a shortage?

Even with crew slightly shorter in number, Maab put the ship on half-duty. She strongly suggested everyone seek out the ship's library. Maab's mother, Orchiir, had chided her for putting a library on board, but fantastic voyages were long things. A knowledgeable crew was a benefit. A compact shelf full of books from wherever the *Bane* traveled, in all the languages thereof.

And so, as the ship sailed, its complement read.

❊ ❊ ❊

Maab peered over tiny round spectacles at Nyim, Amis, and Amnandi. The captain kept herself tucked nearly invisible in a cozy corner. The library, being a small room partitioned off from the galley, smelled delightful.

Nyim had chosen a book discussing the importance of Bilo the Alchemist's observations. "How is it Bilo spoke nothing of dragoon?" he said, having been discussing the works of Bilo with Amnandi.

Amis read the unedited erotic poetry of Bhary of Blanc.

Nyim pressed his questioning. "If he traveled Erah as he said, he made no mention of dragoon."

"Bilo never mentioned gods," Amnandi said, "yet we do not doubt."

"Some do."

Amis, Maab noted, was listening and not merely warming her brain. "Some," Amis said without looking away from her tattered book, "would swear the world disappears when they blink."

"Perhaps Bilo had cause for caution," said Amnandi.

Amis lowered her book. "You afraid, Mr. Stone?"

"I'm concerned."

"I would imagine," said Amnandi, "the captain has considered your concerns and mine, and Amis's, and everyone's. And we remain. Allay your concerns and instead find a reason to be assured."

"Now you've got her talking like her mother," said Amis. "Either of you ever been to the frigid lands?"

Both Nyim and Amnandi indicated no.

"I hope Da doesn't think the ship's lost at sea," Amis said, voice suddenly heavier than intended.

"I've sent birds to all home ports," said Maab.

"Da's a worrier."

"It's not difficult imagining you gave him cause to be," said Nyim.

"My father's an inventor," said Amis. "Scientists are notorious criers."

Nyim leaned to whisper, "And neither of you thinks we're too young for this?"

"We saved an entire village when we were but half this height," said Amnandi.

"Tiny," said Amis.

Nyim closed his book. Maab noted that this was the third time she'd observed Nyim close a book without a marker for place. Excellent memory.

"When I was a child," he said, "my governess told me a dragoon ate the first star before Erah had even formed, a meal that kept it satisfied till the second star appeared, and then the world. And until people appeared on Erah."

"Do you wish Bilo had told you a nursery tale?" said Amnandi.

"I wish merely to know what we can *do* about any of this. Mad kings, gods, Mer, and dragoon?" Then he whispered again. Maab wondered why he thought no one at a distance could hear him. "This is madness, Amnandi."

Amnandi glanced at Maab for signs of madness.

Maab scooched deeper into her cushions, intent on her book.

Then the witch evaluated Amis.

No madness.

"We are sane," she announced.

Youth, Maab thought happily behind her book, *are best guided, not led*.

"My ma," said Amis, "rest her well, used to tell me to live right so we'd have good answers to the curious as ghosts."

"And this mystic?" said Nyim. "What if he's wrong?"

Amis sighed poetically. "We'll still have seen more of Erah than twelve elders and feel good in our old age for it."

Nyim glanced at the captain. She lay her book on her chest and gave a single nod his way.

"Some may well die no matter what's out there," he said.

"Every day, sotter!"

"Young Mr. Stone," said Maab to get the room's attention, "why didn't you leave?"

"Even Keer would have welcomed you," said Amnandi.

All three watched his brain come to a complete stop. Maab understood his heart. Whatever response he weighed, he tried attaching no emotion to his efforts.

His final decision to speak plainly broke them just a tiny bit.

"I have nowhere else to go."

* * *

Wind pushed the *Bane*'s sails as though an active participant in the mission. At one point, Maab thought to ask Amnandi if the assistance was her doing. If the *Bane* could sustain this pace, they'd pass the equatorial line before anyone got old, and then onward toward colder regions.

A skiff approached them. "Captain!" shouted the lookout. "Advising hold. Message on the wind."

"Put us in a circle," Maab said beside her pilot. "I'll not lose this momentum." She cupped her mouth and answered the lookout. "Sound acknowledgment!"

Daoud joined Maab on deck.

"We have a visitation," she said.

"I know."

And almost like magick, Amnandi stood beside her captain.

And beside Amnandi, Amis.

For an instant, Maab felt invincible.

Maab wore thick breeches minus her feathered skirt. She hadn't wanted anyone thinking she was relying on luck for this new stretch of an expanding errand.

She pulled sights from her waistband and scanned the circle her ship made. The skiff was still a fair distance away but closing quickly...without a raised sail in sight.

Maab's heart jumped. New magicks were surely a sign from the goddess!

The ship, as red as a cut, matched speed alongside the *Bane*. Half the crew likely already coveted the sleek vessel. Water churned at either side of the painted wooden craft.

"Zari of the *Cornell*," the sailor announced. "First Mate. Your lot on Keer Isle pointed us your way. You're hunted, Captain. My captain owes you several favors and sends this warning. Ravens as far as Numia have been asking questions about a teardrop ship."

"Captain Beh's sense of honor is unmatched," said Maab. "How old is this word?"

"We heard of it over a week ago. Various boats telling of ravens roosting on masts in the night, speaking riddles. Recounting calamities. Word of Mer being captured and harmed."

"By ravens?"

"Aye! Something foul's intent on you, Captain. Be warned."

"The *Bane* is warned and grateful." She pointed to the unusual boat bobbing. "Speak on your ship."

"A gift from the Isle of Light. We agreed to test it for them. It's a 'motor.' Surely, you'll want one."

The Isle of Light was nearly as fabled as Fabbin Keep. Light favored inventors, however, rather than mystics.

"You caught up to us days out from Keer."

"Aye, I did," the *Cornell's* officer agreed.

"I want one," said Maab. "A steady pace and no lulls."

"Your ship's bigger than the *Cornell*. You'll need two."

"How is it powered?"

"From the sea itself. Isle called it a saline thrust."

"If I send two boats with you, will you take them by the most direct route to Light and speak on our behalf for two of their motors? And two very large ones for the *Bane*?"

"These require quite a bit of framing and fitting."

"I'll worry about that. Have them name their price and know I set the *Bane* against it, providing everything will fit in my boats."

"The motor itself is lightweight; the framing is not. But all are tempered in rubber."

"They get my firstborn for that, too."

"Some assembly required."

"If my team can't figure out a frame, we've no business floating. Will your captain agree to this?"

"We fly the orange flags. I was told to aid."

"Aid, my friend, you have."

SKYE AND MAAB

If calculations were correct—and they'd damn better be—the two boats manned by Niss, Dedoura, Jackson, and Sarantain would cross paths with the widely arcing *Bane* in six days. The *Cornell's* mate had assured Maab that the Isle of Light kept a stockpile of machines from large to small and were simply waiting for the right time to introduce them to the public, doling these particular ones out to a few trusted to evaluate and promote.

"Are we considering this a boon, Captain?" said Skye over dinner as evening settled in the captain's quarters. By then, the ship had calmed from buzzing with great interest to merely being curious. All these new powers in the world: heady stuff. Heady enough, blessed enough, to distract Maab's crew, however temporarily, from the news the messenger dropped on them.

Ravens. Worldwide.

Hunting.

Maab sighed. *A boon.* Skye, being a good mate, knew it was

her job to make her captain sigh. Even still, Maab wished the dear woman had left her the certainty of silence. Maab downed a hot spoonful of soup and took her time chewing its bits of leathery beef before responding. "Let's take anything that doesn't sink us as a boon, Patrice, until we find home port again. Reunite Sarantain with Grucca, Amis with family, and get you teaching Constable Bethune what kisses are meant for."

"It hasn't been a truly *different* voyage, Captain..."

"Those are the ones that wear hardest sometimes on a crew. The fantastic gets mundane." A pocket watch lay on the table. Maab had already tapped it open twice since being served.

"We've plenty of time, Captain," Skye said gently.

"Make sure I stay convinced of that."

"Maab...there *is* no turning back. I say that not because we're pulled to it, but in that the crew—myself first among them—wouldn't consider it. We're in this as surely as if we'd found a babe crying in the woods. The mystic's said something's possible."

"I suppose that's a boon in itself."

Skye crumbled bread into her soup. "It is, woman, and keep it marked." This soup was new. Spicy and sweet. Full of dried beef. Not one of Leena's usual. "What'd Amnandi do to get Leena to try this recipe?"

"She asked."

"Ha!" Skye raised her mug of wine. "To our young, who change worlds with a simple *please*." Skye slugged half, then let silence take the room.

Presently, Maab said, "Did you think we'd be hunting dragoon after delivering kegs of salt to Vale?" She almost made it through without cracking up.

Skye immediately hooted. "If it'd been suggested, I'd have had you fitted with a wig of leeches and confined you to bed. Although... if anyone *was* to find a dragoon, it'd be Maab Pinyasama."

"True. My mother would do handstands."

"We'd be rich."

"Important speeches," said Maab.

"Poems written," said Skye.

"Retiring to nonstop carnalities."

"Never laying foot on deck planking again."

"No, inlaying the planks from this dear ship in our homes." Maab raised the toast. Skye clinked. They lulled into eating again. When done, they dabbed mouths and chins, pushed away from the small table that was more distressed wood than furniture, and stood.

"Do we have time for a walk in the air before our talk with the Mer?" Maab asked.

"Aye."

THE WITCH, THE MYSTIC, AND THE MERFOLK

Oars pushed against calm waters to bring the boat to a halt several strong strokes out from the *Bane*. Though the Mer had made progress with limited trysts with light, the ship remained sparsely lit.

Amnandi docked the oars and dimmed the rowboat's one lantern to its lowest. Her own sight remained lit, but she imagined she saw the mystic's tattoos across from her shifting glacially along his skin in a blue so faint it couldn't be true color.

Beyond them, the ocean.

"We seem to be in circles," Maab said to her, "yet we're getting somewhere. Mystic, will you be silent observer or interrogator?" He was a vague silhouette in the boat to Maab's eyes.

"We'll see."

The watery shush of a head breaking the surface drew gazes outward.

A Mer allowed whorls and branching lines of warm blue to appear on its skin. It had learned that humans preferred visual cues in order to gather their wits. The pattern it repeated indicated it was Rukkai.

"I don't know how many of you still travel with us," said Maab.

Enough.

"You aware ravens are on the hunt?"

Yes.

Maab's rough sigh stretched into a resigned groan. "That's not how alliances work, luv. You need to share information. Not when asked; when you get it."

Slowing thoughts sufficiently to share with you is laborious.

"What's their intent?" Maab asked.

Many thoughts of killing. I have pods monitoring and interceding.

"I wasn't aware Mer and ravens maintained relations," Maab said.

Daoud spoke up. "There's much we don't know."

"Not useful, mystic. Rukkai, what's the likelihood they'll overtake us before we reach cold waters?"

You seek guarantees?

"I seek to not see the bottom of the sea before the next birthday! I want Erah well. I...need help."

We will intervene.

"Without bloodshed?" she asked.

Entirely up to them.

"Are you aware of the ships without sails?"

You refer to the motors?

"Yes. We plan to outfit our ship with them."

"We've not done the science," Daoud said to the Mer.

"We will be the science," said Maab. Amnandi wondered on

the interplay between the two. "It will work. Amnandi, you have questions?"

The witch turned her full attention on the Mer. "Are you aware of the dragoon?"

No.

"How far will you journey with us?" Maab asked.

As far as you do.

"The cold?"

All waters are our waters.

"Then this, my friend, is the plan," Maab said, a plan which, bereft of intricacies, was succinct, flexible, and needing no agreement. It was, quite plainly, the only thing to do.

A FINE CREW

In two days' time of nonstop travel, Niss and Sarantain reached the Isle of Light, glad for one of the first times in their lives to be off the water. They'd seen many amazing things in their collective time sailing, things dead, things alive, things huge and small. But the gigantic floating carcasses they'd passed of deep-sea dwellers left a lingering quality of suffering about them even after death. Skin that bubbled and popped. Ichor extruding through pores like meat through a dirty press. Only two, one a great whale and the other a tangled eel longer than all three of their boats put together.

"Not a single carrion bird," said Niss to the inventors feeding herself, Sarantain, and Jackson. "Not a single scavenging fish. A spreading ring of the same darkness we saw from the ravens, though."

The youngest of the inventors, not much older than Amnandi, drummed disappointed fingers atop the table. "A sample would've been lovely." Her name was Barrow.

"You're welcome to come back with us and dip a cup," said Niss, at which the young scientist perked. She reminded Niss of an older Amis, only scruffier and better fed. Niss would've readily wagered the lady's uneven bangs were short because they had been scorched, not cut.

The contingent from the *Bane* hadn't seen the escort at full capacity, since it kept pace with them the entire trip. Niss redirected her attention to the room's elder. "You say these motors will double our speed?"

Dibbah, Barrow's apparent supervisor, frowned at Niss. "Not say. Guarantee. The math's been done." The elder's wiry gray hair was tied back in a tail so tight, it left her rheumy eyes that much more blazing against skin as dark as a universe.

Niss apologized. "I've never seen much distinction between math and magick and thus far magick's made its own rules."

"To know math is to know the rules in iron," said Dibbah.

Niss saw the energy pushing the elder to want to come along, but appreciated the even-higher expenditure to sit back.

"We could use all the maths we can get," said Sarantain.

"Your captain's on a worthy mission," said Dibbah. "Barrow, take them through the warehouse. Load them with necessary items."

"Yes, ma'am."

It dawned on Niss that Dibbah was not only offering equipment but expertise. "The captain may not have sufficient coin for this."

"My dear, all of Erah funnels coin to us. Lack is rarely a concern."

Niss, Sarantain, Jackson, and Dedoura raised cups of water to the gray-haired woman. "In that case," said Niss as expedition commander, "we offer a promise of debt. When you need us, Dibbah Eti, we will come."

Dibbah returned the salute. "No doubt of it. Barrow will

attend you on your ship."

"Is there actually room for me when you depart?" asked Barrow.

"We'll make the room," said Niss, but pointed a cautionary finger. "If you're serious."

"My friend, look where I live? No one leaves bed until they're satisfied they're properly serious."

Dibbah grunted herself to a stand. "And I guarantee your boats will be ready by morning."

"Pack your necessities," Niss said to Barrow Field's uneven bangs. "We leave two seconds after those motors have been tested."

***

The motors worked perfectly and, to Niss's ready admission, even improved steering.

The components for the *Bane*'s motors took up lots of space but fit, and the few extra items were no issue. Both ships sat comfortable on the water.

And there was no need for fuel.

"Each time you start the motor, it tastes salt and wants more," was how Barrow explained it.

"And there's no magick to it?" Niss asked.

"Perhaps just enough," the young woman had said with a smile, then turned with the pretense of studiously checking straps holding her precious cargo down.

Niss had never had a ship of her own. Being beside Maab was more than enough. Maab Pinyasama was home. But should there ever be a need for Niss Killa to have a separate home, *Perhaps Just Enough* would be its name.

She made her goodbyes to the first mate of the *Cornell* and his blood-red ship. An agreeable sun brightened the day.

"We ship off!" Niss announced, at which a sizeable portion of early-rising math weavers heartily cheered.

* * *

They stopped for a sample.

Sarantain was a quiet, watchful soul by nature. Niss thought nothing of him scanning the sea and sky as Dedoura piloted the other boat, both vessels not quite as fleet as fish but thrumming along nicely, courses true for the *Bane* by way of dead behemoths.

"Have you made allowance for drift?" Barrow asked. She sailed with Niss and Jackson.

"No need," said Niss. "The ichor sets."

"Sets? Atop the ocean? Even kelp masses big as islands drift."

"Luv?"

"Yes?"

"We've experience."

The body of the giant cobalt eel, an animal so rarely spotted it was exalted rather than mythical, floated like the intestines from a god, its pale yellow dorsal sail being the only thing putting the lie to that.

Niss and Sarantain idled their motors while Barrow snapped poles end to end, clamped a glass container to the long pole's tip, and affixed a heavily lined bag to a pulley running from the pole's base to the tip.

"You're entirely certain of your devices?" said Niss. "We prefer not to invite death."

"From what you've told me, this ick surrounded your ship without plague. Beyond that, I've no idea. But I do know substances. I'll have this one's secrets in battle."

"Into the fray, young beauty."

Barrow dropped to her knees foreship, centered her mass, and leaned outward, feeding the sturdy pole bit by bit into the water and letting it come up just under the edge of the black slick surrounding the eel.

The slick behaved as with the lifting of the edge of a blanket, not oozing into the container but sitting on the glass's rim, whole. A solid film. Barrow levered the container's lid shut, severing a circle of ooze, then yanked a thinner pulley system that snapped clamps into locking position atop the glass lip.

"Nothing gets out of that unless it burns its way out," said Barrow. "We know acid's not one of this thing's traits." Tugging the main pulley jerked the bag forward till it rested under the bottle. Barrow disengaged the clamp, the bottle fell in, and the scientific booty was brought onto the boat. She immediately stored the bag in a lightweight metallic box, then prepared another glass and bag.

Niss checked on Sarantain, who glanced over to check on Niss. Then she noticed the puzzled frown on his face.

"Storm's approaching," he said. "This ain't a sky for storms." He directed her eye to the distant eastern horizon, which looked as though the goddess had drawn the faintest charcoal line beneath the clouds then smudged it.

Both sailors pulled sights from their belts. Dedoura was already moving to steer closer to Jackson and Niss.

High clouds slowly obeyed the westerly winds. The smudge did not.

"Wizard," Niss said to Barrow, "have you a better sight than this?"

"In the green sack."

Niss quickly retrieved it and trained it on the mass. The instrument was not only better, it adjusted to astounding clarity. Niss felt able to touch the image.

She did not want to. "That's no storm!" she called across to Sarantain. "Ravens."

Barrow stowed everything safely and nodded at Jackson to restart the motor at the same time as Niss.

"Follow Dedoura," Niss said, steadying herself to take the measure of the cloud. She couldn't read raven faces but she could read the intent of bodies.

Through the scope: searavens thick as a storm, all rigid as spears, gliding fast as arrows, violently slapping the air whenever an updraft gave out. All gaining ground on the two boats faster than the unmoving horizon made their flight appear.

"We can't outrun them," Niss shouted over the motors to Jackson.

"We move anyway."

Niss turned a not-too-hopeful eye to Barrow. "Weapons?"

"Nothing of use."

The graying warrior put the scope away. "Face to the wind," she told the young one. "You don't look back. Do you understand me?"

Barrow nodded and sat amidships, emptying her mind of all thoughts.

"Not the test of the motors any of us would have desired," Niss said to the woman's back. "Unless you've maths we don't know about."

Barrow, over her shoulder, said, "Sometimes, math can get unpredictably dangerous." She snatched a glance upward.

Niss knelt to retrieve her bow and quiver. "Eyes front, luv." *Luv.* A usage she'd picked up from Pinyasama.

I know to whom my heart is bound, hummed Niss as the fine hairs on the back of her tough neck imagined the approach of the baleful mass. Orange flags fluttered wildly on both boats, but there'd be no discourse between parties when the ravens reached them. One didn't travel in numbers like that to talk.

"Do you know songs, girl?"

"None that I can call forth."

"Then have mine." And Niss sang out as clearly, as robustly, as the sea, the wind, and whatever surly gods allowed, wishing her captain could hear her belting it this one last time, and hoping dearly that the kind woman stayed protected always.

I know to whom my heart is bound,
I know 'tis bound for you.
I know to whom my heart is bound,
Let me lash myself to you.
And should we part, I'll send my heart…
To search all worlds for you.

Niss looked across to Sarantain, who must have heard some part of it, because he smiled at her and raised one fist in the air. Niss and Jackson returned the fist, Jackson's other hand never leaving the tiller.

The motors chugged fiercely. Minutes. Then minutes stretching.

Only two boats sailing the Great Goddess's sea. Beautiful weather. Clouds wispy as plant fluff. The sun at their backs. Until it wasn't only two boats.

The quality of the air shifted. Not darkly. In that way of something momentarily sliding past the sun.

The cloud was close enough that those on the sea heard the ravens' anger.

It sounded like a caress.

Not a single caw or screech as the ravens sheared the sky, nothing but thousands of wings swimming atop air, a more-palpable silence than had surrounded the boats for the past minutes.

In the span of seconds: early evening, an evening that stretched outward before all watchful eyes until they stared at the rear of it and the sun returned.

A cloud of ravens, their course sure, their course swift, passing over the boats.

Straight for the *Bane*.

In the sea deep beneath the intervening sky: a dark mass

moving just as swiftly, seen by Niss, and in the same direction.

Niss could do nothing but wish she had a bigger, faster boat.

Or a young witch with portals at her fingertips and eyes made of light.

❉ ❉ ❉

The call went out on the *Bane* toward dusk. "Captain? Incoming airbound, thirty degrees starboard aft!"

Maab pulled her scope and viewed the angle. A thin dart of a cloud undulated against the sienna sky. The *Bane*'s arcing course put the moon in front of the ship. The dart had the setting sun behind it, throwing nothing but beauty and mystery Maab's way.

The scope put reality to the mystery.

"Ms. Skye," Maab said quietly, "weapons ports open, if you please. Full cannon, visible and well lit. Swords and bows on deck. I want this ship to bristle."

Skye, beside the captain, lowered her own scope, just as quietly saying, "Aye," then heading off.

❉ ❉ ❉

Below, Nyim heard Maab. "Crow's nest! Three times hard on the bell."

Three resounding peals grabbed the attention of anyone unaware.

Nyim grabbed at Cedar as she moved rapidly with Leena. "What's that mean? What's happening?"

"Battle stations," Leena answered.

"Where should I hide?"

"Three rings is everyone," Leena explained, "otherwise, none of us lives to dress the wounds of another. Stand ready and *listen*."

Before Nyim could retort, "But you're a merchant ship!" Leena and Cedar were gone.

A rumble of wheels and squeak of ports opening confused him. He hadn't even been aware this ship *had* cannons, but there was no mistaking the weights being shoved into place. Swords and bows appeared in hands as if by magic, but he knew it was merely practiced proficiency.

Amis and Amnandi bore toward him. They wheeled barrels of weapons. Amis had fully stocked quivers and bows, Amnandi rushed a block of wood with swords slotted into it.

"Mate wants you and me on torches," Amis said. "No lights go out."

Amnandi set her block down, threw a portal, and grabbed Nyim's arm. The next moment, they were in ship's stores. She pointed him toward a wheeled barrel, this one with holes rather than slits cut in its top. A small, lidded bucket attached to the barrel's base below the handles sloshed with an acrid liquid.

"The light protects us," said Amnandi.

"From what?"

"Ourselves and fear. Keep them lit."

She threw the return portal. She, Amis, and Nyim stood ready.

Skye pulled the lever that turned the steps into ramps, at which Nyim, Amnandi, and Amis pushed forward.

The most disconcerting thing: the quietude on deck. Archers ringed the entire perimeter of the *Bane*'s teardrop. Without weapons, it might have seemed they were staring at the evening, looking for the first hint of stars. Swords caught bits of gold and purple.

"If you feel overwhelmed, find us," said Amnandi, and was off.

***

The captain herself kept watch on a particular patch of evening, and gradually realized that the vague uneasiness she'd felt a good hour before the bells wasn't due to the monthly bleeding she'd wadded away, but from this soaring concentration of malevolence.

The mystic stood beside her, slowly growing taller.

The cloud gradually evolved wings. The wings sprouted beaks. The bodies—the smallest as large as Amis, the largest impossibly large for any bird—all angled downward and, as one, slapped the air hard enough to thunder.

The scope didn't waver. It was their eyes she wanted to see. Were they ensorcelled or of their own minds?

When the mass moved close enough that the question was answered, the crew heard Maab give the shout for arrows. Twenty bows swung upward.

I have birds as well, she thought, a line from a poem, *who fly as brutally as thee*.

One couldn't observe the world without learning that everything got angry. Everything howled in some way. A green plant would turn yellow. A fish would stiffen a spiky dorsal.

There were a thousand different faces of anger edging the approaching cloud.

Which spoke of a thousand different decisions made to threaten her crew.

Half the arrows were blunt, their oiled ends ready for the kiss of fire.

Nyim and Amis raced the deck, obliging that kiss.

From above, the *Bane* must have looked like a constellation adrift on the sea.

From deck, it seemed the night approached to collect its stars.

Maab bit down to order the water behind her eyes to calm itself. She looked upward at giant Daoud, now a good ten feet, holding a heavy oar as if it were a sparring staff.

She looked at Amnandi, then the rest of her crew. All that knowledge and experience on board, and things still came to holding a big stick.

She would not allow her crew to die as pointless killers. Twenty bows? Even two hundred would have been as effective as a sneeze against the thousands approaching.

"My soul is bound to thee," she said aloud, accepting all sins and faults on behalf of her crew.

It was apology. The next words out of her mouth made it so.

"Arrows to the sea!"

"Captain?" Skye said.

Maab whispered "This won't be won" to her.

Skye, equally low: "We're giving up?"

"We don't sail to die covered in someone else's blood! We won't heal by drinking poison."

"If they die fighting—"

"They die seeing which of them dies first. Look toward. At first, I saw a fight. It's not. It's a cleansing. We may never enjoy an afterlife, but we will live as we do in this one."

"Maab..."

"First volley into the sea. After that, I leave it to the crew. Shout it out; you've a louder voice than me."

Skye hesitated only long enough to see the captain's heart. "First volley into the sea!" her boom reinforced, loosing bow fingers one by one. To Maab: "The ravens might see us as mad."

"Which might not be a bad thing," Maab said to the big woman.

Maab closed her eyes for the beat needed to send a blessing to Mother Ayanda Khumalo. This wasn't a challenge her daughter could meet, and yet the girl ever ready to port people from danger, or to swing a staff, or render magicks perhaps even her mother hadn't seen, showed no fear.

Amnandi stayed too focused to be afraid, Maab knew that from the instant the girl first stepped foot on her ship that first time those seven years ago with her hulking chaperone, Bog. In the intervening years when either Ayanda or Amnandi visited, she'd seen it repeatedly.

The world had to make sense somehow.

A witch made it so as best they could.

This one had the heart of an immortal. If there was a long future, the books of Amnandi Khumalo were already written.

She caught Skye looking at her. Both their faces were wet.

"There's still a chance they'll want to talk," Skye said.

"Or pass on by," said Maab. She wiped at her eyes. "Neither of us are good liars." She caught a flash of blue at her periphery. Amnandi had appeared from the other end of the ship.

"Mer!" The witch ran to the ship's railing and shone her eyes downward. The twilight water was nubbly with heads, a surfacing of underwater life unlike anyone aboard the ship had ever seen.

One could practically step off the *Bane* and walk in any direction.

The waters surrounding the island of Merfolk vibrated, the intensity gradually increasing.

Maab looked to the mystic, hope in her eyes.

He looked to Amnandi for the same.

There would be no defense against this as well.

A massive, wordless shout blasted from the sea, one aimed as precisely at the ravens as an unavoidable arrow.

The outer edge of the storm scattered into midair collisions and squawkings clear as vehement curses.

None, however, fell from the sky, and they regrouped quickly as rain interrupted by thunder.

The mental howl went out louder this time, and it was Maab and her crew who dropped. People fell to their knees, bows clattered from hands, and hands ineffectually covered ears in an attempt to block what wasn't there.

STOP!

RUKKAI

The cloud above split in two. From its middle, five ravens descended, circled the *Bane* as its crew regained their feet, then pirouetted to glide into the waters a prudent distance from the Mer.

The conversation appeared to the humans as unmoving silence punctuated by squawking and random furious flapping.

"We will know what she knows of the dead," the lead raven, one still young despite her powerful bearing, said. Her plumage was tipped in red.

"We will exact vengeance," said another.

"We have pledged a bond with this ship," said Rukkai. "Scratch it, you cut us. Cut it, you impale us. Kill it, you guarantee we hunt."

"The human has declared war on us."

"It was one of your own."

"The human flees."

"She did not even know you pursued."

The speaker for the dead zipped into human-like form. She swam to the line of Mer and grasped the head of one at random. "The deaths…"

A cold sensation of death linked through to each Mer, but more than death. A terrible anguish, one so unfathomable that the departing soul's only response was a miniscule "Why?"

A lament.

Answerable only by unending tears.

Nothing moved for long moments. Even the water seemed to cease flowing between the tight press of Mer bodies. Aboard the ship, only a few paid mind to what was happening. Rukkai felt them. The rest were in extreme pain, their eyes barely focused enough to see one another, let alone the transpirings atop a mournful sea.

There were two who had eyes, focusing all hopes on Rukkai.

Amnandi and the mystic. He who towered over her, over all of them.

He whom Maab had trusted to be a physic. And who now wished he knew the things Rukkai knew.

*＊＊

When the ship recovered, when all were asleep except the mystic and the witch, and the *Bane*'s anchors lay deep in watery silt, when nothing atop the onyx sea gave evidence of a single disturbance in its day, Amnandi whispered to the mystic through the curtain defining his room, "You sensed them. You knew."

His whisper back: "What could anyone on this ship have done? Fretted. An inevitability. Sometimes, death comes quickly."

"I've found that those who say death comes quickly rarely consider that death doesn't have to come at all."

And she left him there because she was angry and tired and dangerous.

TO THE COLD LANDS AND DRAGOONS

When Niss found the *Bane* along its plotted course, they hauled all the pieces of the new equipment and shuffled them into Sarantain's spacious storage depot.

Maab had ordered full stop for the reunion. Sarantain, Cedar, and Barrow made straight for the depot without being told. The goal was to have the *Bane* outfitted by next day's lunch and underway before supper.

Carpentry had the entire crew at its disposal.

Barrow had explained the plans and principles, walking along with Maab to inspect the ship, making calculations in her mind as to the curvatures of the uniquely designed vessel, weight bearings, stress tolerances.

"This will be basic installation, as we're not drydocked, but it will hold," the scientist reported, then curtsied awkwardly while blurting, "Thanking you kindly for permitting me this honor. A field test of this nature is invaluable."

"This is not a test, luv. Your full name?" said Maab.

"Barrow Field."

"Ms. Field, my ship is your home for as long as you see fit."

"Do I have permission to fiddle?"

Maab exchanged a wary glance with Skye. "Fiddle?"

"No matter where one is, no matter what one's doing, there are always bits for improving. I'll do nothing that harms the ship."

"Provide a log of all you do," said the captain.

"I'm told there's a witch on board. We were interrupted before I could be told who. I wish to meet them."

"You already have," said Maab.

"Your carpenters are going over the plans again to make sure all's well and understood. The crew can expect to assist with full installation very soon."

***

And very soon Maab gazed on progress. *My ship*, Maab thought, *has grown fins*. Three, to be precise. Two for stability, one for brute thrust and steering. The three motors mounted directly to the hull were housed under protective metal fins that drew water over and away from the ship. *Shiny flippers. Shiny flippers in the face of doom.*

Right and proper.

There were only three people aboard the ship: Barrow, Sarantain, and Cedar. Everyone else occupied every rowboat, raft, and dinghy the *Bane* held, watching their home from just a bit away. Not that anything untoward was going to happen. Maab wouldn't have allowed *anyone* to remain aboard if there was a chance in her reassured mind of something untoward happening.

But there was still a chance, and there was no way anyone would pretend seeing their big boat flex its flippers wasn't best appreciated as a gawping spectator rather than someone at work.

She sighted Sarantain, at the wheel, trying to ignore all the holes they'd drilled in the ship to feed the various tubes and controls that linked each engine to the rear thrust's command.

Maab raised a horn to her lips and gave a short blow.

Cedar blew *Received*.

And in what felt like forever, she watched the boat move without wind, gaining speed moment by moment in a wide berth around the flotilla, with Cedar calling each increase through her horn. Sarantain steered. Barrow worked arcane bits below.

"Three-quarter speed!" had the ship cleaving the water as though running to meet a lover.

Cheers went out as the great teardrop completed its circle and resumed a lateral course.

The cheers grew into outright hoots and joyful curses as full power pushed the *Bane* as though the goddess herself swam ahead to tow it.

They would reach everywhere in the world in half the time or better.

Maab felt certain that somewhere deep below, in their own way, the Mer cheered for her too.

That thought helped her mood more than she expected.

❋ ❋ ❋

She was a somber ship for two days as ebullience wore off, mortality set in, and thoughts of loved ones far away added weight no matter how swiftly she raced. Maab stayed on deck when needed but scarcely more, instead conferring with the mystic or consulting charts. Skye barely slept, being spotted night or day.

Barrow, whom the three youngest crewmembers had hoped to learn from, spent most of her time with Cedar and Sarantain, checking for stresses, leaks, or outright failures.

People were feeling ghostlike, even Amnandi, who had taken to silence as refuge again.

"Ms. Khumalo," said Maab, "a word."

Night had fallen. Under a clear sky, each star was a dessert offering a different taste. The skeleton crew that served as the night shift, accustomed to seeing the young witch staring upward under such infinite skies, always gave her space. Watching her take joy from distant light was calming.

"You and Skye are both awake," said Amnandi. "She was here barely minutes ago. The mystic knew the ravens approached and said nothing."

"He and I have spoken on that." The captain's pink silks caught Sharda's glow and became suffused. Maab said nothing further, which let Amnandi know the matter was settled.

The two contented themselves with the stars and the crisp air offered by the *Bane*'s passage.

Then: "I offer apology to you, daughter."

"I've chosen every moment of this voyage," said Amnandi.

"Doesn't matter." Maab lifted her gaze from the sea to the firmament. "This is the part of the sky where the constellations slam together. Nothing but a mass of lights trying to outshine each other. Do you see such an attempt as the foolishness it is?"

"I do."

"This world deserves to be worthy of you, luv. If your mother were here..."

"She's on a mountaintop. Totally isolated. Meditating."

"If any harm comes to you..."

"Heart Mother..."

"No, never get formal under beauty like this." Amnandi followed Maab's lead, head firmly to the stars. "I'm fairly sure the gods intended such sights only for poetry and love. I love you, Amnandi Khumalo."

Amnandi didn't care to wonder when tears had entered her own eyes. "To Sharda moon and back?" the young witch asked.

"Sharda moon and back."

✻✻✻

I hate the cold. Those who relish in it make me suspicious. Yet the crew, despite being bundled, is happy. Knowing the Mer swim beneath us contributes to their happiness. We've reached the first of Magrath's Archipelagos. They're still green, but I suspect running across their grass would bring no pleasure. A goods station asked if we'd encountered talk of sea beasts dying, or if we'd seen it ourselves. The shopkeeper said she'd heard rumor of an entire shoal of fish dead along the peninsula, which is where we head next. "No cause for it," she said. "Magrath's waters are pristine."

Maab thanked her with only a "We sail that way," then led us back to the Bane *with our goods. Perhaps Maab thinks the goddess sent us on an individual mission, but the concern in the keeper's voice told me otherwise. We shall see.*

For now, I am safe. We all are. I've taught myself new magicks and learned new maths.

May we prove medicinal as this slow sickness enters the veins of the world. We will not let it reach Afrela; Maab has promised me this.

And with these words, I promise you as well.

✻✻✻

A late-night meeting. Maab, her carpenters, the mystic. Amnandi off to the side, invited to observe.

A convocation of possibilities.

"This seemed very simple to me at the beginning," Maab wanted to say, but the mystic's gaze was too piercing. She didn't need deep splinters being dug from her.

What she would've continued on with, equally simple, was "Seek the physic, find the physic, deliver the physic, continue on with life. See Ayanda again. Have a great feast with her. Go homeward. Show mama-ti my ship's new fins. *Be alive and happy.*"

"Was there no way the ravens might have assisted us?" was what came out.

Sarantain and Cedar watched the exchange with interest. If this voyage planned to shatter their ship, they wanted all necessary preparatory information in advance.

The four sat on crates and ringed a tin brazier trying its best to free sparks from a wire-mesh dome. The deck was quiet, the crew sparse and engaged in their own conversations or deep monologues.

Daoud, far from being dismissive, was sympathetic. "Have you ever known a searaven to be helpful?"

"Once or twice," said Maab.

"And far between," Daoud completed for her. "Their history is full of self-interest and greed. Childishness equated with power." He shook his head. "They would not have helped. The Mer will see us through."

Cedar leaned forward, cast herself inside all the personal space. "As to the Mer, you're putting full trust in them?"

"I've never known a Mer to lie," said Daoud.

"And I've never had a lover worth breakfast, yet I've split a biscuit with more than a few," said Cedar.

"I see them as trustworthy," said Maab, "until we have reason not to."

"That's not saying a lot, Captain," said Cedar. "Pardoning my rough foot."

"We have nothing else to work with," said Maab. "They sensed the same urgency from Erah as this ship and crew did. They've yet to turn back, even though they could've been gone twenty times over and we wouldn't have had a clue. I'm not concerned about the Mer's intentions. Mystic, we are being led by hounds we can't see. What are the chances we can locate a dragoon? And how do we not die in doing so? I've never tugged the tail of an elemental being."

"We know for a fact," Daoud began, but was interrupted by both Sarantain and Cedar's simultaneous:

"Do we?"

"If you've trust in me, you do. Dragoon are fact. As real as that fire."

"Then how can something that large remain unseen?" said Cedar.

"Had you ever seen a mystic before?" Daoud asked.

The old woman shook her head.

"Yet we are everywhere."

"Doing pissing what?" Cedar said. "Pardon, but I've seen the young on this ship exhaust themselves. If this world's rules are that they have to use themselves up before they've truly enjoyed, I don't see mystics as having more influence than the time of day. If all you plan to do is sketch the dragoon when we get to it, I'd like to know that now. Again, begging the captain's pardon."

"Do go on." Maab waved respectfully.

"I mean, just ask this one question to be at peace." Cedar pressed on, tapping the mystic's knee to make sure she had his complete attention. "Do you have any clue how to communicate with a dragoon?"

"A bridge to cross when we get to it," said the mystic.

"That's a facile phrase," said Cedar. "Barely worth me spitting at."

Maab spoke softly. "They'll understand us. If we get to a dragoon and wake it, it will *know*. How could it not?"

"So, we're hoping it's a being of starlight and intellect?" said Cedar. "Be nice to apply such hopes daily."

"We know it is," said Maab, casting eyes toward Daoud's direction for confirmation.

"Why's it not sensing this ick, then?"

"Perhaps it senses everything as a dream," said Daoud, "a dream at times wondrous, at times painful. What escapes regret? Even a stone can have reason to bemoan its placement. Perhaps it needs to be shocked to step outside the usual noise."

"Sarantain," said Maab. "You're too quiet."

"Quietly learning, mum. Cedar's said all I needed. The ship'll be ready for whatever you ask."

Maab touched her heart and forehead in thanks for his silence and affirmation. "*Perhaps* is a vague word," said the captain, "despite being large and ponderous. But it can be a tool of precision as well, as real as a chisel. Perhaps we'll find a dragoon. Perhaps it is aware of the problem and has not acted. Perhaps, very simply and succinctly, all it needs is a nudge."

AMIS WITH AMNANDI

Before rounding a mountainous cape toward open seas, they put into port once again. Tempest Red, a craggy place sometimes mentioned by traveling poets for its wars and feuds from long ago, always seemed embroiled in some fasion for such an out-of-the-way place. It was the last stop to anyone using the colder climes as a shortcut to the tip of the other side of Erah. Furs, boots, lard, mittens—last chance, highest price, because the wind, when it bit there, used molars to grind, not fangs to bite.

Amis and Amnandi, pushing separate wooden carts behind Cedar and Sarantain, bundled extremely well against the teeth. Wraps around both their heads, leathers under tunics and breeches, light jackets covering, and fingered gloves. The only colorful thing Amnandi wore was a blue scarf barely visible below her collar, looped snugly around her neck.

"Would you wager they've done it?" Amis whispered, hoping she was well out of earshot of their elders but unable to contain the question anymore.

"Sarantain is respectful of Grucca."

"I don't mean now. When they were younger."

"I doubt it. They probably didn't know each other when they were 'younger.'"

"There's too much history there. They've done it."

"Not talking is always an option."

"This keeps my mind off the cold."

"So speaking of the sex lives of mentors—"

"Is a meditation, yes." Amis's laugh drew the elders' attention backward.

Amis remarked on Barrow. "I think the scientist is sweet on me. Keeps finding reasons to ask me questions."

"About?"

"To be honest, they're about you, roundabout."

"So perhaps she's interested in me."

"I don't see how," Amis said, genuinely unsure. "Let me ask this: you frightened? I've seen your night wandering. Nothing bothers you."

"I'm bothered by everything."

"Ladies!" Cedar called to their lagging feet. "Pace up." Cedar and Sarantain veered toward an iron shop.

There was no bustle to this place. The townspeople—sparse and quiet—moved in their wraps as though they were parcels on the way to delivery, heads up or down depending on the wind. It was a gray land, more rock than soil, more leaden cloud than inviting sky.

"You'd tell me if you needed me, wouldn't you?" Amis said.

"You're my sister."

"Forever and through all. I'll keep you updated on Barrow's

love for me."

"And Nyim's."

"And Nyim's"

"The Mer?"

"Each sick with need."

They moved close and let their shoulders bump.

"You're a good sister," said Amnandi.

"And I won't let anything happen to you. Unless I'm dead. Let's avoid that."

***

Every witch knew the planet thrived or died according to what lived on it. That was a basic known to even most children. Beneath Erah's crust, who knew? Arteries of heat-carrying lava accelerated surface germination worldwide. Nerve endings made up of spores traveling underground rivers with more tributaries than bee hives had honey relayed one region's health to another. Every lightning strike that made it to the ground was energy fed directly to Erah's heart.

Fools identified themselves in saying the world was not alive, that poetry was lies. But when they or the world showed sickness? Then it was *Comfort me, comfort me, give me stories to make me feel well.* Something Amnandi had heard her entire life.

Give me the heart of the world, give us green things and water and a chance to see the sky. The sun. Day become peaceful night. The universe, she thought.

Give us the universe that we had before.

An elder had wanted to see her.

The quiet lives of Tempest had sent the newcomers on their way well supplied and armed with information. An old woman there, a seer who had dreamed more visions than most people had breaths, got word to the shops to advise the giant, the knife, the staff, and the rain to visit her, and so Sarantain, Cedar, Amnandi and Amis found themselves in her home of stones and mudthatch, sitting on worn cushions around an in-ground fireplace whose smoke churned upward into a great iron belly, then a pipe, and out the roof where winds tore it.

"I've seen disease under the sea itself, eating its way upwards. It lays upon the silt a moment, then races as if freed. A new type of death," the seer told them from behind the smoke of a different kind of pipe.

"Soul sickness," said Amnandi.

"Heed this witch," said the seer, who'd not even seen reason to tell them her name. She emphasized the directive with a finger jabbed toward Amnandi's brain. "Something in the spirit of the world has changed. Do you know the world *anathema*?"

Sarantain, Cedar, and Amis said no. Young Khumalo said yes.

"It's hard to explain it in this paltry trading language," the seer fretted.

"Use your own tongue," said Amnandi. "I will translate." She had kept ear on the snatches of native conversation. The words weren't far removed from Quaddic, which she'd learned during two summers along the Hernan Coast on the more temperate end of Tempest's continent.

The seer released two mellifluous bursts.

"It is like," Amnandi said, "the instant turn of the stomach to long-soured milk. It is the soul of a thing tasting the wrongness of another." The seer's pat atop her hand told her she had translated the meaning well enough. She spoke again.

The seer's pronouncement: a ship on fire, the rising of a great beast, the four of them—the giant, the knife, the staff, and the rain—through uncertain mists.

And feathers. Feathers upon the water. But that could mean so many things.

"I am glad you came," the old woman said.

"Us particularly?" said Cedar. Prophecies unsettled her.

"Anyone. No one here will do it. We've grown small and shriveled. There's something out there. You travel toward it. I *feel* it."

"Is it what we need?" asked Sarantain.

The woman shrugged, a barely perceptible rise and fall of birdlike shoulders.

"But your sight?" said Cedar.

The woman grunted and pulled a wrap tighter around her. Unheard but quite heard, the words *I wish I traveled with you*.

"I wish you well," said the seer.

The four took their leave, saying goodbye to Tempest Red and its muffling cold.

"Why did she want the four of us particularly?" asked Amis.

"There is not always meaning," said Amnandi, "but the vision itself is important. The fact that we were seen may be enough."

"Said like a true witch," said Amis.

"We are all witches."

WE, THE WITCHES

By the time all supply crews made it back to the *Bane*, Skye had personally broken up two fights and been told by Leena of another. Nothing brutal. A shove here, an insult there. But worth bringing to the captain's attention, who, in Skye's eyes, spent far more time in counsel with the mystic and the scientist and considerably less walking the decks for her crew. What person was so learned enough to speak incessantly on things no one could know? True, this wasn't the ship's first quest, but god stuff was always unpredictable. This one even more so, because there was no direct line of sight between problem and goal.

No clear adversary, she mentally ticked off. Unseen allies.

And elementals. Which were older than gods, provided gods weren't fantasies. Every nation on Erah had gods. Some abided them, some found communion with them, some made servants of the very idea of them, most forgot they had been taught about them in the first place. Where Skye was from, a common phrase was *The goddess does not eclipse wages*, which didn't actively disrespect the goddess but it made relations pealingly clear.

She pointed this out as she and Maab oversaw the crew.

"This isn't a warship, Patrice. The crew don't need an adversary."

"This is barely a merchant ship, a freedom this crew loves. But now they're not sure of even that."

"What do you recommend?"

"I've none. Which doesn't help my own disposition."

"Maybe throw a few punches at me?"

"It'd be fun, but no. It satisfies me to make you aware. It wouldn't hurt to have you wandering above decks a bit more. Legends need to be seen."

"I'll give speeches nonstop."

Skye mulled this. "Mutiny sharpens purpose too, I suppose. Taking the captain's leave, if she doesn't mind."

"She looks forward to your next counsel."

***

Nyim had been one of the ones fighting. When Amis saw the swelling blooming at his left cheek, she was incensed. Not two hours off the ship and people were trying to kill him? Had they not seen she favored him? She needed details.

"It wasn't a fight," he said, trying to keep any notes of sulking out of his voice.

"Folks spontaneously bruise where you're from?"

"Mate Skye flung us apart. I lost footing and hit a barrel."

"Were you twirling?"

"I was...not graceful."

"What was it about?"

"I'd rather not say."

"It was about me. Fighting for my honor."

"You have honor?"

She would've hit him but she'd noticed he, like Amnandi, didn't always intend to pair insult with questionable phrases. Which was likely what got him in a non-fight in the first place.

"You see me trying to show concern, yes?" she said. "So, just answer my damned question."

"She insulted my family by saying I had none. I cursed her in my native tongue. She spoke my native tongue..."

"Always assume everybody on this ship knows at least two languages. Maab travels everywhere."

"I had no idea my attacker had ever been anywhere near Afrela, let alone my peoples. It looks like she's never spent a day in the sun, despite being crew on open seas. She's paler than you. I called her a mindless worm."

"Worth getting smacked. And I know who you're talking about. She's not one for anger without provocation. What else you do?"

He shrugged.

"Let me be more precise: what idiocy'd you say to her before or after that?"

"You're influenced by your witch too much. You sound like her."

"Flattery can't confuse me."

"I told her I wouldn't have to do so much cleaning if filthy bastards would do basic minding after themselves. Go ashore, come back without wiping your boots. Drop a little food, know that a mouse or bird will get it. I told her they were the human equivalent of a tow rag."

"You called a seasoned woman of the sea a rope-tied rag we use to wipe our backsides...dangled out a hole into the sea afterward...to be cleaned as the goddess sees fit?"

"The captain has me cleaning the bowsprit way more than anyone else! I've noticed. The pisser's basically the entire floor—

how can they miss?"

"Nyim?"

"What?" he snapped.

"Stop talking before you get the other half of a set."

"You were ready to defend me."

"Amnandi will think before she speaks. Most times. You, you're literally the hole an ass fits in and your words—"

"Literally?"

"I said that to see if you'd offer correction, you golden idiot of immense proportions."

He hesitated.

"Speak. Up," Amis said.

"Apologies."

"If I didn't want to kiss you so much, I'd ask the goddess to strip away your lips."

He was stunned into silence.

"You've pissed me off. I'm on a grand adventure and you've pissed me off."

"Apologies."

"Gonna go talk science to blow off steam."

"I..."

She whirled. "Science, Nyim!"

That meant Barrow. They were on a perilous, no-turning-back mission from this point—actually, had been for several points—so this was no time for delaying honest aims.

"Barrow!" Amis shouted when she found the young woman sorting gears and cogs.

Startled, Barrow looked up, immediately expecting dangerous news.

"You've got designs on Amnandi," said Amis, who then read the deep, unspeaking frown on Barrow's face as dawning comprehension. "Go to her; she calls to you."

"Does she, now?"

"Not as is heard."

"I see," said Barrow.

A flash of blue tinged the edges of their space. As if on cue, Amnandi exited a portal with a wave at Amis but beckoning Barrow. "The captain wants to see us immediately."

No matter what, Erah sowed love. Erah found a way. The short, uncouth, scruffy daughter of Sawyer Dotrig held to that.

"You too," Amnandi told Amis, waiting.

"Oh." Amis entered the portal. The three disappeared.

✸✸✸

Seers. Maab Pinyasama didn't care for them. What they saw wasn't necessarily true, and rarely immediately useful. It often wasn't a matter of interpretation but of Time. A seer could see an exact thing but have no idea if, when, or in what world—for seers had been known to spout ideas from mirror places—the event might occur.

And, at times, the seeing wasn't meant to be a vision but a spur.

Those, to Maab, were the worst.

Sarantain, Cedar, Amnandi, and Amis watched Maab pace. Barrow and Daoud sat quietly at the rear of the captain's quarters, Barrow making notes and Daoud staring over steepled fingers.

"This ship in flames could mean many things," the captain was saying.

"The first being the ship will be on fire," Skye pointed out.

"On fire, perhaps reborn. Vigorously triumphant. Favored. By the goddess, I will take a boon of simple luck," said Maab.

"Or on fire," said the mate.

Maab stopped pacing. "Noted." She studied the four waiting on her. She ticked off on her fingers. "Giant, knife, staff, rain."

"I'm big," said Sarantain.

"Told I can be cutting." This from Cedar.

"I am lean, long, and precise." Amnandi.

"I've no idea," said Amis.

"A volcano, perhaps," said Maab, not to Amis but to every wild thought crowding her. "Where better to seek dragoon than in Erah's first furnaces?"

Sarantain tapped a finger on the tabletop. "Feathers on the water," he said, raising eyebrows at the captain. "Not ambiguous at all."

"We're not going to suddenly realize this trip is dangerous," said Maab. "I'll not tolerate that from this fine bunch."

"A seer knew we were coming and sought us out, Captain," said Sarantain. "That, to me, suggests a powerful vision."

"Daoud?" said Maab, looking over the heads of the crew.

"Pondering," responded the mystic.

Maab arrowed attention toward Barrow. "What does science say? Be as vague as need be."

"If this ship catches fire, there's little my motors can do," said Barrow. "However, from what I know of visions, which is hearsay only, I can guarantee nothing not ablaze will fail at a critical moment."

"Good enough," said Maab.

"We sail?" asked Skye.

The captain nodded.

All stood and made to leave...except the mystic.

"A moment," said Daoud.

Everyone stopped.

"Perhaps we should speak of trust and expectations."

"Our attention is yours," said Maab.

"You came to Fabbin and saw many wonders, things myself and my cohort live with every day, but even we have no guarantees. We run toward voices in the dark same as you, until we find answers. Do we agree to journey together, extending that grace to all of us?"

It did not surprise Maab that Amnandi Khumalo answered first. "We do," she said. All other voices followed.

"We do this for our home," said Daoud. "May the goddess see fit to assist."

"We do this," said Maab, "even if she doesn't. To your posts."

The *Bane* got underway.

***

They encountered two ships mere leagues from Tempest, two ships both as underfed as abandoned pups, equally malnourished in spirit. Both apparently waiting, flying no flags or colors to identify them with a port of origin, which told the watchful eyes on the *Bane* that they were sons of Tempest. It wasn't unheard-of for distant ports to levy unofficial "taxes" on those voyaging their waters. But they generally picked the defenseless. Random explorers meeting accidental deaths were common; small passenger ships making use of the arctic shortcut often reached their final destinations short of personal effects.

The sea knew the stories of the sea.

But it was a hungry dog that attempted to bite a merchant ship or better. Merchants tended to talk about mishaps and were generally prepared to put up a fight.

"Do we steer 'round, Captain?" Skye asked.

"They've set a clear-enough message. We'll speak," said Maab. "Cut engines. Drift." She motioned for her horn. The day was cold, the sky nothing but bits of gray on darker gray. It wasn't conversation weather. "You in need of assistance?" she called out a sensible distance away.

The least scruffy of the gray ships responded. "No, Captain." A scratchy voice, one accustomed to shouting rather than speaking.

"Good sailing to you, then." Maab didn't give the order for engines. She waited.

"That's why we're here," said the gray. "To ensure good sailing for all. You've an interesting ship. I plan to respect that."

"These dogs are well practiced at maintaining flanks on those they converse with," said Skye to her captain. "Just three ships having a momentary bob on desolate, isolated waters."

"It would be interesting to ask you questions about such a unique ship," the scratchy voice said through his horn.

"Should the goddess see fit to arrange port for us together. Till then, Captain?"

A short delay. Maab could tell the grays weren't used to this much talking. "Well, Captain," the scratchy ambassador said, "if you can see your way to sharing a bit of your hold, we can move toward that day."

The *Bane*'s momentum brought the ship gradually closer to the dogs. A crewperson whispered to Skye, who then whispered to Maab.

The dogs' cannons weren't many, but they were well maintained.

"By the amount you traded off," the gray continued, "I'd say we can both leave this transaction peaceful and well."

"You see the flag I bear?" said Maab.

"Hence my patience."

"Amnandi, Sarantain," Maab whispered. "I want their captains. Can you do that?"

Sarantain moved closer to Amnandi.

"When you're ready," Maab whispered.

"The port ship first," Sarantain told Amnandi.

"Your sister ship," Maab called out. "Who speaks for her?"

"I do for both."

"It's a poor ship captained with puppet strings," said Maab. She waited. A moment later, a deeper voice with the same ragged undertones as the first.

"I speak!"

"Will you require a separate levy?"

"We are *family*," the first captain sneered. Maab could tell he thought himself witty. "We share as blessed Mum taught."

Amnandi had already made her way to the crow stack and climbed its lee side. Amis handed her the scope and pointed.

The second captain put on the appearance of being an ugly person when all he needed was to shave and right his posture.

Amnandi climbed down to make her unobtrusive way back to Sarantain, who had moved to the rear of the crew on deck, obscured from any searching eyes on the other ships unless they were looking specifically toward him. But then, all they would see was a head above other heads, a blue blink, and the head gone. A head and very tall, hard body appearing from a shimmering blue rip that opened and closed so adroitly on a gray, scratched deck that the deck's scruffy, bundled captain was barely heard to squawk before being yanked inside a new hole that appeared after a tall Black girl in a colorful headscarf ran from the first and into the second.

Five seconds later, the first gray captain joined his brother at the epicenter of glinting swordpoints.

"Theft's a matter of odds, isn't it, Captain?" Maab said to the scruffier of the two.

The first scratched his beard. "Always."

"You see a ship like this moving on its own, are you not curious? Do you not want to follow? To see what will be seen where it goes? Where's your imagination, sir?" asked Maab.

"Bad crop of imagination this year." He clearly had no plans capitulating, although he stood unbound holding his own hands behind his back, his own sword and ankle daggers already in the hands of Maab's crew. "Took to sea for donations."

Maab walked to within arm's distance of him, her crew moving smoothly aside.

"My ship's still got weapons, Miss," he reminded her.

"Your ship's seen what mine can do. Name yourself."

"Ringgode." He glanced at the other gray, giving the stout, tattered man leave to speak.

"Paool," said the other.

"He goes by *the Walrus*," said Ringgode. "Flops in bed vigorously. Miss."

"We could drop you this instant in cold waters too far from your ships to reach you in time," said Maab.

Keeping eye on both of them, Ringgode, the deeper-voiced one, hadn't stopped searching his surroundings since the instant his brain accepted the strange thing that had happened to him. "This ship. Not official enough or rich enough to commit depravities."

"Threaten you with something stronger, is it?" Maab asked.

"That's the game."

"One of you goes back to your ship, one doesn't. Which of you's the better thief?" She pointed at Paool. "He answers first."

"I am," Paool answered.

Maab trained her hard eyes on the other.

"I lead," Ringgode the first captain said. "He thieves."

"You heard the expression *There's no greater thief than a self-professed leader*?"

Cold air must have snaked up the leader's leg, because Maab surely saw a shiver.

"Then this is what we shall do." She turned to Ringgode. "He stays with us. You'll not follow us or speak of us in any way. Your ships will become fishing ships while I'm away, or kindling when I return."

"This is body theft, Miss," said Ringgode.

"Captain Maab Pinyasama," she said. Skye stood mere feet from her. "We extend free passage to someone and he calls it body theft."

"Manners on the sea aren't what they were, ma'am," said Skye.

"Daughter," Maab called.

Amnandi came forward.

The captain gave a nod to her. "We're done here."

With a flash of blue, any attempt at piracy was over.

"I'm going to assume you know these waters a little better than I do," Maab said to the smelly, disheveled man known as the Walrus as he watched his and his cohort's ships recede across the choppy gray sea. Before he could answer, his hands were tied behind him by Sarantain. As he was led away, he heard Maab say, "Full speed."

❋ ❋ ❋

Ice, no rarity for sailors, was fascinating. Rain may have nourished Erah, but the two extremes, frigidity and fire, created it. Slowly, over the course of days, ice dotted the *Bane* along small sections of railing and between braids of rope. Oils were applied more frequently to both ship and selves. Good-natured insults and other pleasantries were delivered more efficiently. Worries about the Mer's lack of presence filtered to Maab's or Skye's ears here and there, but the captain gave the reassurance that the Mer were as deep swimmers as massive whales, and had likely mapped the sea's invisible currents better than anyone on land had drawn borders on Erah.

It didn't miss Maab's sight that Amnandi had become significantly withdrawn.

Invitations to games got furtive rejections. Humming brought no humming from her. And the ship hadn't heard a note from her koka since...

This damned journey.

Maab made it clear that no one except herself was to speak to Amnandi on this, including and particularly Amis. A witch's privacy was made of stone.

The one person Amnandi wasn't avoiding was the mystic. Maab and Skye both noted it. She was studying him. Nearly stalking, seen by Daoud only when she wished to be.

The *Bane* became a strange zoo for a bit, like those gaudily tented attractions in inland cities that promised intrigue, frights, and animals some had yet to encounter.

Except here, Maab thought, her eyes on gangly Khumalo carrying food to the passenger, who remained bound at all times, one wrist and one ankle tied together with a rope of short-enough length as to make the effectiveness of either limb useless; here, the strange beasts were nerves gradually unraveling.

The girl moved minus her soul.

Maab summoned her to her quarters that afternoon.

Amnandi entered just as the last of the persistent clouds drifted away, leaving the ship and sea bathed in momentary sunlight.

Maab offered no preamble, saying softly, "What's wrong, daughter?"

Amnandi looked at the floor.

"Is it hard to lift your head? Are even your eyes heavier? Come sit."

"May I stand?" Amnandi said, and for the first time in a long time, Maab noticed that despite Amnandi's height, despite Amnandi's abilities, despite the young Khumalo no longer being a child, she was still wholly that: young. Young and constantly surrounded by those who needed some of her to balance their lives.

Maab had forgotten how much stamina it took to be a decent person. "Stand, provided you take my hands."

Amnandi did this without protest. Her hands were larger than Maab's, even less chilly than Maab's, as though witches offered warmth without being asked. But they fit comfortably in the captain's. Their arms formed a bridge under Maab's upraised eyes.

"I need to be in water, mother," Amnandi said, suddenly as close to trembling as Maab had ever felt her.

"This water's cold as death," Maab said.

And then the truth of it for someone so accustomed to speaking only truths. "Meditation has been cloudy. I've been with people too long. Please? I need…"

Maab shushed her, released her, and took her chin in her fingertips to bend her. She kissed Amnandi's forehead as she had seen Amnandi's mother do numerous times, and immediately felt the girl's brief tremor ease. "We've been in motion and you've been constantly needed."

Amnandi nodded.

"A moment, no more," agreed Maab.

***

The sun was muddy as the anchor dropped. Merfolk watched the substantial weight whiz through their ranks.

A second splash drew their attention.

The witch child. Several of them found that they missed her. It had been a long voyage even by Mer standards. The witch child had spent most of it aboard the vessel.

They felt her swim away from the ship. Even encumbered by more fabric than usual, Amnandi welcomed the sea's flow, temperature, shock, and pull, traversing languidly until mere strokes from the massive wooden sweep of the ship, where she twisted to her back, extended her arms, and simply floated while breathing very deeply.

The Merfolk amassed below moved well below the depth of sight from above. The waves of questions, waves of unspoken fears, waves of doubts from the ship and from the child reached them fine enough. But Rukkai and several others continued upward. They formed a ragged circle around the girl, not touching her, perhaps more in touch with her for that, seen from above only as smooth black humps bobbing like temporary islands.

They asked nothing of her. Their silence told her that her silence was fine. More than fine; it was power. And she was welcome to the entire ocean's worth of it.

When they sensed her body give off the tiny electrical signals that presaged movement, they knew she was about to leave. It had been brief, but the water was cold, the hardiest human frail, and daylight—without intending to—could convince one of warmth where there was no warmth and to drift where one shouldn't drift.

Humans were not made to sleep on the water, which was a tragedy the Mer could not fix.

They submerged before she exited her light trance, but she was aware of them, and they of her gratitude.

She swam to a knotted rope that waited for her and climbed aboard. Great chains moved upward.

Rukkai waited, straining its senses. "Get her warm" filtered down to the water; "get her warm and leave her be."

The powerful mechanical flippers spun.

THIEVERY

The thief, tied in the hold of the ship, thought he studied cagily. He did not.

"They let you in that freezing water? I know all about it; I've nothing to do but listen to people talk. What kind of ship is this? You're barely two steps from being a child."

Amnandi remained silent as she withdrew his emptied bowl that next day.

"Is good food, though," he rasped. "Keeps me regular. But you, girl, where're we off to?"

"Don't call me girl. You know my name."

"I can smell the livestock, so you're not hauling passengers. I've heard horses, so you're planning a bit of ground travel." He frowned up at her. Doing so cracked his dried lips even more, but he didn't care. His skin appeared as gray as the sky he lived under. "You questing? This ship on a quest? I didn't think anybody actually did that anymore."

"Your field of experience is narrow."

"Your captain leaves me down here in the cold."

"We work all day in the cold. You're warmer than us."

"You get to move about. I don't."

She said nothing.

"There's a bit of cruelty in you," Paool said, nodding as if setting something important in place. "Always in the quiet ones. Bit of lonely bile. Speaking thereof, I'd like to use the hole."

"No."

He tried to look surprised. Amnandi ignored this.

"Someone escorted you less than an hour ago," she said.

"Nothing gets by you, does it, gir—miss? One of the benefits of magick in your bones. Got my own flavor of magick. The seer is my mother. Twice removed. What I mean is my mum dies, the seer's daughter took me in. Her daughter died; she herself took me in. No magick in my bones, but it's in my head," he said, giving the back of his head three soft whacks against the post he was tethered to. "You ever kill anyone, miss? From what I'm told, quests involve a lot of death."

By this point, Amnandi was crouched before him, hands hanging loosely over her knees, bottom inches off the dead wood of the deck, her entire demeanor saying she could hold this position for hours. Without falter.

The thief shrank a bit when she cocked her head to one side and squinted at his eyes.

She was studying him! He didn't like that. Had nowhere to back up to, so instead, he shifted his butt a smidge away from her, but the motion didn't break the spell.

His adoptive third ma had told him of this day, of the day he'd have a witch pry his soul loose.

But that same old ma was also a liar who'd rather spin a web than sit quietly with her boredom. Not always but enough to remind the thief now that he was on a ship—something he knew—and he was faced with a girl—someone to manipulate. His ma could've said he'd rule a nation one day, and it'd add up to him shipwrecked with island crabs.

He made his face as slack and dull as possible while the girl stared at him.

She leaned in just a bit more. "Are you asking for an end?" she said. To his ears, the accent clipped the words, made them sharp at entry. This was an actual witch, his unseen constricting scrotum reminded him. A witch on water, which likely heightened her magicks. Ma had always said magicks were part and parcel of the goddess, not that anyone in Tempest gave half a thought to goddesses, sprites, celestials, or wraiths. The supernatural either took its place with them under the cold gray...or it stayed entirely the hell out of mind and out of the way.

He was on a boat, yes, but he was tied up. This was a girl, yes, a young woman, but a witch no less. She'd asked him in his own language if he was asking her for death, something he didn't doubt she could deliver.

Paool Tuteb answered quite slowly, "Making no requests of you, miss."

Amnandi stood as though he'd ceased to exist, spun the bowl to an easy rest between her forearm and side, and left.

The thief wondered how many nearby eyes had paid attention to that exchange. He pulled his hood over his face and sealed himself neck to foot in the thick blanket, thinking he heard the witch say, "Make it snow," but that was likely imagination, and imagination was but wishful thinking, same as he and his brother had thought this ship would be an easy wage.

Thievery might not have been his best destiny.

* * *

Maab regretted having crossed the galley to access the lower deck to groom the horses the minute she heard Leena's voice. Leena hadn't said a word to her on the way but stopped her on the return.

"Will we be bringing on more mouths to feed, Captain?" Leena said.

For a change, there was nobody else in the galley.

"You need to speak as family again?" Maab said.

"I do."

"As family, we prevented a pointless battle and are on our way. As family, my choices as captain don't fall under your review."

"As family, is there a point we turn around?"

"I don't know, Leena. I honestly do not know. This seemed simple."

"Amnandi has been watching you for guidance. This is your story, Maab. She *needs* to see what you do. You don't have the right to endanger us, but we have the right to choose, and we have chosen. When this becomes foolish or overly dangerous, listen to someone besides your heart." She gripped her sister-in-law by the shoulders. "Not every physic requires a full dosage before symptoms ease. Maybe we've done enough already. Maybe this is now a different story to tell. Stop shaking your head; you don't know it isn't. That feather sarong of yours is no guarantee of mysteries."

"Have I ever said it was?"

"You act like it. Sister, my wonderful, loving sister, know when to go home. It's all me or Skye or anyone on the crew who hasn't said...wants said."

"A widespread concern?"

"No. But we *are* heading for an eternal elemental. That's damn new territory, I'd say."

"It's a boring ship with only one destination...but I understand."

Leena released her and dried non-wet hands on her apron, her signal that a conversation was duly over.

"Don't decrease the thief's portions," said Maab.

"Nobody on my ship goes unnourished. Except its captain. You're getting a bit stringy. Used to be a bit of jiggle to the rear guard."

"My portion of jiggle will always be sufficient to any aims I have. Is there anything else before I cross paths with Skye for additional berating of my lack of ass?" Maab made to move off.

"A new song," the cook suggested. "'The Lovelorn Dance' is getting old."

＊＊＊

Maab started the song out of the blue by doing nothing more than stomping on the deck.

"I have never known a journey that I would not take with you, nor a drink nor meal nor song I would not share." She did not sing this. She boomed it, just as fully and boldly as if she'd been hours at a festival. The foot kept a steady four-four rhythm.

"Should we travel to a place where you've no trust for me nor me for you, we have left Erah for the unknowable worlds with one wish: to go back home."

Crew nearby picked up the next verse, letting the movement of their faces rouse blood to their hands and shake tingles away. Two voices at first, low in starting but quickly gaining volume.

"To journey home, we crash through stars, we bore through Sharda Moon

We fool the gods into believing we're kin

We make twilight of impending doom

For in half-light, half-dreams, we awake the dearest fate..."

"And in our full dream we what?!" shouted Maab, whirling so that each of the feathers atop her breeches flew.

"OUR DEAREST HOME WE MAKE!" boomed back, ten voices strong.

"Again!" shouted Maab.

"*Our dearest home we make!*" The entire deck.

"As you damn well were, dear loves!" She marched off to find her scientist to once again be assured every gear and cog was in place, functioning properly and—if need be—functioning beyond its means.

There were four more verses to the song. The crew continued as a single voice.

***

By the second night after Amnandi's swim, it was too cold for sleeping as deeply in the ship where they'd put the thief. Skye moved Paool to the carpentry section, where he remained tethered to an even-thicker post, and was frequently glared at by Sarantain and Cedar when they didn't outright ignore him.

"This is a ship of fools," the thief might seethe amidst sawing sessions, sawdust like persistent insects at his mouth and eyes. "Your captain dresses as a bird and thinks songs take the place of action. You've pups so clumsy, it's a wonder they haven't sunk the damn boat." He would wait, then, to see if anything he said got a reaction. Not necessarily anger. Anything. To be unseen was torment.

But a full day of seething was strenuous. After about eight hours, genuine questions settled on him.

"What's she going to do with me, for true?"

"What she said, you piratous piece of shite," said Cedar.

"You'll be dropped off when we're done," rumbled Sarantain.

"Your every mutter doesn't have to sound like it rolled down a mountain, Big Man," said Paool. "I know my place with you." He looked to Cedar. "And with you." She split logs with an axe so sharp, there was barely effort. "I've no quarrel with either of you."

"We fly the orange flag and you see fit to rob us?" Sarantain said, holding a borer that could easily drill through skulls or unmoving planks.

"We see fit to rob everybody."

The thief didn't know the various interplays of Sarantain's scarred jaw. Cedar laid a dirty hand on the big man's shoulder.

"There'd have been no violence had you complied," the thief asserted.

Sarantain set down the borer and crossed to the gray man occupying corner space in his workshop. He lowered to get face to face with him. "I have a husband waiting for me. Would you assure him of no violence? Can you cross the leagues and tell him I'd return to him unharmed minus a few wages?"

"I've had a witch kneel in my face. You don't scare me any more than she did. The measure of your captain is weakness. Leave me unharmed? I should have fish picking around a pike through my chest to get at breakfast."

Sarantain slapped him hard. The hulking carpenter gave the wide-eyed thief his full attention. "There is a *code* to the sea. I've spent decades teaching this to any youth who come aboard. The orange flag is inviolate."

"The orange flag would've served as a tablecloth for a good meal I too rarely eat," the thief spat back. "Speak to me no further, or I will scream for your captain."

Sarantain stood stiffly. The creak of his worn leather apron spoke an entire lifetime. Crossing back to his workbench, he said, "Feed him a dowel if he opens his mouth again."

"The cold has made you vicious, luv," said Cedar.

"I'll have tea later."

❊❊❊

The ship was equipped with six metal stoves for heating: a large one for the animals and five to move around as needed. The metal boxes sat on metal plates twice as big as the box bottoms.

Two warmed the deck of the *Bane*, one aft, one midship. Crew rotated their duties around rubbing their hands and faces at fire striking at the mesh grates.

Small ice floes dotted the water like whittled shavings from something much grander. The *Bane*'s passage spread them outward, but the ice always found a way to re-join in its wake.

Nyim shivered in front of a heater. "I'm not used to the cold," he said, teeth chattering. "I've"—he pulled a deep breath of warmth into his lungs—"I've never seen ice before, not like this."

Amis's gloved hands were jammed under her pits. "My da's told me about mountains of it. He's never seen them, me neither, but folks have sketched them. He's got all the books on Erah."

"I know of icebergs. I've just never seen ice on water...that I can stand on."

Amnandi hadn't joined them at the fire. Amis hadn't seen her since breakfast, and Nyim hadn't for an entire day. "You'll be back in Afrelan heat before you know it," said Amis.

"You've been there?"

"No. Nandi's told me."

"Would you like to?"

"I plan to see the whole of the world before I'm done."

"And then settle on your farm."

"Marks for listening, Mr. Young Sir."

The first mate approached, pulling off huge mittens and blowing on her hands. Amis, Nyim, and unusually quiet Barrow made space for her.

"How much longer before temperate weather?" Nyim asked.

"Two days' hard sail at the least. More if this ice gets romantic."

"Romantic?"

"Hugs the ship. A brittle floe's a lot different than thick chunks," said Skye.

"But no icebergs?" he said.

Skye sniffed, then dried her nose on her thick sleeve. "You don't need me spoiling everything that's to come, do you?" She lobbed a wink at Amis.

"No, ma'am," Nyim agreed.

"According to our new guide, in days we should see land. The course he suggested keeps us well away from big ice."

"To trust a thief..." said Nyim, more than a bit disgusted.

"He's on the same ship that we are. We go down, my ghost kicks his ghost that much deeper."

"Captain Pinyasama is an odd one," Nyim said, adding quickly, "I say this with respect."

"Very much so," said the mate, "and I take it as an honor that you recognize it. Means I'm on the right ship."

"What happens when we reach land?" Nyim asked.

"Not just land but particular land," said Skye.

"The captain thinks to use magick to approach the dragoon," said Barrow, the only thing any of them had heard the scientist say all day.

"We seek volcanoes, young sir," Skye said to Nyim. "Pray your boots are padded well, warm, and that they be made for walking."

FOOD

The sun shone fiercely for a welcome change, as though to prove primacy in this place of slippery rock and hard shadows. It hadn't warmed the tips of anyone's nose yet, but the brightness made seeing everyone's breath less irksome.

Two parties walked the shore, one to pack snow in rain barrels, the other to hunt small game. The *Bane*'s larders held well, but extra meat was always a benefit, particularly now that a colder environ would preserve, leaving the salted for later days. There was no place on Erah where one couldn't track small prints toward dinner. Sailors learned early to appreciate meals instead of asking what they were eating.

The prints the parties found, however, were larger than they expected.

"Bird prints, captain," one reported after hustling back to the ship. "Size of mine."

"Bedamned ravens are following us," said Maab. "Any sign

they might still be there?"

"Multiple prints, bare human feet, wing marks, but no sight or sound of them. But it's all fresh. Wind hadn't even blown snow over them."

"We haven't seen anything in the skies," Maab said. Her shore parties had been kept in constant view. She glanced upward, shielding her eyes against the sun.

"The tracks didn't leave the shore," said the scout.

"Lower the metal pole for Rukkai," Maab ordered. "Bang it hard. Niss, Amnandi, and Dedoura, come ashore with me. Bring lots of scrap wood, matches, and oil."

***

Rich flames licked higher and sootier than the frigid island had ever seen, with smoke visible in all directions. As further inducement, Maab had Niss loose flaming arrows towards the inland crags, falling laughably short of the rocks and promontories but wholly on target.

Maab waited. She glanced at the trail Rukkai had made hauling itself ashore. It hadn't made a sound in any of their heads yet. The way it lay full out on the snow made Maab think of the thief and his partner. A walrus. Said to prefer cold climes and be ferociously territorial. She'd never seen one. Maybe they were all Mer.

She'd learned from the Mer that patience was ferocity.

After several lengthy, silent moments, Amnandi spoke. "Movement." She pointed westerly. First one, then two beatings of wings, then two ravens moved toward them so fast they were avian blurs.

Maab's hands went to her bow. The entire party armed, backs to each other in a widely spaced circle, pivot feet dug into the hard soil beneath the blowing snow. The ravens fought the wind, Maab knew, a minor advantage to her party. The breath of Erah moved erratically here, in fits and starts, gusts and sighs. It was cold. When it came, it demanded heat.

Rukkai rose to its full height but remained impassive.

The ravens flew with the sun in their eyes. Clearly, the birds hadn't thought this through. A second advantage yielding the possibility of a third.

Two landed with full plumage showing, then a production made of throwing snow clods into the air with the forceful scratching of talons. A raven minus feigned indignance was rarely a raven. Both shapeshifters raised wings and strained their beaks toward the humans.

All bows were nocked. Across the short distance Maab informed the birds, "I guarantee at least one of these will find its mark."

The quick eyes of the ravens sized up the archers. The human-sized birds settled down.

"Shall we speak?" Maab said.

In two blinks, two naked men of Maab's height waited on her next words. The pale blue-gray skin of the one complemented the warm, honey-sun tones of the other. Both were hairless, both completely black-eyed, but each with random flecks in their skin which caught the light, somewhat like the Mer.

Maab found herself infinitely grateful for Rukkai's presence.

"A witch," said the honeyed one. He cast those swallowing black eyes on each as he spoke. "A myrrddon," at Rukkai. He ignored the landing party. "The usual human murderers."

But at Maab: "The swimming bird. Your ship is even shaped like one."

"Then I'm in good standing." She flared her arms out, then set her bow down. She took a step forward.

The honey-toned raven noted the archers. "They remain armed."

"That's because we're not stupid," said Maab. She made sure she had the eye of the both ravens, then walked several steps forward.

She stopped short of her flanking arrowers' trajectories.

Both ravens approached.

"I thank you for not interfering," Maab said. "I'd thank you better for making yourselves useful." When she saw that they were intent on merely staring at her, she went on. "Aid us."

"What do you seek?"

"The answer to a deep hatred. One sown by your own kin."

"Hatred is common," said Honey.

"As grass," the blue-gray one added.

"This time, it's grasses made of godstuff. Haven't you felt the shift in your moods? Haven't you noticed things sickly that ought to thrive? Things dying that ought to be ancient?"

"We are not here for poetry, human."

"Hear this, then: something makes things grow. I imagine a dragoon is part of that, some vital part of the air, dirt, and water, just as Sharda moon gives us dreams and the sun brings warmth." She jabbed a pointing finger northward. "*Help. Us.* Scout ahead. We seek volcanoes, the livelier the better. Find several that churn blood. If we're to find a dragoon, it *will* be there."

The depthless eyes of the ravens gave away nothing. The two lithe bodies pivoted away in a blur of transformation, taking flight once more, back the way they'd come. But unhurried. Paced for watching.

And Maab watched.

She retrieved her bow and continued to watch until the ravens became small, then gone. Nothing but brackish outcroppings aged with haphazard snow.

"We come back with barrels," Maab said. "We gather what we came here for. We leave."

But her feet remained rooted on the tenuous horizon the

ravens had melted into.

As Maab watched, a flock of ravens rose. The scattered birds flew away from the humans, the boat, and the Merfolk undoubtedly beneath the sea.

※※※

The thief guided them successfully away from a coral spike, a perpetual whirlpool, two known behemoth breeding grounds, and the shoals of bergs that hadn't fully risen yet.

When they hit new waters, his usefulness was over.

The *Bane* was half a day out from the last spotting of the ravens.

Crewmates were at one point or other heard humming "The Homegoing Song." The mechanical flippers tirelessly churned the ship forward. The mystic extended himself to his utmost via private meditation. Those who pined continued to pine.

Those who were Amnandi made themselves oblivious to pining, ennui, fear, or anger. Even during duties, Amnandi Khumalo focused herself on one thing: embodying heat. Initially, people thought feeling warmer around her was a trick of the mind, but enough cold crew reported it as actual warmth. No one but Amis was bold enough to touch her, and Amis had found Amnandi's cheek so warm against the flat of her hand that she immediately laid that hand to her friend's forehead.

The same heat, but Amnandi's eyes showed no sign of sickness.

"What're you doing?" Amis asked, face to face, Amnandi seated over an empty bowl of stew, Amis standing at the table.

"Accustoming my body to the flow of energy."

"Burning yourself up," said Amis. She took a seat. "This harmful?"

"I—" Amnandi had to think a moment and continued honestly, "don't know."

"Magick is stupid. You can control it up and down?"

Amnandi nodded.

"And stop? Just be you?"

"Again: yes."

"Captain know about this?"

"No. She doesn't need to."

"You and your experimenting. Glowing eyeballs, breathing like a fish, living oven—" Amis waggled a finger like an ancient elder. "You weary me, Amnandi Khumalo."

"From the one who got us attacked by a wraith as children," Amnandi reminded.

"We're not kids anymore, Nandi. We're not supposed to be stupid. What if something in you fizzles out before we need you?"

"It won't."

"You promise?"

"No. I'm only giving you odds."

"Odds is math." Their other childhood friend, Bettany, excelled 2at maths. Amis did not. "Give me your sensibility. At the very least, start letting us know that you're experimenting on yourself. I don't want to learn about you trying to fly by me having to lasso you."

Barrow entered the mess, served herself a bowl, and sat at the far end of the massive bench table. She ate quietly.

"What's on your mind, scientist?" Amis called down.

Barrow glanced up, tapped her bowl with her spoon, and returned to the food.

"Stew's not that fascinating," Amis whispered to Amnandi. She stood. "Leaving you to your heat. And you"—she narrowed her eyes at Amnandi—"don't leave it burning."

With Amis gone, Amnandi had no reason to stay. She raised to return her bowl to the rinse station.

Barrow eyed her nowhere near as surreptitiously as she thought.

Amis had implied in confidence that Amnandi fascinated her. Amnandi approached.

"A favor?" Amnandi asked.

"Of course."

"Take my hand." They clasped. Amnandi saw immediate surprise flash across Barrow's face.

"You doing that?" Barrow said. "On purpose?"

"It's me. Have you studied the internals of the body?"

"A bit."

"How am I doing this?"

Barrow looked flustered. "I've no idea— It's—"

"Magick."

"Magick," Barrow said, giving it the extra consonant pronunciation. "You're better off asking the mystic."

Amnandi maintained contact. Her lovely face softened, drawing warmth into Barrow's eyes. "Do we always need answers?"

"No," said Barrow. "Not everything is a question."

"You may study me later for magick. It would be good to know."

Barrow smiled upward. "If we know each other long enough, we might get a book out of it. *Barrow's Almanac of Magick.*"

"Who would say no to this?"

Many would say no, Amnandi knew, and surely so did Barrow, but thoughts of yesses as wind whistled and turbines thrummed loud served infinitely better.

SPIRITUS A

Three sets of three sleek bodies split off in a trident, streaking toward a shrieking whale. The beast, young and huge, would clearly become an elder of the sea, outliving most in the water or on land by several lifetimes.

Its strong double flukes pushed it erratically but unerringly for the silencing base of an iceberg.

Rukkai's mate reached it first, attaching themselves over one eye of the plunging beast. Rukkai matched that action over the other eye, placing the whale in total darkness. The two of them radiated calmness to it. The third in their triad affixed itself to the whale's crown.

The remaining triads found purchase along various parts of the great whale's body, fighting currents and the massive sudden corkscrews the young male made, not to throw them off; they didn't believe the whale had any awareness of them. Passionate violence had seized it, with the only satisfactory release being its own death. Blood and tissue from various wounds made by lesser obstacles attracted smaller fish to either come see, to bear witness, or to taste. Their fish minds, unadapted to insanity, would not shriek, but they'd know hunger. And get hungrier. Until there was nothing left to eat but themselves.

At which point they might grow teeth outside their teeth.

Rukkai felt consuming terror from the whale, a screaming realization that it was already prey, that it was death in the way its fluke had broken the back of a calf too playful while the whale's inner vision shrank to a pinpoint. The panicked whale had then dived, the water itself threatening to keep its blowhole sealed forever, followed by the streaking Mer.

Mer who sang a song of peace to it. Calmed its strained muscles with gentle electrical impulses, insinuated themselves into its awareness, and reminded it that even a behemoth couldn't split an iceberg.

The whale stopped twisting. It slowed. The iceberg loomed large, perhaps only a few more insistent fluke strokes away. Even this slower speed would leave enough blood and snapped bones to allow the whale to settle on the sea floor, drift into the dark, and eventually disappear.

Unless it turned.

Turn, Rukkai sang.

Turned hard and fast.

Turn.

The whale did not want to turn.

Please.

The great body twisted left, pushed hard, nearly shaking loose several Mer along its spine and at the base of its flukes, missing the broken diamond of the iceberg by a single length of its own body.

Not much, considering, and not a lot, but enough.

The Mer remained attached to the whale as it got its bearings, Rukkai and mate Von uncovering the eyes. They whispered truths of the sea at the sides of its head.

It had been a long voyage beneath the sleek hull of the ship. They had done this over and over: whales, octopi, glittering shoals attacking themselves.

Erah was going insane in pieces.

It hadn't affected the humans yet—or had it?—and Rukkai's own Merfolk continued to be as level and attuned as ever—maybe? Rukkai had been too busy to take full measure of those in its own extended pod, let alone attempt to contact Mer around the world to assess if this calamity were indeed worldwide, which there was no reason to think it wasn't.

But there was no reason to think it *was*.

Faced with this prospect of limbo, Rukkai, Von, and the exhausted others with them did what came naturally: they cared for others. Compassion was no answer to either the malady or the question of its scope, but it helped Mer move among the currents, keep pace with the *Bane*'s goings-on, and perhaps sowed the seeds for some unknowable day when even the Mer would need balms.

After the whale, they continued their search for underwater volcanoes.

⁂

The honey raven had assumed leadership of the flock. The flock, being highly out of their comfort, didn't complain. Once they all felt their feet under them again, they would. Honey knew it. The way of things was the way of things, and no raven admitted to being ruled by another, despite giving the title of King fairly regularly. A king was a mark of commonality and civilization; otherwise, ravenhood might be seen to be a hodgepodge of interests, particularly by the humans who were as disorganized and feeble-minded as pebbles tossed by surf.

He was burnished gold, freckled in obsidian chips that caught the light perfectly when he paraded in human form. Kings often stayed more human than raven, and though he was no king, it was prudent to behave as one.

There were fourteen ravens arrayed around him, all in their avian forms except one. The blue-gray one, hoping to appear authoritative, mimicked the gold, whose name was Edrickl.

Edrickl spoke briskly. "The strongest fliers take the greatest distance. Argue amongst yourselves about who's the strongest, I don't care, but leave the moment I complete my requests." He paused to allow for squabbling. Surprisingly, there was little. "We fly short-range, mid-range, and long-range. We will have the answers these humans need by the time they catch up to us. We let them labor or die."

"As long as it benefits us," said Deneb the blue-gray.

"As long as it benefits us," Edrickl reinforced. "If any of you succumb to sickness or madness, returning to us will mean your deaths."

Squawking and a bristling of feathers meant everyone intended the same for him.

"The more...wearied of us," Edrickl announced with the effort of diplomacy, "will fly short. I will fly mid to serve as the gathering point."

Two others assumed human form, both as pale as a rolled-back eye, flecked in ruby and disdain. "We fly mid as well. We will receive reports."

The Bone Brothers. Rarely apart. Young and vicious. They had followed the *Bane* after the main body of the avenging raven cloud storm departed, solely because they hadn't flown all that way to *not* kill somebody. The *Bane* was full of soft people; the brothers merely needed to be patient.

The ones flying short knew to remain silent.

Edrickl hoped this entire enterprise wasn't foolishness. To go down in the annals of Ravendom as a fool was a terrible thing.

SPIRITUS B

The mystic had it.

He burst into the captain's quarters as Skye stood to leave.

"Stay," he urged. He looked exceedingly rested. His tattoos appeared more vibrant, as if freshly inked. "How long have we traveled this current course?"

"You mean since you last woke up?" said Skye.

"Half the day," said Maab.

"Then we're deep in a zone of huge contentment. I've sensed it in dreams, meditations, and visions. We brushed the edge of it and I almost awoke, it was so unexpected. What has the witch felt?"

"She's been at ease," said Maab. "In talks with Barrow, composing music, tending her duties."

"Yes, influenced by it but not understanding it," said Daoud. Did they understand him? Coming out of a liminal meditative state so sure of things made him...unsure. Thoughts convinced him he'd spoken the necessary words. Words themselves felt incomplete. But sure.

He pulled the reins on a rush of thoughts. "Am. I. Babbling?"

"Not yet," said Maab. "Continue."

"What thing is content that has ever dealt with us, with peoples across Erah? Nothing. I could net a fish right now that would curse my forebears. And yet...I *feel* it. Contentment. Something that was here before us and lives apart from us. We travel within the sphere of influence of a dragoon."

"Can you verify it, give us a location?"

"I'll need to go into a deeper dreaming than I've done in a while," he said, half of his mind already reaching for that tantalizing, desirous state.

"I'd sleep with you if I thought it would help. I mean that in all ways," said Maab.

"I'd certainly accept," said Daoud. "But this is less comfort of the body and more awareness of distinctions. I must compartmentalize all that I experience during the meditative state to sift for valuable specifics." Did they understand? Did he?

The captain indicated to the mate to escort the man back to his bed.

"Come on, giant," said Skye, gently guiding Daoud by the elbow. "To your dreams. Your eyes are too wild to be sensible to us."

"But you understand the hope here, don't you?" he asked, moving off.

"I do," Skye assured him. "The captain does."

"We should dream," he muttered, snared again in the edges of his half-aware mind. "We should dream."

* * *

That night, the *Bane* dropped anchor. Merfolk's bobbing heads surrounded the ship. Torchlight spread across their dark bodies, giving the appearance of the sea mirroring the universe.

Now and then, the wisps of an aurora.

If nothing else, every person on board would take the night they convened with the Mer to their old age.

Rukkai was on board. Its mate Von as well, and four others, the most any Mer stood on the *Bane*'s deck. Introductions had been succinct. No one in attendance was there for social reasons.

Torches on high kept watch for ravens even though the light was so swallowed that Niss and Dedoura in the crow's nest wouldn't see a dark wing unless it brushed their cheeks. Maab intentionally made sure no one on deck carried a single weapon. If the birds came, they came. If they didn't, they didn't.

The Mer, no longer bothered by the torchlight, remained rigidly glistening shapes while slight breezes drew fire splashes across them. Their thoughts no longer caused the crew to sing.

"Our mystic has reason to believe we're in the presence of an eternal. Have you felt anything?" Maab asked Rukkai. "He senses it in dreams."

We do not dream.

"But you've other means?"

It may be that we have always sensed it but perceived it as the world.

"I understand."

If so, you and I have never traveled alone.

The crew deserved words from the captain. Good words.

"We've sailed hard for many days," Maab said, addressing each spirit on the *Bane*, "each of us in our own thoughts. There've been discomforts; there've been worries. None of those are over. Our instincts, however, have been rewarded. We got here, to this anchored spot, because it was where we needed to be. Going forward, we journey not only toward something new. No one's been promised glory or riches. We may now be in the glory of eternals. Do. We. Go. Forward?"

The shout of assent was so sharp, it might have cracked an ice floe.

"Rukkai, now that you know there's something to sense for, sense well. Stay close. This ship is now guided by dreams; there's no predictable direction to take."

Each Mer on deck wanted to know if Amnandi had sensed anything, and flooded the captain and crew with that query.

Maab waved her forward.

"I...am unsure?" the traveling witch said. "Is that answer allowed?"

"Allowed and preferred as honest," said Maab. "We rest here the night. No sentries. Everyone belowdecks, where it's warmest. Gamble, drink, read, then dream. How well should we dream, Mate Skye?"

"Till we've sent enough jeweled thoughts to Sharda to bring her down."

"A poet has spoken! Tomorrow"—Maab quieted, her theatrics pristine; she swiveled her head slowly, even turned full-body around—"goddess willing, we find what we have looked for with the help we've had. If there's a greater blessing than that, we're not meant for it." She faced the Mer. "Rukkai, thank you. I'll dream for us both."

Each Mer lowered themselves and quietly slid across the rough deck to the rail. Five *plip*s announced their return to the water.

Belowdecks that night, there was no gambling. Drinking was, by unanimous unspoken agreement, restricted to hot ciders and teas. Several varying holy books belonged to several varying members of the crew, and those members read silently. Most enjoyed the comforts of hushed conversations and the coziness of bodies at rest literally everywhere. Skye composed poems.

Tucked in his usual spot, away from the general murmur and life of the crew, now with additional curtains to deaden sound, the mystic slept. Amnandi and Amis, inside the enclosure, watched over the dreamer.

∗∗∗

Just before dawn, Amnandi was awakened by Amis shaking her.

Part of her already knew why Amis was concerned.

"He's crying," said Amis. "And smiling. Should we get the captain?"

An answer would wait. Amnandi rolled to her feet, wrapping her heavy blanket like a caterpillar's shawl over her head and shoulders. A tear slalomed a salt track down Daoud's face before hitting the scruff of new beard. The pillow was wet.

Amnandi leaned closer. His breathing: normal. A hand to his heart: stable and unhurried even through the multiple layers of clothing and blankets. The smile: as though he found amusement in something small, private, and perfect.

Perhaps something beautiful.

"He's been like that awhile. I watched before I woke you up," said Amis. She stifled a hard yawn.

"I know. I'll watch again. Sleep," she instructed Amis. "Dream."

"Everybody's pushing dreams," Amis said, moving toward the pallet. "It's a curse. I'll wind up dreaming about chores or sermons. You sure no captain?"

"I'll wake her if need be."

"And me, too," said Amis, although the words were muffled by the blanket wrapped so quickly around her head. "Wake me, too."

Watching someone dream was fascinating. Entire lives existed beneath the thin skin of the forehead from one breath to the next. Amnandi sometimes found it easier to speak to someone when they were dreaming. Less subterfuge. Less worry. Lots of space for the silences that fostered clarity. She found that most times when people spoke, nothing of value was said.

More teardrops slowly built to dripping points at the corner of Daoud's eyes. It took seventeen seconds for the next to appear. The slight amusement on his face faded, returned, faded, returned, but never blossomed. His eyes rolled behind his lids like a tongue probing a cheek for the day's leftover spices. Amnandi had always wanted to know what she looked like asleep but would, sadly, never experience it in quite this way.

Compared to the things she did know, that omission was minor at best. Witches were privy to concepts others weren't. Galaxies. Black holes. Quantum barriers. Her mind had touched the minds of Amnandis of several iterations, not solely during dreams. What better mirror stood beside that?

Even her mother had never crossed those particular veils. Amnandi wondered if the mystic had.

This smiling and crying: was he there now with his other selves? Had one of them told him a valuable secret? Did he feel loved?

Was he at rest?

Seventeen seconds. Another tear.

Not the worst night, counting the tracks of someone's tears while they smiled and dreamed. As time went on, though, he didn't stir. That in itself wasn't immediately alarming. What finally furrowed Amnandi's brow and got her on her feet to the captain was his unchanging expression.

To smile for that long a time was evidence of panic, subterfuge, or terror.

* * *

"Is he dead?" asked Amis.

"He's breathing, Amis," said Amnandi.

"I mean mystically dead."

"Shush," said Maab.

Leena, ship's acting doctor since their last stop at Keer, approached diagnostics by shaking him vigorously, then peeling open his eyes, counting his breaths with a mirror under his nose, and checking his pulse at wrists, neck, and ankles. "You ever meditate this deeply?" she asked Amnandi.

"No."

Mate Skye bent nearer to study his face. "That's an odd expression. Captain...should we get Rukkai?"

"Rather not clang the sea awake if I don't have to. We'll give him more time. If no change, we'll wake him."

"How?" said Amis.

"A dunk in the sea does wonders," said Maab.

By noon meal of that same day, the call went out to wake him. Amnandi had, however, formulated a theory and a plan during the intervening hours, one more delicate than tossing a bald, tattooed man overboard. She remembered her mother entering a sleeping person's dreams once to remind them where their immediate life was. All it had required was meditation, quietude, and solitude. It couldn't have been more difficult than Amnandi traveling the veils.

Could it?

"That's what we need to know, luv," said Maab. "What's your gut say?"

"I don't sense danger in an attempt," said Amnandi. "People never hold one another in the dreaming unless both want to stay."

"That conjecture or knowledge?" said Maab. By now, several tried to peer around the curtains to learn what was going on. For now, Maab, Skye, Amis, Amnandi and Barrow crowded around the beatific sleeper's body.

Sarantain stood just outside the heavy burlap, his scarred arms folded, not quite guarding the mystic's "room" but guarding it.

The ship moved along at half-speed, which was a good sign. The captain expected this incident to be temporary.

Duties up top were performed without worry.

Amnandi had to wonder whether what she knew was conjecture or knowledge. "Both?" Amnandi said. Knowledge: she had seen her mother do it. Conjecture: she had not been taught precisely how. But thoughts were thoughts whether awake or at rest; they were the filaments by which all communication was made possible. Thoughts traveled deeper than words. They drilled into existence.

In this, she knew where she needed to go, whom she needed to speak to, and what she needed to do. "I'm in no danger, I promise you."

Even Amis relaxed.

"Speaking to one another in dreams is actually somewhat easy," said the young witch. "Translation, however, is what my mother calls 'a bear.'"

MUNDI

She prepared by eating a sweet bun because she was hungry, chased by the kind of strong, bitter tea she hated but her mother drank for inward balance. She was warm enough in her seated meditative position, but Amis draped another blanket across her shoulders.

With that small action, Amnandi's smile—behind closed eyes—matched Daoud's.

Everyone but Maab exited.

In ten minutes, Amnandi's breathing matched the mystic's. In twenty—unbeknownst to Maab—their hearts. At twenty-two, the witch dropped soul-long through the veil behind which Daoud existed.

In it, heat and the total absence of light.

His idea of paradise?

His essence greeted hers, as if he had been waiting, then he disappeared. The sweet darkness of this new universe splashed against her like waves moving her toward a deeper sea.

She flowed.

Daoud appeared again and, before she could experience him fully, was gone again.

Did he consider this guidance?

Guidance sometimes took forever.

In that instance of impatience, she requested the presence of her others, and since the dreaming had no contract with linear time, they were there. Each had long been given a name according to colors each preferred: Amnandi Green, Blue, Black, Red, Brown, and Yellow. There were likely infinite colors, but throughout her childhood, *these* were the ones who permitted contact. Her veil selves. Her first sisters.

Even though she had spent so little time with them in recent years, they knew her mind instantly. She knew theirs.

Amnandi Green wore jade yarn threaded into the intricate knots of heavy dreads.

Amnandi Red's fabric combination of reds and oranges made her a sun. Her headwrap was a river of crimson scarves.

Blue: bejeweled. Always bejeweled. The only one of them to ever wear jewelry, even as children. A lapis stone on a simple cord around her neck. Aquamarine bangles at her wrists. Her clothing, topaz with a finer sheen than ice.

Amnandi herself, wrapped in grays, still a bit cold, still somewhat unsure.

Her selves ringed her.

"This mystic," said Green. "A jokester."

"Perhaps at heart," said Amnandi.

"No. Entirely."

Blue peered closely at Amnandi. "How did you miss that fact?"

"Nevertheless," said Red, "we shall use that knowledge to our advantage."

They felt an easing in their souls, just the tiniest ever-present constriction loosening.

The mystic appeared far away from them, but there was no distance in dreams. Where he was, they were.

No time, no distance, but there was intention, and he intended to be half a thought ahead of their perceptions, popping in and out.

"Have you noted a pattern in any of his actions?" asked Green.

"Not as yet," said Amnandi.

"Let us sit and wait," said Yellow.

Black and Brown agreed.

They sat. They waited.

It took no time at all.

It took a great deal of time.

Necessary time.

Learning of other worlds. Green's world had undergone a plague that Amnandi, Unina, and the elders of three communities of Afrela came together to overcome. Plagues and foolishness moved together at swift speeds. Red had become a traveling counselor—which was already a witch's trade—but specifically for children, who were very rarely treated as if they had worries or concerns outside their small bodies. Her unina Ayanda Khumalo journeyed with her primarily to sight-see and record notes on magick used by animals.

Blue was in love. With that world's Barrow, no less, having met in a pub where Blue sought out Bog the Unsmiling.

The universe was but a question and an answer.

There were no secrets; there was only life stretched infinitely long. Everything was out in the open.

That was the mystic's joke. Irony was the source of his smile. Everything was knowable.

What was life—no matter what one did in it—if one never saw its underpinnings?

The pattern became clear: he appeared where he thought they

thought they wanted him to be. He wasn't a guide there. Not at all.

Merely an amusement.

A circle of mindful witches aligned their minds.

Finally: within the circle, where their intent was to hold him there in tight embrace.

Daoud would see, as the coven of witches now did, quite purely, quite clearly, shockingly and simply, the dragoon for what it was: a traveler.

Its destination: everywhere.

Outside this space, the mystic awoke. Instantly. Fully. He asked to be helped topside to feel the cold and watch gusts ripple frigid waters into small works of art. Maab held him under one arm, Skye at the other, and they silently waited for him to fill with himself again.

They were in the presence of dragoon.

He met Amnandi's eyes.

You find, Amnandi told herself, *what you are looking for*.

So very simple.

Daoud, in a whisper, said, "This is our chance to burn."

***

When the ravens found the largest, most active volcano in the region, they reported on it and unceremoniously left.

Maab neither watched them go nor entertained a regret. Ruminating on the short-sighted was for later, when full and rested.

"I'm holding you to those motors, Ms. Barrow," she said to Barrow, the *Bane* at full speed.

"They'll hold."

To Skye: "The crew?"

"Ready. And you?"

The mischievous look in Maab's eyes said it all. The steely

smile she gave Skye added a little extra zing. "We'll be witches in our way."

They would reach the target mountain by nightfall. Momentous things and nightfall often went hand in hand. Adventure happened as it happened, a few times under the gods' influence, most times not. The ship would once again cease motion at night, but there'd be no rest. Maab would put everyone through paces. Equipment would be checked and rechecked as thoroughly as she expected each person to attend a crewmate. She'd been on a mountain or two in her life. A mountain didn't care about years of experience elsewhere; it cared about being paid attention to as large lonesome things often did.

And this mountain, according to the ravens, was more confused. In places, barren and dried of any possibility of living things; in places, greener than some of the tropical isles; yet many others, ice and snow in the forms of knives and ghostly shrouds. There was no logic, the golden one had complained, to the mountain.

There'd never been, Maab thought.

And a mountain that was also a volcano? Doubly its own law.

✳✳✳

Two Mer slowly guided two rowboats around shoals and rocks. Whether they were tired or cautious, Maab couldn't be sure, but her heart sent thanks. The mountain had innumerable roots in the water ready to crack a boat's ribs. When the two boats made land, the Merfolk waited a moment to be sure the humans had their footing, then the two slick bodies were obscured by the spray of a sudden wave hitting a large rock. They disappeared.

The deeps were full of underwater entrances, tunnels, and vortices.

Maab, now without her feathered sarong, took a deep breath.

She set her sights and set off.

With her: the witch for her magick and her mind; the mystic for sensitivity, mysticism, and height; old Cedar, who had climbed numerous mountains between turns at sea; Sarantain for sheer stubbornness against odds; Niss in case of a need for death.

Six, Maab had argued to Skye during the previous long night, was just as good for finding an elemental as six thousand.

Maab had no course or plan.

There was "up."

"Not gonna have the young lady pop us about?" Cedar wondered, her breath a cloud through the scarf circling her head and neck.

"No magick till needed," said Maab. A pack on her back containing rope, medicines, extra gloves, boots and clothing, spikes, food and water, and various knives weighed almost as much as she did. There was no indication that it mattered.

Amnandi followed right behind her.

Four heavy packs brought up the rear.

***

Any god giving the world cold like this was misguided. There was nothing enjoyable about walking through its air, crunching atop its snow, or living in it. Where was the joy? Tempest Red bred thieves because of it—

There, Amnandi stopped herself. She was a witch, able to warm herself. Hatred of the elements was foolish.

We must see where we are with each step.

She would remember to write that down. They weren't late yet for her return home. Unina would enjoy reading her daughter's thoughts; she always had. Hearing them, reading them, theorizing with her. Mother Khumalo, as she'd come to be known around many parts of Erah, was nothing but one big conversation, and

Amnandi loved her for that. The world presented nothing but questions, and the younger Khumalo had taken it upon herself to know the answers to as many of them as she could find out.

Snow thrown by the wind clung to her lashes and the oval of her hood.

She wouldn't allow herself something so minor as the foolishness of weather complaints. She would see this through, because that's what every single witch she had ever met did. Most of Afrela thrived because of love and respect for them. During all her travels with Unina, Amnandi had met witches who were not witches, mages without knowledge of a single written spell, and healers of land and spirit. It was foolish to think she was doing anything that others hadn't done since before she was born. In heat, in cold, in love, in war, from Afrela to Eurola to Tyn and back. She watched the sure, snowy footsteps of Maab Pinyasama and felt nothing but a solid connection to doing what must be done. She had gladly put herself in Maab's shadow for months. How else was learning to take place? A bit of Maab's hair showed from beneath her hat; Maab didn't care. Now and then, the captain's breath came out in ragged puffs; it didn't affect her mind or stride. This small star of a woman was as much a guiding light as any constellation fixed in a midnight sky.

Perhaps it's not the cold that bothers you, child, Amnandi told herself. She walked in strong footsteps. Sarantain and Niss behind her carried her own march along. Even the mystic buoyed her. She was somewhere she'd never been before, needing thoughts and abilities she might not have but which were absolutely necessary one way or another.

An elemental.

What if I am not enough? was never a question she'd had to entertain before. Unina had made sure she was.

And here? Now? Answer yourself, child. When there are doubts you must give yourself answers.

A shipload of people have made sure you are enough.

Snow is no more daunting than sand, and rocks are rocks everywhere. What comes, comes.

She spent no more time on thoughts. A witch's life was one of listening and watching. Right now no one spoke, which seemed to quicken paces. They made good time up the mountain slope throughout the day, pitched camp without incident at dusk, and set out again the next morning.

The avalanche which came the next afternoon, while not wholly unexpected, was entirely unwelcome. The thunderous *crack* and rush of it didn't eclipse the immediate shout of "Of damned course!" from Maab.

TIME

First Mate Patrice Skye had been told: "Wait two days. We'll send up a signal balloon. If not spotted, proceed as you see best."

What she saw best was, after a day and a half, assembling a crew and heading ashore. Nyim and Amis immediately volunteered, followed by Leena and Barrow. Skye's instructions upon leaving Dedoura in command: "You do not leave until every one of our bodies is on board and fed."

The tracks were easy enough to follow. Snow slept undisturbed everywhere except where the preceding group had gone. Footprints seemed odd in this place that felt as welcoming as a boneyard. Those signs of life altered Skye's impression of time. She shook off the sense that she was studying the distant past. The physicality of the shake landed her in the present. The snow seemed to get a little deeper every ten feet, and the wind's teeth got sharp.

If that's a challenge, bites heal, Skye told the mountain. *Do better.* She leaned in to a sudden gust, her eyes tight for warmth.

Each person with her carried a collapsible canvas sled on their back. If it came to dragging Maab and crew out, they were prepared.

It was a short march to their first barren patch. Hard dirt, igneous rock, not even dead scrub. The patch sloped upward, plateaued, then sloped up again for a good distance to properly become part of the mountain, even if still a decent trek from the actual base. Skye knew Maab's mind; her bird woman would keep to as straight a line as possible until the terrain told her otherwise.

Gray sunlight shone through a large cleave in the butte. From the ship, attentive scopes had watched Maab head straight for that light, then the party disappeared. Now tracking would begin in earnest. The cleave was wide enough to permit broad shoulders but not much else. Skye went through first, listening to the movements of her party. Nyim had difficulty with the snow. Amis reached back a hand to help him up the widely spaced crags serving as steps. "Thank you," he said. Barrow and Leena followed immediately, silently, the first no doubt taking in what she could of the geology with whatever part of her brain not focused on footing, and the cook worried.

Skye gritted her teeth at their actual doctor having elected to remain on sunny Keer Island. Beyond unfortunate, but he was old, tired, and frail, and Skye had seen him teach Maab's older kin a lot.

"May you be unneeded," Skye had told her when Leena volunteered.

The cook had readily agreed.

Through the cleft, a snowy plain. Pieces of the mountain loomed tall all around them, high spires and sheared tops as evidence of ancient turmoil and cataclysm. Those older things tended to speak of newer dangers; each in the party kept watchful eye. There wasn't a single hissing vent in sight, but Erah was apparently infamous for keeping secrets beneath.

Skye stopped to survey. Six sets of tracks through her scope led clearly toward another cleft. It seemed this island was nothing but spikes dropped from the moon, herding the curious toward the distant mother of all mountains that looked thick enough to swallow Sharda.

Midway, snow gave way to rocky ground. Tracks disappeared.

It would be a long walk.

***

"We should've brought horses." Nyim was at least half-serious with this. He handed Amis her waterskin back after refilling his and hers with pristine snow.

"We take care of our horses," Amis answered. "This isn't a land for horses. You might want to watch your step a bit better. I've seen you catch rocks several times. Nobody wants to waste bandages on a rescuer."

"You'd leave me, wouldn't you?" he said, trying not to betray a bit of a smile.

"In half a thought." Amis shook her canteen vigorously to slosh the snow. Walking in the cold leeched moisture just as well as high heat; this climate merely stored water on a chilly layer from neck to arse rather than a salty, warm stew. They both took hard drinks, then tucked their skins inside their coats.

Nyim gave a glance at Skye and Leena sitting side by side a ways off on a cracked boulder. Barrow sat alone. "What do you suppose they're talking about?"

"Them? Not a word between them while we've rested."

"I hadn't noticed."

Amis stood with a grunt because one was supposed to stand with a grunt when carrying packs. Rest time was nearly over.

"Well. You're gonna have to work on that." She walked toward the two boulders where the rest of her party sat. Skye and the cook dismounted.

***

Not a single hare print. No feathers, signs of nests or burrows, no animal call hoping for response from a friend or warning of an enemy. The ravens specifying this site simply meant they had sighted it. A possibility, nothing more. The Mer might have sensed something was odd here, and the mystic put weight behind dreams, but Skye trusted the languages of life itself, and life was not extending bountiful greetings. Perhaps there were grazers on the unseen parts where grass grew; sailors sowed seeds just as well as a bird's bowels. Perhaps, Skye mused while ice specks whipped at her cheeks, whole flocks of stout, wooly sheep had acclimated to this place, a place that felt remote by choice. Maybe they were even tended by magickal beings.

But as things looked, this island, which Skye had named "Earth," a strange word she had learned from Amnandi (who herself had learned it from a dream), gave every impression of needing anyone setting foot on it to go away and forget. But the dream Earth, Amnandi had said, felt like an isolated place, so the name fit.

The only indicators that the entire land wasn't entirely frozen in time and space were the occasional signs of recent change: a fresh crater from a boulder drop; gales chiseling snow and ice into sharp fingers showing the way the winds had gone; a bald spot up high being clear evidence of an avalanche.

An avalanche from which snow and chunks of soil now and then continued to cascade.

Skye's stomach churned.

The height: mid-slope, near enough to the ground to have

moved at the speed of a team of horses.

Large enough to have easily buried six people.

❋❋❋

The oddest thing about watching Amnandi tremble to maintain the shield around them was no one, not Maab, not the mystic, not Niss, Sarantain, or Cedar, could do a single thing to help her. Amnandi had shouted at them not to distract her, approach her, or touch her.

Which meant they watched as the thin teen of a girl maintained a blue energetic dome between their bodies and the weight of the world.

Sarantain and Cedar couldn't build anything.

Niss and Maab had no clear strategy.

Daoud had immediately volunteered to enlarge his body and bear the load to allow Amnandi to port everyone out, but this was not an instance where heroes would suffice. The weight would snap his back like a twig.

Occasionally someone's stomach grumbled, which would have been comical except it meant Amnandi had held a mountain long enough for them to get hungry.

Instead, Daoud sat and tried to radiate warmth inside the enclosure so that the girl wouldn't have to waste such energy, although he had barely learned the technique from her.

Tunneling out and under? Freezing, suffocation, crushed.

Gathering tight to Amnandi to port? The witch had already calculated the time between releasing the protection spell and throwing a portal. Someone would live, someone would die.

Amnandi's eyes were closed, her head bowed. Water dripped from her face. Some was sweat. Some wasn't.

The energies leaving her body vibrated her to her bones. Her party had been too scattered to have ported them all to safety in time. She'd shouted "Come!" to bring them that much closer, throwing the protection spell instinctively, an instantaneous blanket that she'd been able to draw inward as they moved into a tight circle around her. But what had been protection was now a trap.

Traps, the daughter of Ayanda Khumalo mentally shouted in her own face, *have ways of escape!*

Hold.

Think.

THINK!

Part of her brain had kept track of how long they been under. She relieved it of that duty. Somewhere behind her closed eyes was a solution. Mother always told her, "Think less of what you want and more of what is" on the matter of solutions. What was wanted often blinded.

Daoud, in meditation, continued to do his best to reach anyone on the ship.

He heard Amnandi whisper his name.

"Grow above me. Hands and knees over me."

The move would kill him.

He didn't hesitate.

"Everyone beneath him. Hold him up." To Daoud: "Grow only as tall as the shortest upreached hands." Amnandi's entire body shuddered. "I'm going to contract the shell to meet your back. Slowly. Stages. When I throw the portal, everyone in. I'll double the shield. Daoud in. As fast as possible. Then I."

"Aye," said Maab.

"Controlling this is...not easy."

"I know, luv. We're ready," said Maab.

"When I say go..." said Amnandi.

It felt like ages for the blue light to rest atop Daoud's back.

"Go."

Amnandi dropped her arms, threw the widest, most powerful

portal she could, pried her eyes open to see Maab, Sarantain, Niss, and Cedar leap from buttressing Daoud's body, felt him violently contract just enough to fit into the portal while simultaneously throwing himself into it, and then the witch threw an angled shield to allow the split second needed to place herself within the portal…

…as everyone ejected into air above snow. Amnandi had no idea how high. She hoped she hadn't miscalculated. She hoped the snow wasn't a thin layer atop stone.

She had no energy to do more than count five bodies falling a short distance, feel relieved about that, then pass out.

***

The brilliant flash of blue immediately caught all eyes against Earth's unending drabness.

Gods bless the color of magick was the first thought in Skye's mind as her body took off at a run toward the illumination not too far up a distant slope but still a climb. Still far too much time to think the worst.

They ran hard. At a point, Skye ordered them to stop. An exhausted party would be more danger than help. She cleared space and started a fire, one larger than it needed to be. The six of them drank, and paced, and stared ahead. Skye forced them to chew jerky. What the eye saw from a distance, the foot knew would take time to reach. It might be possible to reach the spot before light faded.

It depended on how well her team ran.

"Ready?" she said, second winds in place.

They took off before she did.

And left the fire burning.

***

Maab struggled upright in the snow and did a head count. The motion created a mini avalanche as she sat up. Sarantain's knees and boots. Cedar's tan, furry hat. Niss already on her feet, performing a similar check. A pit where Daoud, still larger than normal, cradled what Maab knew to be Amnandi by the girl's burlap pack against her thick gray coat.

The clever girl had given them as soft a landing as she could, as far down from the source of higher instability as she could. She'd set them hours behind where they'd been, but they were alive to take those steps.

Huge triumph, as far as Maab was concerned.

She looked back the way they'd come. Smoke.

She rushed to Amnandi, felt the strength of her pulse, breathed Amnandi's breath as her own, then dropped to her knees to rummage supplies from her pack, ripping off her gloves with her teeth one by one, seeking a balloon, folding out its large paper-lantern top, affixing its three-wick base to it, and hoping not a single god had any interest in the irony of wet matches.

The wicks caught. Heat built, filling the waxed paper's head with the desire to fly.

Fully puffed, the bright red lantern accordioned to nearly as tall as Maab but weighed less than her finger. She tapped it to give it rise, and sent it off, praying the wind behaved. Then she cleared a large circle of snow, revealing dark rock and hard ground underneath. A fire to answer a fire.

Daoud gently extricated himself and unconscious Amnandi from the soft crater he'd created. Sarantain and Cedar approached Maab, pulling kindling from their packs.

A fire to say Maab had been foolish.

A fire around which to wait.

***

Both parties barely contained themselves when each came into view. Amnandi's still being unconscious tempered Skye's team's enthusiasm as they rushed to Maab's camp and took in the scene.

Amis bumped into Skye's heavy arm and used that physical contact to stop herself from panicking forward. If she had learned nothing else from Amnandi's mother and Amnandi herself, it was patience. Even if one had to force it.

Amis had taught herself that sometimes in this world of wonders, there was simply nothing for her to do.

Leena moved forward. "Injuries?"

"None," Maab said, ignoring her own facial scrapes and what was likely a remarkable bruise on her left hip under the layers of breeches.

"None physical," Leena corrected. "The girl burned herself out."

All eyes went to Daoud, who kept Amnandi enfolded. He did his best to feed her his energy, offering up not only his body heat but the rhythm of his breathing. Patterns recognized patterns, and whatever forces were within her would respond in kind.

"Barrow?" Leena said, feeling useless, hoping for a learned suggestion, but the scientist's face held the same rueful uselessness as her own.

"Make the fire bigger," said Amis, already pulling her pack around for her kindling.

"Don't waste it," said Cedar, the *We've a long way* clear in her voice.

The group sought enough sizeable rocks to roll around the fire as seats.

The fire snapped and cracked the slow-burning lumber. Flames sent up smoke. The smoke, Maab hoped, reached the lantern. The lantern would be seen by the watchful *Bane*.

Eventually, her eleven from the *Bane* would return to the ship.

***

They pitched two sailcloth tents once it became clear they'd be in that spot for the night. Each tent was large enough to hold six. Amnandi had barely stirred beyond the rising and falling of her chest for breath. Small charcoal burners gave what passed for heat within the spaces, sending errant ash and acrid smoke toward the vented apex. The tents being floored meant no one had to contend with wet sleeping rolls.

Conversation remained extremely limited. The lack of night sounds drew everyone even closer to the coals glowing orange then white in a series of refuelings.

The sky was full of the moon and stars, but those celestial sights remained out in the cold. Unseen for now. Unfelt in the heart. The captain's tent focused entirely on Amnandi. Barrow had ceded her space to Amis, who'd clearly meant to remain at Amnandi's side. In the first mate's tent, silence reigned in order to hear each whisper and stirring from the other.

Not even on the darkest, most stagnant sea had isolation felt like such a trap as this isle of elementals, and it was no secret that all eleven of them wondered if the isle was even that.

Daoud had returned to standard Daoud. He held Amnandi as best he could in his lap, while her long legs trailed the fabric floor. Her booted feet touched Amis's upright feet, although the rest of Amis slept an uneasy but unavoidable sleep. At some point, every one of them succumbed. Sarantain and Cedar slouched shoulder to shoulder atop their bedrolls, not yet supine. Niss, barely breathing lest she miss something, dozed under a wrap. Maab had eventually curled near the coals directly across from Daoud. The source of heat gave off just enough light for halves of shadows to stand against the night. Daoud had stopped studying the edges of these shadows some time ago. His eyes were closed, his mind active. The open mind was a library of information it didn't necessarily realize it had access to. He let his wander.

He and Amnandi were closest to the coals. When he opened his eyes, he studied the spirit of her face. He saw in her the wise old woman he hoped she might become.

Open your eyes, child, he wordlessly requested, wondering now if he was seeing the mother in the daughter's face. From the regard Maab, Amnandi, even Amis had for the matron, his meeting Ayanda Khumalo would be a great pleasure.

He longed for the opportunity.

But no future was assured.

Open your eyes, child, he thought again, less request, more plea. Her future needed her.

At some point he dozed, but not for long; the coals had barely changed in their metal bowl. The duration would likely have been longer if not for Amnandi moving. A tiny shift of a shoulder. Daoud was about to extend a foot to nudge Maab.

Amnandi's gloved hand atop his squeezed. He stopped.

Though she didn't voice it, he knew she meant for the others to sleep.

She squinted her eyes open and murmured to him so that he had to bring his head closer, but he'd heard every word.

"Tell me how you do that," she'd said.

Becoming a giant was the easiest thing in the world to do, including all clothing and effects upon the body. If she recalled the question in the morning, he'd take it upon himself to tell her. It wasn't that different from witchery. In fact, they were likely the same thing. New words such as *quantum artistry* would enter her world.

But she had immediately drifted back to sleep as softly as a sigh.

***

Nervous ebullience felt odd, but there they were. And a feast would have been proper, but rations were on hand.

The groups crowded into one tent.

"A sharp twist of wind, an ice crack—who knows?" said Maab. "I've no idea what caused the fall. One moment, fine; the next, the mountain roared at us."

"Tried to liquefy our bones with vibrations," Cedar embellished. "From now on, I go nowhere without a witch." She raised her cup to Amnandi. "How you feelin', dear?"

All the attention concentrated on Amnandi in that pungent space was absolutely overwhelming. Amnandi wanted to say so, but first she needed to say, "I won't be able to do that again soon," in case anyone wanted a logical reason to turn around now. She had given herself several such reasons on the road to consciousness.

Leena had been looking her over authoritatively. "She's got her appetite, no fever. Eyes look clear. A little weakness, but that's to be expected."

"A lot of weakness," Amnandi corrected.

"Dear, what you consider weak, a lot of us would wish to be our best day," said the cook, then to other adults within the tent, "Am I wrong?"

"No," said Maab, feeling the bruise along her hip singing its song every time she moved. "This is an extraordinary young woman in whose grace we travel. And that's *without* witchery," but Maab saw the slight duck of Amnandi's head so she sailed on. "We've had breakfast but no one got any rest. Try for a bit of decompression now. Amnandi, if you're up for it, we leave by early afternoon, cease before sunset."

At Amnandi's nod, Maab ushered the extra people out of the tent, mix-and-matching parties for comfort.

She, Daoud, Amis, Nyim, and Leena remained with Amnandi. The normally vocal youngsters kept a subdued silence, speaking only when spoken to, and even then in quick, studious phrases.

This is but a test of life, Maab wanted to tell them, leaving them, however, to get the feel of that themselves. Life was frequently an oddly formed terror soothingly shaped. It was a certainty that neither Nyim nor Amis had ever thought they'd be sitting in a cold tent on a frozen island so far from their homes it might have been another world, worrying about a witch during a mercy mission on behalf of either the goddess, the world, or a natural combination of the two, whereas Amnandi had probably entertained such a thought before she'd fully weaned. But the young ones needed their silence. They needed to see Amnandi eating thawed jerky and drinking from Leena's precious stock of powdered spices heated in a tin of water.

And when it was time to go, they all needed to pick up and do so. There wasn't a single journey that wasn't oddly shaped.

At the appointed hour, Maab asked Amnandi if she felt ready to go.

Amnandi said no.

They waited some more.

The next time Maab asked, Amnandi said yes. Camp broke quickly. Maab stood proud to see the swiftness and efficiency in Amis's ties, the dogged sincerity in Nyim's foldings, and the absolute effortlessness of the *Bane*'s more-seasoned complement.

No one in the wider world would know that this attempt to heal a part of Erah had been undertaken, a fact which didn't stop a single tab, snap, or buckle from fastening as the packs became packs again, as weights shifted to find the right balances on backs, and as bearers' footprints drove a trail into the snow.

SHRINKAGE

Maab was pleased to see Nyim and Amis not letting Amnandi out of their sight. There was a lot of ground to cover. Their attention on her shifted focus from that.

The avalanche effectively sealed the pass the captain had wanted to take. Going around wasn't particularly arduous, but it added time to their journey, which meant even more exposure to this island's hungry, shifting winds.

What was it about the cold that shrank perspectives in ways the heat never did? True, each extreme exacted distinct physical requirements, and the mind did indeed follow the body, but cold changed one's *nature*. Cold sent thoughts into a realm of withholding; it branded fellow travelers as adversaries. Maab had seen her share of crimes, some committed near her, some to her, some viewed from a distance. No crime under a burning sun ever felt so brutal as one committed where the assailant's breath left a trail of guilt.

Base instincts survived in the cold.

Daoud, ahead of the group by a few feet, raised a hand to signal a stop. He pulled his scarf away from his nose, closed his eyes, and tested the wind. He faced Maab with confirmation. "Ash."

Maab tasted with her nose as well. The rest of the group followed suit. Hints of ash unmistakably threaded into the breeze when it walked rather than ran. No sign of ash in the sky, though, no smoke or clear fire, only the mild acrid perfume every nose in existence experienced as ingrained memory.

"This wind circles and twists so much, it could carry scent of our own camp to us," Leena complained. "What's the source?"

"Ahead of us and east," Daoud said.

"The volcano for certain?" said Maab. "You getting any sense of warmth?"

"No. Just the scent. A scent barely there."

"It's there, though, and so will we be. I take that as an invitation," said Maab.

Daoud agreed. He covered his nose and jaw again. Their course shifted eastward as much as the land allowed.

❋❋❋

Cedar emerged from behind an outcropping.

"Bathroom breaks are the most arduous part of any adventure," Cedar joked, patting herself for warmth after hers. "Any you young ladies bleeding now?"

A round of *Nos* answered her.

"If you do, backs to the wind. Still freeze your butt off, but it helps keep you from cursing family." She gave a wink to Amis before kicking snow at Nyim and Daoud. "Tucked to your navels, I'll bet. If you're lucky, you'll make a decent woman of yourselves before this voyage ends."

Neither male laughed. Neither grunted, either.

Emotional limbo. Cedar hated that. "It's cold, gentlemen," she elaborated. "Sarantain, how cold is it?"

"Cold enough to be evil."

"This is what cold has forever done," agreed Cedar. "Taught the body to conserve piss and poo for as long as possible to get us thinking of them as important."

"Poetry, that is," said Skye, readjusting her large pack after their brief wait.

"Backs to the wind for you three, too, lest there be a sudden rain," said Cedar to the male portion of their group of eleven.

"They know how to relieve themselves, Cedar," said Maab.

Cedar slipped arms into her pack straps and hunched the load to her bony shoulders. "Ha! No man has ever peed properly. Marks of honor for them to be as inefficient as possible."

"I did once," said Sarantain after a glance at the high climb not too far off, then at the younger people. "Spent a month wandering a wilderness in search of myself afterward."

Cedar moved a little more surefooted than the youngsters to overtake Amis and Nyim, directing a look over her shoulder at them. "My lead, young ones." She had been through cold mountain lands like this one before, where the only firm ground existed under the step you'd just taken. The wind kept the snow at a thin dry layer here or scattered from the ground altogether, which led to overconfidence. The youngsters didn't need to learn a sprained ankle could be just as fatal as an avalanche.

She called back over that same shoulder, "Mystic! Give us a boon!"

Daoud shielded his eyes against the sun to scan the broken horizon. Nothing to be seen; he knew that. Nothing to be heard; they all knew that, but still the scent of ash. In the nose and in the brain, ash, existing more between thoughts than anything else.

"We walk the right path," said the human-sized giant.

The sun was at its sighing point. Soon, the day star would feel heavy enough to drop. Slanting rays slid rare umber and pale gray draperies across jutting stone, with the highest stone, the volcano itself, absorbing more than its share. It became beautiful.

"Keep eyes for signs of caves," Maab ordered. "If we can sleep out of the wind with a larger fire burning, so be it." She pulled her scope and scanned as well. Gold splashed against the volcanic range, then autumn's best orange, all suffused by rock so dark it stood outside age. The mountain filled the captain's vision.

"Does it give the impression it had always been there and always would be?" asked Cedar. "It should."

This pleased the captain. She replaced her scope, walked backward a few steps to see her whole crew, turned to lay a hand on Amnandi's shoulder, then put their faces side-by-side back into the wind.

FOR ALL OF US

The land was full of pocks: in rocks, in the ground itself, on the sides of outcroppings and odd formations. A volcano may have considered itself a god, but air still influenced its designs. The cave that cut into the rough shale of the mountainside was more a widened cleft—as though someone had sliced rocky cake. The impending night winds blew across rather than into it.

"Not quite homey," said Niss, surprising them all because she had said less than ten words the entire time, with those being more directional grunts than words.

"I'm learning to receive blessings with gratitude and satiation," said Nyim, pushing past her for the not-too-deep interior out of the elements. He knelt to pull out his lantern. Before he could light it, illumination flared to all crags.

"Amnandi..." Maab said with a slight shake of her head.

The light dimmed, crossed paths with Nyim's lantern catching, and faded.

This was the first anyone had noted the difference between warm witch light and stark fire light. Something deep in each person immediately preferred witch light but settled for the familiar flame.

The first order of business: erecting a tarp to serve as an additional wind-block while also leaving space for smoke to draw outward. "Nyim, Amis, that's you," said Skye.

Two coal fires. One near the mouth, one midway for the group to sleep behind, bodies in close huddle. Niss and Barrow handled the coals.

Sarantain screwed dowels together into a tall tripod. He hung Nyim's lantern from it, lifting the cave's light upward, giving them a sky.

Leena, Maab, and Cedar tended the cooking: iron pot placed atop one set of coals, flat iron pan for the other, tin pot for the water and spices her sister-in-law turned to broth.

Daoud's task was to mind Amnandi. Amnandi's, to sit with Daoud.

Night came down. Not a single sound of jungle, sea, desert, or plain. Only a sightless wind ceaselessly circling a quiet island.

Warmed jerky, dehydrated fruits and vegetables, hot broth, and a chance to exchange their heavy coats for thick blankets in the heat of the coals and the surrounding warmed stone helped set aside worry for a while.

"What do you think is happening back on the ship?" Nyim asked the captain.

"The thief has probably commandeered it and set the *Bane* to plundering. My grandmother always said she meant to be a pirate."

"To Elder Pinyasama," said Skye, raising an empty mug.

Maab returned the salute.

"Dedoura likely has the ship on permanent alert," said Maab. "That or she's convinced the Mer to drill holes in the mountainside to bring us closer to the dragoon."

"Crew's eating tarts and being lewd," said Leena, hiding her smile behind a hand.

Sarantain flicked a pebble against Cedar's boot. "Bothering our tools," he said, receiving an agreeing nod.

"They figured a way," said Barrow, "for the ship to fly."

The cave took a moment to think on that and smile.

Despite circumstances, it was well proven that the ability to smile in a cave made people ridiculously happy.

In Maab's mind, the figure of her grandmother, such a robust woman.

"The first time I ever set foot on a ship," said Maab, "I wasn't much older than Amnandi, her first trip on the *Bane*. Do you remember that, luv?" She felt Amnandi's yes against her shoulder. "I'd tried to get your mother to sail with me; she said will her daughter do? You bounced on that ship as if you meant to own it. And no one in Erah's history has *ever* been so thoroughly chaperoned. Sarantain, Bog, Grucca. Myself, Patrice, Leena— essentially the entire ship. Your first adventure on your own." Maab gave a gentle laugh, bringing her arm even snugger around Amnandi. "Are we ever alone? No. My first time, my mother hadn't received the ship from Gran Dear yet; Mother and I were visiting after Dear had returned from one of her longest voyages ever. Nearly six months! Yes, I'd been on the ship as a child before that, but it meant nothing to me; I was too young. I didn't see it as its own world until the day Mother assumed command and took a ride along the entire shore of Myrrai and back. With me staring at how big the world was the whole time, and more so: *that I was in it*. That may have been the first time the goddess and I spoke to each other. She said hello. No words whatsoever." Maab quieted with the remembrance.

"I grew up in hilly land," said Skye. "Among meat. Herds so widespread, the ground bounced when they moved. I could see the sea from certain hills. Home sat in the valley. I was a farmer till I grew of age. Every child's that. Then..." she said, and gave a lovely pause, her eyes sparkling with mischief under the light.

"Then?" said Amis.

"Then, a teacher. I taught words and poems and how to use them for good. How to root out blather and lies. How to turn words into food."

Amis slurred out, "We are all magick," closer to sleep than all of them. She had managed to plant herself between Cedar and Sarantain. They, in turn, had covered her in half their blankets although she was already wrapped in her own, head covered by the hood of her coat, warm and dry from the coals. They were all in coats, layers, boots, and gloves again, under blankets sturdy as sailcloth, as comfortable as they could be atop their bedrolls.

It had been a long day.

Amis yawned. Then Nyim. Then even Niss.

Bed soon.

"I think," said Skye, "I took to the sea to learn new languages. New words."

Cedar tapped Sarantain's knee. "Me, was for love. How old were we, Sarantain? Our first jobs on two different ships. We met at port, woodworking even then, our carpenters buying goods. Wisps of our current greatness. I showed you a notebook full of ideas; you showed me a toy cart you'd made. Said your niece had made you keep it with you at all times till you got home to return it to her. The most wee, beautiful bit of wood. Where is it now?"

"Lost to time, goddess," said Sarantain.

"Make another," she said.

"Give it to you?"

"To me. I'll see you home."

One of their long-burning logs cracked and coughed fireflies, none near enough to anything to be a danger.

Barrow, all had noted by now, was always comfortable

listening. Or observing. Right now, her eyes were closed, but trained ears hearing her breathing knew she was awake, for however briefly.

Daoud sat farthest away, meditating.

After a few moments of silence, nothing but breathing throughout. Of the eleven in the cave, ten were asleep.

Daoud rose, went outside, and stripped to grow as tall as he could. While he could do so with clothing, he generally preferred not. It was energy he could use elsewhere, such as heating, although at this size, the cold wouldn't affect him too much. He became large enough to sense all manner of things crossing through his consciousness, bumping into thoughts, or plip-drip dropping from a billion stars above. The plips became a trickle, the trickle a stream, the stream a river, and the river—he hoped— the essence of him hoped (this was not his soul but something older)—it hoped the river looped infinitely toward a source.

***

Subconsciously, each elder crewperson knew when to check on the fires. Sarantain had done it right before all had dozed, Cedar followed up while he slept, Maab peered out of one eye some indeterminate time later, and now Skye, who had felt a tiny dip in warmth. The lantern was out, but by now all eyes had adjusted to the coals' glow, slight but valiant. Skye knew where the shapes belonged regardless of how the bodies contorted.

The mass in the corner was missing. Boots and clothing were by the flap, situated orderly. Stars shone crisp through the vent gap. There was another glow. Blue. Not bright but enough to settle on the air and draw the eye. It came from around the lee of the cave, where the mass of the mountainside acted as a wind break. She made her way there quietly. The thought of drawing a weapon hadn't entered her mind yet.

Daoud glowed. Skye, taking him in from his folded legs to, at least thirty feet above, his unfurrowed forehead, amended her observation: his tattoos glowed. No one who made their trade at sea hadn't seen a phosphorescent animal. Daoud looked as though he'd swum through a field of phosphorescent jellyfish and emerged with their tendrils plastered all over him. The maths of wiry squiggles, curves, and dashes that collided with one another were alight. The strokes were thickest at his legs, narrower leading up from belly to chest, and thinnest at his shoulders, arms, and head, of which Skye saw only the shaved sides, not the top. She'd seen the tattoos on those sides before. They were not what she now saw glowing. The current pattern was more complex, as though the swirls had evolved.

His head was upturned, as if he'd fallen asleep watching for something from above.

She watched. He'd done nothing to indicate he was aware of her presence. She, on the other hand, had immediately noted the rise and fall of his chest courtesy of the movement of the blue lights, although his diaphragm barely moved. She removed a glove and touched the side of his thigh as though the side of a new structure. The flesh between the long, coarse hairs was neither warm nor cold.

She circled him, thanking the goddess that his privates remained hidden from view by dint of his extreme height and crossed legs seeming like huge crossbeams. He had taken the time to clear a wide circle of snow, rocks, or other debris from around him. A ceremony, then. Something mystical that required solitude, nudity, and gigantic stature.

He hadn't even stirred after she touched him.

Although she and Daoud rarely conversed aboard the ship, any foot touching a plank of the *Bane* fell under her care. That was how a ship functioned; otherwise, its captain got nothing done, decided nowhere to go, nor tied reason to impulse to seek new fascinations at sea.

The first mate watched over all.

Skye returned to the cave, gathered her pack as quietly as could be, assured Niss and Maab that all was well, and re-emerged into the cold.

She sat far enough from Daoud that if he suddenly stood, he wouldn't injure her, and near enough that he might feel the warmth of the fire she had built between him and her. She had no idea if the heat benefitted him, but it couldn't hurt. His body blocked a good portion of wind. Skye pulled her blanket over her already-hooded head. She hugged her knees and took one last look at the sky. Constellations looked strange from this angle of the world.

Strange sky. A naked giant sitting in the cold without freezing. A naked giant glowing undersea blue. And whose tattoos sought communion with unknown things.

And though the island had yet to produce a single animal, she would watch over this man.

Strange and stranger, but she, thinking of her captain, the *Bane*, and assorted tales from the two witches she knew in her life, had seen stranger things.

The mate wasn't aware of when she'd fallen asleep but she was instantly aware as Daoud picked her up under her knees and back, carried her into the cave, set her down, retrieved the expandable metal disc to snuff the outdoor coals so as not to waste them, then returned.

She allowed herself to sleep, and was glad to see he was clothed come morning.

❉❉❉

"From the way this volcano formed and how the winds circle it, Cedar thinks we can corkscrew up the mountain rather than a vertical climb. I won't say no to that," said Maab.

"Not as *much* climbing," said Cedar.

"I'm rested enough to port when necessary," said Amnandi, knowing that if she hadn't added "when necessary," Maab would have protested.

"Neither of you useless magicians can turn into a bird?" quipped Cedar.

Amnandi and Daoud checked each other, just in case.

"No," they said.

Maab's frown had barely left her face since awakening. "I need to know what the Mer are doing. They need to know what we're doing. I *think* if the Mer actually managed to contact a dragoon, Daoud would know it. Cedar estimates we can reach the volcano's rim before night tomorrow. I would prefer to find another way into it. I hate rappelling."

Skye stepped forward and raised her voice. "Everyone! What guarantee do we have that we'll find anything?"

"None," said both Nyim and Amis.

"And who leaves here dismayed by that?" the mate went on.

Not a murmur, not a motion.

Maab set her pack. "We march."

❋❋❋

They hadn't counted, but after a certain number of steps, the ground ceased being part of something larger and was instead an instance of looped time. Not only the ground but handholds gripped to pull oneself onto a ledge; breaths expelled from a jump across minor chasms; ropes used and spikes set to keep an entire human chain intact. All repetitions.

And yet, there was less of the mountain ahead of them.

Daylight had been favorable. The low sun slipped the clouds just enough to clarify the way without casting annoying glares off the patchy snow. The wind had formed natural, twisting ramps, rough but manageable. No one except Daoud and Amnandi truly detected the ash, but the logic of the situation was compelling. Too many things had drawn them there for this island to be insignificant.

Daoud had explained that he wasn't so much following the scent of the ash as the memory of it, a memory of Erah so new its malleable skin was nothing but possibility. A deep memory of the dragoon encircling the world head to tail, slowing the planet's wild spinning using energies not a single life on Erah could evolve to understand. Memories of the burning dragoon in sync with the world condensing, becoming compact, solid, and no longer solely a dream.

A dragoon, Daoud gradually realized, existed solely as memory but an infinite one, a cycle of contained being. By that logic, everything Maab and all within this hardy group did was preordained, but he didn't say this. Outside of Fabbin, people behaved odd with "preordained." Even within Fabbin, predestination paradoxes were the main thing driving mystics to heavy drinking and eventual homelessness, for if life was all part of a greater memory, then the ends were already written, which certainly led to determined nihilism and ruin.

Daoud focused. If this cold land and the adventure they undertook *were* the dragoon's memory, it was not yet his. He braced himself, pressing his back to the rock. He dug heels into pocks, hands tight on a rope as Sarantain's own gigantic body made its way up a steep incline between them and the next level, the rest of the party prepared to follow like beads on a string. It was not yet their memory, either. They, like him, enjoyed hope.

Daoud willed that enjoyment into arms twice their usual size as, one by one, ten more people climbed a knotted rope to him, then past him, moving carefully until the final of them, Maab, gained the ledge. He shrank. Maab paused to pull her flask from her coat and gave him a long drink of body-warmed water after the tiring but successful climb. She remained with him as the others slowly moved off.

He felt rested after a few seconds of air. The two followed.

Maab said, "It's not lost on me, mystic, that to go deep into the world we have to go high up and over."

He was certain her thighs ached, her feet screamed, and she definitely smelled like meat left in rain. She walked ahead of him, but he hoped she heard the smile in his voice when he said, "Yes, true. Our universe enjoys jokes. Very esoteric." He thought: *How else to heal a dream of death but with one of laughing life?*

✻✻✻

"It's an actual physical being?" Amis said to the back of Amnandi's hood after Daoud had briefed everyone. The sun had fallen by another finger's width in the sky.

"It could be," said Amnandi. "If enough of it came to remember what it was."

"A supposition"—this from Nyim, walking beside Amis—"which you learned only ten minutes ago. This could be madness."

Amnandi didn't turn to offer the shrug she gave. "We'll see. My skin hasn't stopped tingling since I woke up."

Adults—proper adults, unlike themselves—ahead of them. Adults behind them. The youths spoke with the solemnity of a library space but didn't pretend no one else could hear them.

Leena's voice came quickly from behind. "You feeling any other symptoms?"

"No, ma'am." Amnandi considered things a moment. "This feels less a symptom and more...reverence. Some part of me recognizes wonder here."

"As long as there's no cough or pain," the cook said flatly.

"What if the Mer have already been successful? How would we know?" Nyim said.

"We'll know when we speak to the Mer of the dragoon," said Amnandi.

"You can't—" he began.

At this the young witch turned. "You would entertain what I can do?"

"She's a witch, you know," said Amis.

"I don't even entertain what I can do," said Amnandi.

Unina would be amazed at this trip during a later and thorough telling. Amnandi regretted she hadn't had as much time for proper journaling as she'd liked, particularly in light of the captain's request to do so. She would find a way to make amends.

The island's constant bite of chilly wind lessened the higher they went, strange since altitude generally gave circulation free run. The occasional gust struck but it had little spirit in it, perhaps expending energy elsewhere.

Relative calm made people wary. They walked on. The more Amnandi thought, the more the tingling she experienced edged toward a slight itch. A witch appreciated caution, but apprehension rarely felt useful.

A silly young man telling her, the daughter of Ayanda Khumalo, what she couldn't?

Immensely tiring.

Everything was tiring. Amnandi wanted to be at home as much as anyone.

"Captain? I should rest," she said.

Maab held the flat of her hand to the sun. The muddy eye had sunk another finger's width. Two more hours before dusk. They stood upon an expanse of flat, if not sheltered, land. A good time for decisions.

"We bed here," said Maab.

The crew fell to setting up camp with pointed focus. Anxiety, fatigue, repression—the encampment was thick with it.

During supper: muted conversations in separate tents. The sky giving way to shadow.

At night, the nightmares about the Mer came.

When all awoke in the morning, the night was written on their faces. They compared dreams. In one, the Mer were humans who visited the camp and remorselessly slaughtered them. Another, the goddess gathered all Mer to boil them. Ravens in Nyim's dream asked him to betray the Mer, and he did. Easily.

"If they're in danger," said Amis, "what can we do?"

"Nothing," said Maab, and left it at that. She stood, weary of sitting on rocks. "Break camp," she ordered. "We make the rim today."

NIGHTMARES

Sickness in sufficient quantities never failed to protect itself. Mer generally swam in circles while they slept. They never dreamed. This group, asleep, swam slowly en masse straight toward the base of the island, outwardly a placid procession. Inwardly, each shrieked.

Minds beset by dreams. Their entire realities inverted, their sense of themselves gone. Sickness fed off the dragoon's radiating energy and attacked, opening the peace of sleep to allow phantasms.

The connective threads between the pod allowed death to creep. Convulsions flared, not stopping the procession of Mer but jarring the group into jagged waves. Now and then, a very violent shake, then nothingness. No somnambulant swimming. Just falling. A Mer here, a Mer there, motionless, sinking from the line, limp, the others continuing as if the slowly drifting Mer had never existed.

Rukkai and mates Von and Tem formed the tip of a macabre parade that moved inexorably toward a huge pocket at the base of the volcano, dreams of rot, loss, fear, betrayal, lusts, death, hatred, and waste torturing them. Dreams that crawled along the Mer's brains like ravenous crabs to pick their meat apart.

This was a surface world disease. Rukkai sent this subconscious knowledge through the tattered link, its body flashing sporadically, tics and shakes erupting from head to tail tips. For all their screeching of superiority, ravens loved pretending to be human. They cultivated hatred as though tending crops. Rukkai tried to tell each beset soul that the illness that infected the Raven King infected the human world and was amplified through proximity to an elemental.

Rukkai's mind twisted around to snap at itself, teeth vicious as a shark's. Wasn't an elemental in all things? Wasn't surface disease everywhere? Hadn't Mer swum through every murder, lie, every act of greed the entire surface spent countless waking hours perfecting?

THESE DREAMS ARE THEIR WORLD, Rukkai's mind boomed. *THE DRAGOON HAS NO PLACE IN THIS.*

A crab flayed skin from a memory. The silver flesh beneath became a dream of seeing a young Mer trapped in a net, hauled out of the water, and returned to the sea in pieces.

Rukkai shook. Hard. Muscles tore.

Dreams were cowardly things. They came in the dark when the mind waned. They brought pain and confusion, their sole goal to consume without feeding, the opposite of nourishment. The dreams came in astounding numbers, an unending wave of chittering mouths.

They demanded Rukkai remain asleep.

Rukkai's mates bumped into it. Or Rukkai into them. Even asleep, bodies knew the energy of those they loved. Even attacked in a coma, touch provided memory of real life. There was more than internal strife, more than anguish. The contact was so fleet it barely registered, but it sparked. Rukkai's thoughts pierced somnolence like a needle seeking starlight, not enough to see anything but enough to remind the mind that reality surrounded it. Potent and ready to be touched.

The crabs surged Rukkai, surged this new pinprick of thought traveling the mass of Mer bodies. They snapped at neurons, pathways, observations, and intentions, severing some but missing many, too many.

The thought of Merfolk circling the base of that island until every one of them gradually sank spurred consciousness; awareness quieted howls; instances of quietude brought actual battle: the Mer minds weren't defenseless, even when asleep. Sleep was a time for gathering energies.

Rukkai felt for how many lives had already settled into the silt. There were dozens of flat spaces in its mind, gaps in the link. Never to be art again. Never to swim.

Rage so intense that the entire deep section of the sea lit blue exploded the length and breadth of the sleeping line, obliterating these leeching, strange usurpers of peace. The burst of consciousness was likely felt as far away as Tempest, and likely straight through the deeps to the dragoon itself.

For the entire sea floor moved.

***

The entire world moved.

Amnandi had to think on that, think on sudden waves, sudden flooding, sudden earthquakes, storms.

While Daoud watched her.

Amnandi sat. She rested. She allowed Daoud's worried scrutiny. She observed the others. No sign of awareness from them. The island had not moved for them.

Had it reached her mother?

She wanted to tell everyone that on some level, the dragoon was aware of them. But she wasn't sure. She wasn't even sure that what she'd felt was what she'd felt. Everything in her head and body stewed.

Improbably, she wanted to laugh. They had come so far without a single clue what to do! She supposed that was life, yes, but a witch wasn't accustomed to admitting inescapably particular truth so freely. Everyone on the *Bane* had set out with goals, and none of them included perching on a chilly volcano or solitarily bobbing atop a frigid sea. Improbability had brought a young witch into contact with a giant, a prince, an inventor, and made family of the Mer.

Improbability was a wondrous thing.

A quaking world was an alive world, as conscious as ever but on the verge—perhaps—of speaking directly.

What a glorious thing that would be.

Was Daoud keeping eye to see when or if she would tell the captain what she'd felt? There was no way he hadn't felt it himself. He seemed more attuned to certain aspects of Erah than herself. Perhaps he wanted confirmation?

She met his eyes straight on and held them.

There. Confirmation.

He rose, crossed to where Maab and Skye conferred, and spoke very quietly to them, which drew nothing but attention their way.

"Speak loud enough for everyone," said Cedar.

"Something's underfoot," he repeated.

"Big?"

Words wouldn't quite describe it, so instead, he nodded.

***

It's been said that evolution follows no moral imperative, that energy makes no decisions, only begets actions.

I suspect that both of those are traps. That which changes without regard for compassion becomes a machine, no more complicated than a waterwheel despite its number of parts. If energy abets such change, it is a waste.

Trapped, we despoil what Erah has given.

I look at Amis and see that my sister might become a great teacher of love. She's never failed at comforting me, and has asked nothing for herself for the exchange.

Maab Pinyasama would muscle the moon aside to give us a section of sky for new stars. She suggested without saying a word that I write as we souls rested. Forgive my brevity, Unina, and forgive any distress I have caused you. I think not only of this journey.

The boy, Nyim, has not become a man. I watch him courting the possibility, which pleases me for Amis's sake. Their futures are hinted at and toyed with; they both know it. And though he is a prince, which is itself a worthless farce, he may leave his accumulated fears to be a person.

I feel I could write the stories of all my compatriots, not because it may be my last opportunity but because the people are so clear in my heart. So close to the rim, the warmth Daoud felt, we all feel. For Cedar, Sarantain, and Niss, that warmth is the promise of loved ones. For Barrow, excitement. Daoud has new knowledge to take back to his thinkers. As for our first mate and ship's cook, I believe they are both composing poetry in their own ways.

The sense of these ten is not of an end but that they will wake up tomorrow. Not hope. A given.

I feel pleased for them in a way I don't know how to process, Unina.

I need them to be happy.

I have time to seek out the horrors Erah faces when I leave here. There's a thief aboard our ship who's caused much misery. He will do so no longer. I will study predators so thoroughly, they become prey. You have prepared me.

What hasn't been said by anyone yet is the next part of this journey is for me alone. It cannot be otherwise.

I am prepared.

She tucked the journal and pencil nub into her secret sleeve.

No one did anything without reason, even the Raven King. Reasons were common. Intentions raised the bar. To travel Erah without clear intent insulted the pebbles, grass, sea, and clouds. Ten cold, hardy people in her eyesight intended to share life with others. What was higher intention than that?

She remembered something her mother had told her before the two of them set out on their first voyage. *The purpose of life is to speak to the world.* If Erah moved again, it would do so while she moved through it. *Greetings,* she would say to the dragoon in whatever way it understood her, *my name is Amnandi Khumalo. The world is sick. Can you help heal it?*

❊ ❊ ❊

The blue light faded as the last of them, Cedar, exited the portal. A chasm had been too wide to leap, their view of the rim too near to consider finding another way around. Magicks, Cedar had told everyone, set her teeth on edge. She patted her thighs to be sure they carried the usual weight. "No one who's earned wrinkles and scars has done so without encountering unpredictability clothed in certainty at least several times." However, none of the others ahead of her had been halved by the magick. "This it, then?" They stood upon a craggy, pocked circle which could have swallowed Sharda moon and come back for more. It wasn't a rim as much as it was a vast field ringing a sudden hole. "Mystic, we true in it?"

"Aye," said Daoud, barely registering the presence of anyone besides himself and Amnandi. Cedar's question might as well have come from an errant memory of people. Amnandi glowed green, blue, red, black, brown, gold, in that precise sequence, over and over, soft as gauze and as gentle to his eyes as his brother's hug. Obviously, no one else saw this; otherwise, Maab wouldn't stand there sighting along the rim, Skye wouldn't be silently checking the interior well-being of each of the party, Maab's sister-in-law wouldn't be wasting time praying, and Amis and Nyim wouldn't continue to fail to realize how deeply under everyone's protection they truly were. Green, blue, red, black, brown, gold. Daoud wondered if he glowed as well. Amnandi hadn't looked his way yet. She remained beside Maab.

Then Cedar's phrasing of the question he'd absently answered hit him. *Are we true in it?*

Are we real? To experience life demanded truth; anything else was tragic farce. No one loved, laughed, or cared without truth. No one journeyed a foot to heal another if things were unreal.

One existed through all things by being true in all experiences. It was a simple epiphany, a brief, tiny, welcome one, but he would remember to thank Cedar, once again solidified in his mind, meaningfully and sincerely.

Amnandi faced him at that moment—and he was sure that was no accident—and with the surprised widening of her eyes confirmed that he, too, glowed. He waggled a finger to indicate her own status. She nodded and went back to conferring with Maab.

The mystic wasn't trained in auras, but he was sure each heart around him glowed unseen in its own way. He wished there was time to classify the rainbows surrounding himself and the witch, but that was clearly a task for another time. Possibly never. What they faced was not to be repeated.

Cedar knelt and unslung her pack. "We don't have as much daylight shining into that hole as I'd like." She pulled a short torch, gave it an extra soak of oils, and told everyone else to step back in case the sucker exploded. She trotted to the innermost edge of the rim, dropped to hands and knees, and released the torch into the gloom. She followed this with a large stone at hand, peering into the gloom and listening for any and every thing. A great yawn, a stirring, a growl. The scrape of climbing claws. They were the possibilities everyone had voiced.

Daoud and Amnandi, of course, had not stepped back.

The flame struck a ledge but remained lit. The stone fell in utter silence until it met additional stone, clattered into the abyss again, *tock*ed for several long seconds, went silent even longer, with one last strike before nothing.

"Sucker's deep," she shouted over her shoulder. She stood, trying not to wince at the aches and accumulated stiffness. "We knew it, but now we know it won't explode when we're dangling eleven fires full." Daoud and Amnandi followed her back to the halfway point where Maab had everyone unpack. "I'm thinking noon tomorrow's a good time to go down, Captain," the old carpenter said. "Pour as much light down its throat as it can handle."

"And hope the goddess leads us well," said Maab.

"Not goin' that far with it, your grace," said Cedar.

"Perhaps you should," said Daoud.

***

There wasn't a volcano or large-enough cave that didn't at some point welcome the sea. Water found a way. Water made itself comfortable widening spaces, smoothing surfaces, permitting living things to wander.

Living things were not always beneficial.

The Merfolk battled tiny creatures.

The tiny creatures' advantage was that they were numerous. Their long stingers were annoying, but their suckers, once they attached, excreted an even more potent toxin that left burning scars as the Mer spun against stone to scrape them off.

The tiny squid-like things had the feeding avarice of humans. Small bodies continued to swarm into the underwater cavern the Mer occupied, effectively cutting off escape toward open sea, and the cavern's connective point facing the deeper interior of the volcano was too narrow to allow more than a few large bodies through at a time.

A line of Mer formed revolving shield walls of themselves to allow the youngest and the elderly to proceed as unscathed as possible, the shielders only dropping out when so covered they couldn't bear it, twisting along the walls until free, then darting behind the wall to escape. Rukkai was nearly covered. Its two mates the same. The whole *wall* was a mass of stinging tendrils.

But the wall would stand. Those through the exit were already snapping coral and stone or gathering other debris to plug the entrance; dozens more had ingested enough silt to belch out a small hillock. Even if a handful of the small red creatures got through, they'd be quickly snagged and ripped apart. That silent thought traveled through the line. Snagged, ripped apart, and then the Mer would go on their way, trailing wounds and blood to who knew what else. The humans had a phrase: the wine-dark sea. Human poetry. Poetry solely because humans truly didn't know the constant sacrifices of the deeps.

Every cavern made something bleed.

Below the *Bane*, Rukkai and the Mer had lost so much blood.

***

Midnight.

A moon blocked by clouds.

A young woman, all her companions asleep save one.

Amnandi stood at the precipice. Daoud sat among the sleepers some distance behind her.

She wouldn't do anything, not yet. But she wanted whatever was down there to know she would be on her way soon.

She allowed only one word to fill her: *Prepare.*

Exhaustion precluded lookouts. Even Amnandi and Daoud finally slept fully in the deeps. No one heard the downbeat of wings, didn't feel the air's static charge as clawed feet transformed into softer flesh, and legs which appeared spindly yet were strong enough to carry off sleepers lengthened, thickened, and smoothed themselves over knees.

The smell, however, disturbed the group enough to cause stirring. One by one, Maab's crew exited their shelters. It was a cold morning. Distressingly so. A blade dipped in ice would at least have a hilt made of wood to remind one of the possibility of warmth, not like this sudden enveloping leech made of knives that cut away heat in swift strokes.

Maab glared at the ravens as though the birds themselves had brought ill winds.

Edrickl the Gold and Deneb the Blue hadn't changed a bit. Still naked, still imperious.

"You smell like ass dipped in ammonia, then preserved by the cold," said Cedar.

Maab made note to thank her for voicing that assessment.

Not that any of the shivering humans smelled much better, but ammonia brought its own bite.

"These waters are not fit for plunging!" Edrickl snapped.

"You two are used to Erah's more-temperate treatment," said Maab. "You followed us a long way for very little reason, or you came back for even more of one. For honest answers, we can provide you warmer waters and a chance to dry."

"Lies is all they'll give, captain," said Cedar.

"Truth is however we see it, human," said the Gold. He pointed straight at Cedar but addressed Maab. "We will not allow that one to speak."

"Ya smelly bastard."

"Cedar," Maab said.

"Aye," the carpenter relented.

It was lost on no one that during this brief exchange, the ravens had shifted their positions fully downwind. And now that the cold had slapped any remaining blurs of sleep from everyone, it was clear the ravens *had* changed. Their movements: worried. Their eyes: either unfocused, never still, or both conditions at once. Their luster: covered by a sheen of pain.

They were afraid. Fear had as much to do with their unfortunate odor as extreme flight, exertion, and excrement. Fear was the source of their return, and if they were back, certainly there were others.

"How many are with you?" asked Maab.

The Gold held a hand up, splaying all three fingers.

Maab indicated the rim. "Any chance of you flying in there and telling us what you see?"

"Are we carrier fowl for human messages?" chittered Deneb the Blue.

"You really aren't carved for this weather," Maab noted. "What if we offer you coverings?"

"Clothing is your admission of inadequacy," said Deneb. "We will—"

"Freeze," Maab cut him off. She shrugged. "My simple barter shouldn't be so offensive. We have blankets. Heavy ones. You can roll them up and carry them as you fly, even if your intention is a straight line home and not into the mouth of a volcano. But I beg my detour. One brief flight. I would value your impressions."

Deneb stamped the ground with curled toes, forgetting for a moment they weren't strong gouging talons. "Humans seek servitude of everything Sharda sees! You are plague."

"Hush, Deneb," said Edrickl.

"They are plague!"

"And we are cold," said Edrickl. Edrickl moved toward Maab

and crew, already beginning to change. With a hop, he was airborne and over their heads, blue Deneb following immediately. The two massive ravens angled past the inner lip of the rim and disappeared.

"Blankets," said Maab. "Warm them near the fire" was the last thing the ravens heard of the humans.

* * *

They flew deep. Darkness was no hindrance, their eyes being sharp as scythes. Fear kept them silent; fear made them swift. A new poison had entered Erah; Edrickl and Deneb felt its alien progression as if they'd imbibed it from a vial themselves. A new form of hatred that meant for ravenkind to become ash alongside everything else, like the particles stirring in the tiniest swirls from crevices in their wake. Ash was evidence of things spent, but as far as Blue and Gold were concerned, ravens were the true spark of the world. The two sped through nothingness in a downward corkscrew that hugged the walls as closely as possible. A tomb was a tomb, no matter how large or grand, and an inactive volcano was merely a tomb for dried, useless things that would be forgotten well through the last light of Erah's sun. The quicker they were out of there, the quicker... The quicker. Speed was a raven's right, was it not?

The quicker they would no longer be afraid.

Neither knew where such honesty came from, but both were sure each shared it. Adamantly not speaking such truth was equally assured. They glided with a velocity that would have shamed lightning. Edrickl swooped upward first, blasting out of the hole moments from when they'd entered, followed by Deneb, both into high, lung-clearing arcs and an enforced slow descent. The humans would wait upon them.

Edrickl touched down, changed, was given a blanket and

silence. Deneb, the same.

The diminutive sprites twisted themselves in the warmed blankets and allowed heat to speak comforts to them.

After a long moment, and only because a sense of propriety seized him, Edrickl said, "It is a hole. We saw nothing; we smelled nothing."

"You weren't down long enough to cross a fart traveling upwards!" said Cedar. Maab waved her aside.

"Impressions?" said the captain. "What'd you *feel?*"

Humans had never been fit for the internal lives of ravens. Yet blankets were warm around their small bodies and tucked underfoot.

But then Edrickl was bolstered by remembering that humans feared everything, even—or especially—things that ignored them or outright had no use for them. There hadn't been a raven on Erah who'd ever feared the moon, and yet these gangly bipeds still held festivals to mollify Sharda toward benevolence.

"I felt—" A glance at Deneb confirmed Deneb had felt it too. "We felt...unbothered."

"By threats? Dangers?" said Maab.

"Chaos. The chaos all around."

"We knew flying outward would bring us to you, back to chaos, but we didn't care. And not," said Deneb with clear inner distress, "in the way we usually don't care."

"What about obvious dangers to us?" said Maab.

"You're climbing into a volcano," said Edrickl.

"No carved stairs, no magick?" said Maab.

"It is what you expected. A hole. Dead."

"Will you be our eyes?"

This human, the Gold admitted as warmth slowly seeped away from the blanket, had style. She wasn't as bland as the muscled warriors Edrickl usually faced, nowhere near as cocky as a mage; she actually appeared to move with purpose, very nearly witch-like, and at this, Edrickl glanced at Amnandi. If any human received respect among ravens, it was a witch. A witch's daughter, doubly so. The power that a mother devoted to daughter was not wrongly compared to every unseen power that worked to maintain Erah's shape, be it clouds molding mountains, rivers cutting land into fit pieces, or utter foolishness—as was here—in seeking to contact a dragoon. The most powerful witches used the unknown as an effective magick. It guided them in ways that always proved interesting.

The witch stared at him. She was calm, placid, vivid. A danger. A shield.

Edrickl relented against his better nature. "I will be your eyes. For a short while. I depart as I please."

"I wouldn't ask more," said Maab.

"Isn't one of your lies that a human said that to Sharda moon, then asked more, and was promptly cast here to see her only from afar?"

"Myths. They're called myths," said the captain.

"A lie that encourages, renamed with honors," said Edrickl. "Convenient for your lot."

Maab splayed her hands. "Convenience is our downfall," she said, clearly hoping it would please Edrickl.

"Well said," said the raven.

BLACK, WHOLE, SUN

Rukkai advised rest. Many didn't want to. Motivations drawing them pulled harder and harder, especially after the hideous dreaming that left everyone rattled and confused. Rest might mean succumbing.

Not again.

The compromise came in slowing. They swam cisterns very slowly, rolled through caves, crossed rocky stretches of magma frozen into its own torment of perpetual dreaming. Wounds constantly announced their presence. Even those who stopped when they could absolutely go no farther without a moment to themselves stopped with the mindset that they were still moving.

They sensed a need to understand something. Not to

understand their plight; plights were common. This pulling need was the determination to grasp the monumental *why* of anything that felt...wrong? Was that the concept? Had the dragoon unwittingly joined them by sensing that perhaps too much about Erah—or even Erah and other worlds; Merfolk knew the universe to be seas within seas—existed in a fundamentally wrong state, with "wrong" defined as so far from what the state could aspire to be as to be unrecognizable as what the gods knew to be reality?

Such thoughts slowed some as much as their wounds and fatigue. Rightfully so. Every part of Rukkai wanted to stop. To learn that a sleeper was never asleep but perpetually confused? It could crush consciousness to dust. But the combination of sudden dreaming and stretching ennui signified high powers at hand. Rukkai moved via instinct. The movement felt like the deepest, most personal surge toward real warmth.

Rukkai hadn't sensed the witch since they'd separated, not that she and the humans were vital. It definitely hadn't seemed they were. The part of its mind it would have devoted to watching out for vibrations or scintillance from her was better devoted to healing itself, anyway.

The scarred explorer pushed its way through a large fissure, widening existing wounds and creating new ones. Despite their layer of blubber, the cold made even the most superficial cuts hurt, but pain was too commonplace to bother with now. The fissure opened into a huge chamber, one totally dry.

It would be a slog getting across that.

However, Rukkai detected a shift in the atmosphere. Something about this cavern exhibited a possibility the other spaces they'd traversed inside the lattice of eruptions had lacked: intent.

Its mates entered and felt Rukkai's hesitation. Their ever-probing senses picked up something too.

Within this pitch darkness, they were not alone.

What they perceived should not have existed there. Its oddness halted them in confusion.

I smell bird, said Rukkai.

Each Mer that had made it through the crack agreed.

They concentrated their senses, their blue sigils brightening not so they could see but so they could *feel*. In the quiet darkness, the Mer felt the eyes, the hushed breathing, and the practiced stillness surrounding them from cave walls to ceiling, followed by the mass rustle of feathers moving as one.

✻✻✻

Getting inside wasn't difficult; keeping things illumined worth a damn was. The volcanic hole ate light like a delicacy. The *Bane*'s teams descended with assembled glass-enclosed torches that fit into sconces with a metal loop for the rope so that a lowering hand was free yet guided the light all the same. Not a single person complained about the heat near their faces. Whatever warmth Daoud had sensed remained primarily of the mind and not the body.

Amnandi flared her eyes. The sleek forms of the ravens dashed through her beam. It was the only way to keep track of them. Amnandi's ears and head felt stuffed. Gold and Blue intentionally stayed out of range of the torches.

As with any volcano, there were ledges formed from different levels of eruptions. Not as good as carved stairways, but they served as resting points. Noon landed upon them.

The eleven travelers had sidled downward in two lines for safety's sake and now rested side by side, nearly at the limit of the sun's hazy reach.

They rested in the types of silence that spoke clearly: Nyim handing Amis dried fruit, she passing her halved jerky to him; Barrow near Daoud, doing her best to nonchalantly study his markings by torchlight; Maab and Skye on either side of Amnandi, both pretending to conserve their strength; Niss, Leena, and Sarantain ushering Cedar closer to them to share all their warmth.

Offer life life. Whether it flourished afterward was its own concern.

Amnandi wondered if, in giving themselves to the dragoon, would its energies know what to do or simply register their group as the background noise of all reality? Would it register them at all? Would even her mother have the answer to that?

Her mother had sat in caves of unknowing like this before.

Even before Amnandi's birth, Ayanda Khumalo had healed what needed healing and battled sprites, wights, revenants, brutes, and—far more often—evil humans, when all she'd wanted was to see the world with her given eyes.

Imagination provided her mother's comforting voice. *"A witch is never not a witch. Nurture yourself with that."*

I will, the witch told herself.

A witch protected multiple fronts from danger: friends, Erah, the innocent, the foolish (far, far too often the foolish), family. The energetic lattice constructed by what some called the gods, some called nature, but most chose to subconsciously ignore in favor of lovers, hearth, and intriguing meals required it.

Of the eleven gathered, only two were in any way prepared to commune with such energies in a fashion that might make a difference. Everyone knew this. And yet everyone sat on a dimly lit rocky ledge in the middle of a cold waste, prepared to go forward.

Who *wasn't* a witch, then?

Muscles stiffened at long pauses. Maab gave the signal to get up, check one another, and proceed.

Downward.

***

Was a sense of relief an understatement to how they felt reaching a space where they could walk again? It was. The volcano even took pity on their eyes. Phosphorescent lichen lined surfaces but stung the nose with a peppery fugue. Barrow remarked that such growth was highly unusual, to which many in the group exclaimed, "*That's* what you find unusual?"

Nyim whispered toward Amis's ear, "I expect to find treasure here. Jewels and gold."

"Not a tall tale, boy," snapped Cedar.

"Daoud," said Maab, "offer me something encouraging."

"None of us are dead," he said.

"That we know of," Amnandi pointed out.

"Not as helpful as you think, luv," Maab informed the witch. "All right. This glow gives us surer footing. The ground is wide and amenable. My arms hurt like anchors. A single additional ache in my back will snap bone. I smell like Sarantain during summer exercise. That sum it up for everyone?" Nods and murmurs answered. "Then we continue either out of stupidity or the goodness of our hearts. Amnandi, lead on. We follow and keep our answers private."

Maab noted the ravens, perched and nearly invisible against the softly glowing rock, moving antsy, likely weighing options to flee. They'd safely led her team to sections of the volcano that didn't require dangling or arm muscles, had even retrieved ropes and spikes from the descent for multiple use.

She knew the ravens thought she liked to talk too much. "A song from anyone?" she said. "Daoud?"

"Mystics don't sing," he said.

"Mystics can't sing, more like," said Cedar. "Heads up butts lend poor acoustics."

"I love you," Amis blurted to Cedar.

BREATHE IN

The Mer were tired and not inclined to fight, instead releasing a massive collective electrical burst as the dripping cavern suddenly grew wings. The defense would have merely tired the Mer out during the squid onslaught, but here it was enough voltage to stun, confuse, and give pause. The only electricity ravens were familiar with was lightning, and they weren't foolish enough to fly close to that. Loose feathers drifted as ravens immediately twisted away, knocking into one another, clawing anyone nearby to get out of their way.

WE HAVE NO WAR WITH YOU! broadcast Rukkai as loudly and vehemently as possible. If these birds were going to be idiots—constantly—they'd already found the Mer's patience tested to its breaking point. Ravens enjoyed their personal shallow rivers and ponds; the Mer would show them how deep the waters truly went.

Shrieks bounded throughout the chamber, enough noise to wake a dragoon, the eternal current, and Life Everlasting itself.

The Mer formed a circle, then a dome. Their pronged flukes were prepared to whip out as lances.

Rukkai waited for either silence or attack.

The ravens found roost again, settling as much as their indignation allowed.

The ravens from the island, the Bone Brothers Hza and Dza, anonymous in the stir, spoke for the group.

"You have stolen us from our homes for this!"

WE HAVE HAD NO SEEKING OF YOU!

"Were we to sit idly while you killed us? More of us!"

You killed you.

"You would have done the same! Or would you have done worse? If you leave here, do we do this again? We will not be hunted!"

BE. SILENT!

Even the stone seemed stunned. Neither Mer nor raven let a heavy breath escape. Rukkai's dapples and stripes blazed so blue that its body, elongating from the top of the dome, shone as a beacon. Its appendages twitched as though wanting to strike anything that moved.

EVEN WHEN WE COME TO HEAL, YOU PARADE AS POISON! BRING YOUR POISON TO ME! screamed Rukkai.

Neither Bone Brother had flown all this way to miss out on blood. They swooped Rukkai from opposite sides of the space.

Rukkai whirled, the tips of its appendages honed to knife points, and slashed a wingtip off the first, gouged a cut across the belly of the other. The brothers wheeled away but didn't land. They circled.

And circled.

The more they circled, the more they convinced themselves they had time.

The Merfolk held position. The roosted ravens watched.

The first Bone broke the pattern first. He dove so swiftly

and suddenly toward Rukkai that Rukkai's senses experienced a moment of blindness. Talons dug into Rukkai's back. Surely, the raven knew that close-quarters combat against a Mer was suicide. Rukkai immediately twisted, wrapping the bird's neck and legs to prevent his claws going deeper. Rukkai yanked the bird away, then held him out of beak's range, ready to snap his neck. The bold raven could have been dead before another caw.

Rukkai flung the bird away as hard and far as possible.

The second hadn't attacked.

But both clearly wanted to die.

If it was not possible to heal, if not possible to repair themselves, they chose death. When they were afraid, they chose violence. It was why the humans had so many fearful stories of the Great Searavens. Of how a raven would steal a babe for a perceived slight. How they gutted trespassers or the honestly lost. Why nothing in the sea or air was to be trusted, for ravens claimed both. There were stories about the Mer, too, but only because the template had been laid. Mer usually kept dealings with humans extremely rare for reasons consistently reinforced by scores of land dwellers.

The entire raven culture had intentionally sown its fears across much of Erah. And the fact that they were literally able to make themselves invisible to humans didn't help. The pretense may have been that ravens were quiet and aloof, but at all times they—from river raven to swamp bird to mad king—*whispered fears to the sleeping*.

They made sure to be part of everyone's story.

And now the second, Dza, circled.

Hza flapped and screeched but didn't move itself forward.

Rukkai's mates peeled themselves from the dome. Three blue beacons crowned the heights. In a flash, they leaped outward, straight for the circling raven.

They missed.

❊❊❊

When the second Bone Brother flew into the tunnel Amnandi had just exited, he nearly collided with the witch. He did, however, get snagged in the blankets of Blue and Gold as he tried to blast between them.

"Lights high!" Maab shouted. Raised lanterns cast the thrashing bird in a net it could not escape. Edrickl and Deneb shed their blankets to ensnare the raven even further. Daoud grew bigger to scratch the tunnel ceiling with his hunched shoulders and trapped the bird in his gloved hands. Maab still planned to find out how he grew his clothing—a fascinating advantage toward future adventures—but it would wait. The raven's head looked like a chick's poking out of Daoud's sizable hands.

"Bring violence and my crew feasts on squab," Maab said. "Do we understand each other?" She stood close to the panicked bird. Her lantern reflected the wildness in his eyes.

"That's disgusting," said Edrickl.

"Quiet! I don't like being followed. Daoud, if you feel a single prick, clap for joy." She wheeled on Deneb and Edrickl. "This one's known to you?"

"He is the elder of two brothers. Dza. A nuisance," said Edrickl.

"A danger," Deneb corrected.

"Danger," Maab repeated softly. She moved even closer, keeping her face within pecking range. "What scared the piss out of you, Danger?" Eye to eye without a single blink. "Where've you been sneaking about, and what's out there? My good friend is going to relax his grip just enough to give you space to transform for a fruitful conversation."

Daoud relaxed, felt the transformation commence, and set the raven down, bringing himself back to normal size at the same time.

A hairless orange-flecked small man stared back at them, trying to pretend he was neither cold nor afraid, nor helplessly outclassed. The mannish part seemed odd. Usually a changed raven, unless extremely old, held some aspect of youth about them, either in attitude or look. This one carried too many marks of self-inflicted wounds and regrets, particularly in how he tried to glower at them but not meet their eyes.

Maab kept him well introduced to hers. Her brilliant brown eyes spoke for her between pauses.

He was in no way an elder. The Bone Brother's head swiveled toward every noise: Edrickl and Deneb swirling their blankets back on; Niss shifting her warrior position to offer a clear line of flight for one of the two daggers in her hands; the accelerated breathing of two of the youngsters; the absolute unruffled silence of the witch. From the twitch in his eyes, Maab saw that last kept the raven wariest.

He measured his odds in calming breaths.

"You will address me properly," he said. "Dza Bone."

"Dza," said Maab, "questions have been put to you. Grace me answers."

"Your demons have flown into a rage," he said. "Waterlogged slugs."

Maab's impulse to grab his shoulders was stopped only by her remembrance of how ravens hated any unbidden familiarity via touch. "Mer are here? Guide us."

"I will not."

"That was not a request!" Her eyes speared Edrickl and Deneb. "This one's in your charge. If he leads us wrong—"

"You bluff," said Deneb the Blue.

"Yet sometimes I'm plain as day. Give me a direction," she said to Dza Bone, "beyond the one you just came in."

"Your human senses don't hear it yet?" said Dza.

At this, Amnandi and Daoud devoted attention outward for several heartbeats, thirty at least.

And when they heard it, they didn't hear it. They felt it.

Intention surging atop movement. Deep but insistent.

It felt like water, they said.

"I advise returning to higher spaces," the Bone Brother said urgently.

The tunnel they'd traversed was a long one, and any thought of going backward galled each member of the party, but the fear in the wavering raven spoke louder.

And the rumble, just in those few seconds, felt decidedly closer.

The instant Amnandi threw the portal, everyone knew what to do. She was the last to enter, pleased to see people continuing to run on the other side, heading for the far opening of a cavern that still smelled of campfire smoke.

All three ravens took to flight and the uppermost reaches they could find.

"High ground!" Amnandi shouted, and threw the portal leading to the top of this dark, deep bowl they'd clambered down but an hour before. When they reached the lip, they watched the fissure. Having gone into it, it opened into a proper tunnel. Watching it, or watching the darkness where that space rested, for it was too far into gloom for anyone but the ravens and Amnandi to discern, made pulses race. Gradually, sound accompanied the grainy blackness. A roar of souls. Madness battering at walls, cracking stones with fists, leaving toothmarks on the ground. The avalanche had felt like the anger of the gods. The power and speed of the rushing flood filled not only the cavern but battered between the spaces of thought itself, filling brains with an ancient, well-proven fear.

The Mer brought the sea.

A water column shot through the fissure in hard gouts, biting the edges to widen the space. And then, within that stream, Mer. They were invisible save for fleet strips of blue that appeared and disappeared.

The fissure gave way, the resulting explosion as if the entire sea entered by invitation. Water slammed the sides of the cavern and swept back on itself in an ever-faster swirl, churning and bashing and filling half the space until the lights of the Mer, significantly closer, were clearer, then quickly higher still until a wan blue cast painted the volcano walls.

Everyone, both human and raven, did the only thing available to them: waited. While waiting? Marvel at what the goddess could do.

✳ ✳ ✳

Tears welled in Amnandi's eyes.

The Mer were sublimely beautiful as they swam. Blue hues moved slowly, some languidly as if exhausted beyond any telling, some haltingly as if in pain deeper than most souls dwelled. The water filling the sealed crater rested a good stone's drop below the ridge. The Mer did nothing but circle. The onlookers watched lights cluster around a single glow, or a lone spark go through intricate twists off by itself, or groups glowing in unison, the entire view splashes of brilliant cerulean paint.

The pain from the pool was overwhelming. With Amnandi facing forward, no one saw her cry. The Merfolk remained silent, not a single thought rising above the water. She wanted to be among them, not to speak but to swim as needed. To orient herself to their world. To become a vital reason to exist beyond having been born. To touch another being with the light of her soul if by no other means available. She kept a litany of these aspirations going in her mind to ground herself, otherwise she would have dived.

When it became clear the Mer had no intention saying anything or exiting, Sarantain, Cedar, and Barrow made three fires. The eleven explorers gathered around two of the blazes, the three ravens the other. Leena had tossed the Bone Brother a rolled blanket.

Amnandi continued to watch the flashes.

There was far too much pain coming from that pool.

✻✻✻

Conversation through motion and light. Each Mer checked on how each was doing, what each needed. More Mer slowly filed in. There was no rush. The crack of the ancient cistern above their heads during their slaughter of the ravens after Hza Bone had led an all-out attack was nothing less than the goddess's woe.

Rukkai didn't think on the specifics of what had happened. Those thoughts were poison. Its long body flowed among its family, healing and speaking without touching. Anguish, as powerful a poison as any, saturated the pool. Their intricate dances, as they circled and mirrored one another in a massive ball of Mer, connected them in ways no Mer would consider explaining to others.

They intended to spend their time in these frigid waters speaking their healing until they had nothing left to say.

ALL IN

Thirty minutes later, a wet slap against rock. Hard minutes after that, a final slap. Rukkai pulled itself up and over the ledge.

The raven between Deneb and Edrickl retreated a step behind its fellow ravens.

Rukkai ignored the action and slid in tired lurches toward the captain. It raised itself to its full height, becoming a tower of heavy flesh directly in front of Maab. It had never stood so closely before. It made no motion. It said nothing.

Pinyasama knew why.

She took the one step between them, wrapped her arms as far around its thick body as she could, then leaned a cheek into its cold, tough flesh, joining in healing in the fashion Mer knew humans were capable of. "Friend...I'm sorry," Maab said, and held Rukkai until a tear hit its skin.

As Maab pulled back, Amnandi came forward. The sudden

warmth to the air spoke of her intent. Rukkai, inside her mind, stopped her.

Save your strength, child.

Amnandi's torch cast even more light on Rukkai. Welts, pecks, scratches, gouges. A latticework of injuries. Did Rukkai study her and Maab for the same? The bruises, cuts, and aches each person wore hadn't produced a word between any of them except as needed if Leena decided ministrations were in order.

Everyone hurt and was cold and was tired and was hungry, but they—to a sentient being; Mer, human, unexpected raven— were *there*.

The spot felt sacred for that.

The raven behind Deneb and Edrickl broke the silence. "Where is my brother? What of—"

"Gone," said Maab, turning toward the raven, being sure to catch Niss's eye. A dagger hadn't left Niss's hand since Dza had entered their company.

The sea has them, as had begun this. Had you left us alone, it would not, said Rukkai, *be*—he jabbed—*so.*

Dza considered his position. Like Edrickl and Deneb, he had wrapped the blanket around him, delaying flight by precious seconds. As humans so often did, guile had been hidden behind warmth, a brilliant means of taking advantage. Either decision, attack or flee, would see the sharp end of something enter him and come out the other side before a wing could cup the air.

He appreciated the ridiculous perfection of the situation. Nor did he respond to the Mer. As far as Dza Bone was concerned, it was assured he would exit this dark mouth. The dead were forgotten easily enough.

Had I left them alone.

Dza shook this thought off. Introspection was for those weak to action.

Maab swiped her eyes with the back of her glove. "We made

it this far," she said to Rukkai. "That should be worth a banquet somewhere. Have you...found food along the way?"

Not enough. We survive.

In the space of that second, Maab fretted an entire lifetime. She had no food to give them, no means to tend their wounds, and only words to speak with. She had no idea what the Mer had done, there and before, for Erah unseen. "What now?" she asked. There was no going in that water for her or her crew. Another route would mean another cold night. "Do you sense...anything?"

"I do," said Daoud from behind.

"And I," said Amnandi.

We will search and return. We will be swift.

Very swift. Awkwardness had barely set in among the gathered when multiple slaps against igneous rock issued upward. Amnandi cast eyes over the edge. Rukkai and its mates moved in unison, sharing the same exhaustion, pained but steady. When they reached the top, each stood tall.

A crack leads deep below, Rukkai told Maab. *This is not for you.*

"My love, I didn't voyage to be of no use," said Maab.

It is too deep, too cold, and you cannot breathe.

"I can," said Amnandi. She looked at Maab, at Amis, at Sarantain and Leena.

None spoke otherwise.

"Bring her back," Maab told Rukkai, with a nod of assent to Amnandi.

Amnandi doffed her coat, outer clothing, and boots, leaving the layer of protective wrappings and socks underneath. Icy air slapped any suddenly exposed skin it found.

Cold and heat are merely nerve functions, she told herself, already drawing the breath for the inward warming spell.

She had been afraid precisely seven times in her life...and each had felt like what she felt now, except now wasn't exactly fear. It was excitement. A magnetic insistence pulled at every fiber of her to receive something, yet also pulled her forward.

One must give for another to receive. The giver was below.

Amnandi let Rukkai know she was ready. Each Mer turned and leapt for the water.

The daughter of Ayanda Khumalo parted the surface with barely a sound.

A moment later, Amis moaning, then a whimper from the small, dirty girl that, despite the immediate attempt to control, forced itself out of her in warm drops.

❉ ❉ ❉

For the first leg, Rukkai directed Amnandi to hold one of its fluke whips. She was to move as Rukkai moved, twist as it twisted. Amnandi kept her eyes closed except for brief blasts of light to place location in memory. She attuned herself to Rukkai's water stream, its pitches and variances. The downward course was so jagged, it was a slalom along lightning that had somehow trapped itself underground, spent now of all energy. Eternal and dark.

Holding Rukkai conserved her own energy, which conserved air. She used these reserves for warmth. The lightning crack twisted for eternity in her mind, which she broke into manageable chunks. The Mer would not have brought her past her limits; she knew this. She knew also that they expected her to be resourceful.

The passage was wide enough for the Mer to swim single file. Two or three humans may have been able to do it side by side. She would have liked to have had Maab and Amis flanking her, except they would certainly have drowned or frozen by now, a thought Amnandi immediately pushed away, though the shadowy afterimage of bodies sinking into darkness remained.

Fear has no place here. It is not needed. It is not wanted. After several repetitions, she believed it.

Rukkai dipped suddenly. Their speed increased. Her gloved

hand tightened.

This, then, the second leg.

The water felt warmer. Not warm. Warmer. By a hair. The deeper they went, more tunnels, one of them a straight line for what felt like ages.

And then a shiver of light. The sensation against her lids was so faint and so unexpected, she almost dismissed it. Rukkai's water stream had changed, too. They were now swimming more or less horizontally. Now angling up. She opened her eyes to illumination spreading upon the water's vast surface, but it hadn't felt like they'd traveled back to open sea. There was the matter of temperature, for one, and the quality of the light, for another. It was golden. Not sun-gold or even straw-gold. Gold. Gold as if the air above had filled with trillions upon trillions of radiant metallic particles settled atop the surface they moved toward. She let go of Rukkai.

She broke the surface, spied a horizon visible through the oddly luminescent sky, and submerged again. They existed *within*. She floated just a moment, picked a site ahead of her, and threw a portal. She'd never tried one underwater. The energies and shape of the portal shifted into rainbow colors and oblongs but never contracted so small she couldn't enter.

She appeared in the spot she'd selected, threw another portal, and exited well ahead of her guides. In this way, she reached shore before the Mer did but had stayed visible to them. They'd catch up.

The temperature difference outside the water was so marked, she shivered hard, skin sheathed in goosebumps.

Again, not warm. Warmer. Compared to what her body had acclimated to over the last several days, balmy.

Sky overhead. No wind. No trace of a mountain.

She raced across perfect sand before whipping back to greet Rukkai, Von, and Tem beaching themselves. "A portal?"

We suspected during examination but did not enter.

We wanted you.

You see spaces.

She cast another portal that blazed upon the sand. It maintained its usual circular shape but spat reds, yellows, greens, whites, blacks, and all the shades between rather than solely its brilliant blue. Silently drawing the energies back into herself, Amnandi turned toward the Mer. The gateway faded, taking its colors with it. The Mer, under this golden air, looked like living monoliths, each possessed of a universal secret. She wondered whether an attempt by them to glow would dress them in prisms.

Something about this space amplified energies and played with light. She wondered if she could transport to the opposite end of the universe. Portals were functions of thought, memory, time, and desire. The universe was designed for constant motion. Her mind whirled so fast amidst this gold that consciousness might as well have pinged between all her selves at so extreme a rate, they all shared it as one.

She was aware of each of them, and they of her.

Without thinking of it, she sent a cascade of soul heat down herself. Her skin and clothing dried in seconds.

"Is this the dream world?" she asked Rukkai.

Mer do not dream.

"Is this place familiar to you at all?"

No.

"It is very real," said Amnandi Green from behind her.

Amnandi turned toward her. "Do you wish to be here?"

"No," said her other.

"Goodbye."

"Goodbye."

In the next blink, the other parts of her rainbow, each appearing, each holding her with the word *sister* in their wide, fascinated eyes. Each content at deciding this was not where they wished to be.

Amnandi wouldn't begrudge them. This story was hers. They

had their own, which she was sure they attended to.

But how glorious they were.

The next breath had her in Green's existence, where Amnandi Green—appearing several years older than Amnandi herself now—faced an enormous bear that had terrorized a local forest for a full season. It was fearful of the increased scent of humans constantly around it.

Amnandi Red taught children to draw sustenance from a cloudy red sky.

Amnandi Blue flew. Amnandi hadn't known Blue could do that.

Amnandi's mind connected with Amnandi Gold's.

Is this a dream? she asked again, this time of Gold.

It could be if you want it to be, Gold, the same age as her, answered.

Amnandi didn't want that. She preferred reality packed with things to discover.

Is this the dragoon? A point of confluence? It would make sense. She thought it would, then she had to caution herself that what she thought here folded back upon itself. Paradoxes and self-fulfilling prophecies were the bane of witches, no matter how small or how consequential.

This was real. Real enough. She was dry. Her selves had been there. Footprints remained in the sand.

Amnandi Gold left, silently and without regret.

The Mer stood at vigil.

Amnandi may have been assured of reality, but not of time. Her sojourns with her selves had seemed to cover various years within a single moment.

Her fingers tingled with the urge to cast a portal to bring Amis along in the delicious joke they shared. From one step to another: someplace else.

Amis popped through the blazing portal the very next instant.

And screamed, a pain that carried along Amis's every tendon

and thought. A scream of a universe's birth.

Amnandi sent Amis back. Amnandi's wild eyes searched for explanation from the Mer, for comfort.

They had none.

What had she done? What had she done to her sister? She cast a thought to this golden portal space to send her to Amis.

Maab held Amis in a tight hug.

Cedar saw Amnandi. "Child, what is happening?"

"She was not prepared," said Amnandi.

"You found a portal?" Maab said over Amis's hair.

"A cavern that turns thoughts to things." Amnandi threw her own portal. "I'll be back."

The portal exited underwater. She threw the next, then the next, popping along the route Rukkai had led, stopping at the golden hue. This time, she wanted to study the feel of passage, to see if the golden light pressed against her mind or soul in a known way.

But there was nothing. Simply emergence into light.

How could this be? An entire stretch of sea and land as a portal? Rukkai and the others still stood as monoliths. The odd amber light suffused everything with honey. And of "everything" there was only unending beach ahead of her and unending sea behind.

Fascinating.

"If this is part of the dragoon's dream," she said aloud to give the space form and purpose, "I will see the dragoon."

Unlike the portals, there was no transference of energies; there was only a blink...

...then the opened eye.

And a dragoon, appearing as a blue woman with a smudge of red bisecting her lower lip, lips the gold of mountain pears sticky with sunlight, the same gold even swirling across her bare shoulders in constant clashing motion, vines braiding from her head as roots from deep-soil loam, and her eyes, the dragoon's eyes full of clouds at one point, starlight another, insect-faceted for the next blink, then empty of all again. The eyes settled surely and with great attention upon Amnandi from a height of four hundred ancient trees linked end to end.

Amnandi felt each exhalation of the dragoon as a warm breeze. Her neck craned as far back as it could to take in the being's enormity, not even realizing when her breathing synchronized with the other's. The dragoon's pristine face waited the space of a large, very patient blink.

"You do that for my benefit," said Amnandi. An elemental being wouldn't need tear ducts or even eyes to moisten. "A dream of a body creates a body." Heat from the dragoon's blue skin loosened the witch's tight muscles and soothed deep aches. "The body believes what it needs to believe in order to function."

"You recite knowables to me," the dragoon said, despite the red dot on her lips never separating.

"I need to hear my voice," said Amnandi. "Are you the goddess as well?"

"I used to be. She will be me in time."

"And you will be?"

"Another world." The word for *world* for dragoons was *galaxy*. Amnandi felt it translated into an expansion so fast, complete, and bright, it frightened her. She recoiled, hoping she couldn't become that deep or that wide. So much life, so many threads, so many things to believe in order to weave a cohesive reality.

A star forming inside her brain set her skull boiling. Amnandi fell to her knees, hands on her stubbled head to ram healing and comfort into the burning space.

The sensation eased but not of her doing. She flowed into the new star, the new star gained planets, the planets married moons, their moons entranced microbes, the microbes formed committees...

And, finally, people.

But they didn't feel like people as she knew them; they were concepts given flesh, or information taught to hug and kiss.

The elemental shared Amnandi's head again. "What will you be?" The dragoon was genuinely curious; Amnandi felt it. Its question waited as patiently as a moonrise for her answer.

"I don't know. Our world is sick."

"The body heals."

"Not always."

"I am the body. I am all."

"We can't see that. We need your energy, a different form of it, to travel the world. The goddess is unable to contain the newest plague. She's dying."

"Gods die as often as needed."

"You don't hear me!" Amnandi shouted, then pulled all emotions back. She knew there hadn't been a single word spoken. She knew there was no giant. Communication occurred on a deeper level than even the mind. It played out as music along the silvery filaments of her soul, creating harmonics that reached out in every direction to the edge of *every*thing.

She hadn't known it was possible to feel so utterly lost, so alone, alone amongst beetles, grass, seedlings, glasshawks, doves, ravens, parents, lovers, dreams, enemies, the dead, and friends. To exist as part of them but not of them confused every atom she possessed.

Apparently, to ask a question of the universe meant the universe having questions as well. "What are you?" was its question.

Amnandi squeezed her eyes shut in regret. That question hurt.

She opened her eyes. Rukkai, Von, and Tem stood immobile but glowing so blue now, they were practically a single light. As one, they suddenly took note of her presence, sped to her, and caught her in a rush of appendages before her unconscious form hit the ground.

✻✻✻

She had grown up believing that when the goddess spoke, the world listened and things grew, yet it was the voice of an elemental asking the simplest question that rendered her useless. She could hear and see everything, although strangely, there was no sense of smell.

Eternity was odorless?

That seemed unlikely.

Tem and Von hovered over her while Rukkai went back to Maab. Amnandi wished Rukkai hadn't. There was nothing Maab could do but worry and fret. Fretting was the evolution of concern into apoplexy. That was a witchism Amnandi had come up with herself after a solid year of knowing Amis. Unina had given an approving laugh when told it, then jotted it in her journal, Amnandi's first addition to her mother's Book of Things.

A witch found joy in knowledge, sadness in ignorance, and an overriding meditative calm in truth.

What was true here?

She could not move. If she panicked, she would fret.

She could not speak. Her chest rose and fell in message of well-being on her behalf. Von and Tem heard.

She was on her back, her arms at her sides, fingers splayed atop the gritty sand. She felt the texture and warmth underneath her. The world was substantial.

Above her, sky. A sky as bright as the clearest noon yet not a single evidence of a sun.

And then she remembered: this place was a nexus point.

It was only real because she, Von, and Tem needed it to be.

Her mind, like a broken bone setting, was not yet ready to bear her weight.

So, what she needed was time. She counted her breaths and waited.

***

"What can we do?" was the only thing Maab found to ask Rukkai. When she put it to the Mer for the third time, Skye stepped in.

"None of us can breathe long enough to get there," the mate said. She'd even looked to the mystic, but he just shook his head dourly. Skye wheeled on Barrow. "Scientist. Anything useful in your bag?"

Barrow mirrored the mystic. "Not even enough to cobble something."

"Then we find another way around," said Skye.

Maab straightened her back. "No. We don't." She speared Edrickl, Deneb, and Dza. "Ravens. You spend a great deal of time underwater." Maab went to Amnandi's pack, rooting for a tightly wrapped, waterproof bundle. She unrolled the bundle, removed all but a few items, then rerolled it. "Two of you go. One of you dies, I want another pair of hands. These packets are teas. Meant to be steeped. Dry will have to do. Crunch the leaves up and wad them in her mouth. Make a paste of a bit of it and rub it along her nostrils. Watch her breathing. If it quickens gradually, more in her mouth. If sudden, remove all from her mouth and roll her to her side."

"Let the Mer do it," said Edrickl.

"Which of you goes!" snapped Maab, ending all debate.

Edrickl's delicate finger pointed at Dza.

The stubby end of Rukkai's appendage motioned the ravens over as Rukkai twisted into a launch that carried it over the chasm's edge and into a brief splash.

Midair, Edrickl clamped the small bundle into his newly

formed beak, sliced the water simultaneously with Dza, and arrowed as fast as he could after Rukkai.

✳✳✳

I am surrounded by people and I can't move.

The sting of yuffa bark hit the tip of her tongue, then filled her cheek. Completely of their own volition, her eyes flashed open. Autonomics were fascinating. When twin acrid flares ringed her nose, tear ducts opened wide. Amnandi was one who genuinely enjoyed a good cry from time to time. This instance seemed a waste.

The scent always reminded her of someone meticulously lining up rows of fireworks, then lighting them all at once. Maab recalling Amnandi's medicines reminded Amnandi that Maab cared so much for her that she would find a way among all things possible.

And for the impossible, there was Unina.

A long, controlled pull of air bellowed the young witch's lungs.

She tested her brain. A toe twitched. The left pinky toe. She was coming back from infinity.

Ravens attended her, which was fantastic in itself. Perhaps reality had very little to do with infinite things? Or infinite things had nothing to do with reality?

And a nexus was where the two met in a single blurred spin?

She saw the face of the raven, Edrickl, looming over her, his head cocking to and fro to determine her level of fitness. Dza, a Bone Brother. Behind him, all three Mer, their prodigious bodies ready to tower down at the slightest misstep.

She moved another toe, patient to let her brain reset at its own pace. Once she returned to Maab (and Maab duly fretted over her), rested a bit, thought a bit, prepped herself quite a bit more, she'd have a much better grasp on things. She would tell everyone that the elemental was on curiously familiar terms, which would amaze the entire crew.

The dragoon, dragon, Endra'hoonj was quite real, Amnandi would reassure. Definitely powerful enough to help them. They just had to ask the right questions, as she planned most assuredly to confront eternity again.

***

At one point during soup, Amnandi heard Amis mention, "Was she dead?" Amnandi ate at the farthest point away from everyone to quicken a full return to her own head.

"Sister," she called to Amis, who trotted over.

Amis Dotrig's normally dirty face was now filthy, a combination of smudges, tear streaks, nose runnings, dried blood, and terror from inadvertently being teleported into a space designed for whirring minds.

"I wasn't dead," Amnandi said, feeling way more mysterious than she wanted. "Death is surprise. I was never that surprised."

"Don't tell me riddles."

"I believe what I say. I will die some day and I hope you are not there to see it, but understand my feelings on it before I go back—alone—to see the dragoon." Amnandi spoke softly, as always, but she knew Maab was listening. The entire cavern listened. She knew they each thought a variation of *Amnandi only thinks she'll go alone.*

She knew she would *be* alone.

"Death is simply disbelief of one's circumstance. I am open to...many things."

"You are not making this better, Khumalo of Afrela."

And that *was* the life of a witch, wasn't it? Better. For everyone. Amnandi tipped the wooden bowl to down the last of her soup. She called everyone over. "We would never have gotten here without all of us, so I give these gifts to you. Sarantain, you are the most amazing parent who has yet to raise a child. Nyim, Amis: trust in what you've learned. Skye, you are your namesake, forever floating. Endless exploration. Niss, you are perfect. Barrow, you are needed. Maab…" There, her voice cracked. She'd known it would. She continued. "Mother. Unina Pinyasama. Thank you." Darkness hid so many glistening eyes, including her own. "Daoud. Ever growing. I am certain that, in some manner, we are not yet done here." She fixed the ravens with her stare. "It is time you matured past what you've taught yourself." To Cedar: "You have never given up on anyone. Please continue that."

"You asking me to promise?" said Cedar.

"No, merely expressing hopes."

Maab said, "Your mother told me hope was powerful magick. She's softer than fur but won't admit it. Here's to all the hopes in this space tonight. Here's to journeying well."

"Hail and agreed," said Skye.

"Hail and agreed," came a round of quiet mutterings from everyone else except the ravens, who found prudence in silence.

"Rukkai," said Amnandi, although she knew Rukkai swam silently in the waters below her. She directed her intentions downward as strongly as she could. "My wish for you is nothing but rest." She fell silent herself.

Maab gave everyone their moments of stony reflection.

"You done, luv?" the captain said after that short beat. Amnandi didn't have to say anything for Maab to know that she was. "Rest is a good place to end on." Maab addressed the group. "She needs it undisturbed. Understood?"

"Aye," said Amis.

No other spokesperson was needed. The group dispersed, Maab included, but Maab stayed within earshot in case she heard Amnandi cry.

Amnandi settled, meditated, and eventually slept after hearing Maab tell Skye and Sarantain, "If she can leave, she can come back."

The young Khumalo took that as a guarantee.

***

Part of the witch wanted to experiment to see if the portion of the elemental that brushed against Erah would reach into the energies of her portal and draw her directly to it, but this wasn't a time for experimenting. At least, not in that way. She would get there strictly alongside Rukkai. It was likely they could both use the time to think.

Amnandi's thoughts turned, not surprisingly, on her friends rather than the approaching encounter, on what she'd told them. Her first group summation! Mother did it all the time, with a way of cutting through wasteful, unnecessary layers to expose a more necessary truth. Amnandi was seventeen years old. Did she have the right to attempt such?

But she hadn't attempted to speak wisdom, solely what she saw. Wasn't that what Unina did? To see someone is wisdom, all else folly. That's not something Unina told her, but it felt like it would have been. *"We create the art of our lives using others; it is important, then, to note their shapes and variations, yes?"*

She missed her mother greatly. The cool, tough skin of Rukkai was a solid comfort, but if Ayanda Khumalo had been beside her? Mother and daughter would have made the elemental flesh. Would have reminded it to walk Erah's continents and swim its oceans in search of all the lives that lived each blind day of the planet. Awareness was necessary. Sickness was too often invisible.

Unina would have shown the dragoon that a grand scheme was useless if the foundations were unfit.

Rukkai swam so fast, the currents passed like tubes. The experience felt very much like birth but with more twists and dives. Perhaps people should enter life that way, twisting, sliding, dipping, caroming, to prepare them for grand days ahead.

Perhaps I should not worry if I am attempting to distract myself too much.

And so she didn't. She let herself be pulled through Erah's blood toward what she hoped would allow itself to be Erah's heart. As far as she knew, no witch had ever approached the gods for direct intervention. Nor an elemental. But there was always room for firsts.

She found that quite fortunate.

***

She asked Rukkai and the others to stay in the gold-suffused waters. She alone would tread the sand. This culmination was not a matter of will, it was hope and intention.

She dried herself as before to see if that trick still worked. Step by step, she tried new things. She improved her hearing. She clothed herself in the last garments she'd seen her mother in: lightning-blue headscarf, the loose red robe, the gold ancestor rings. And if this was to be illusion, she wanted the effort to feel properly grand.

A volcano.

A volcano would do.

One alive and warm. Surrounded not by snow but by grasses. Tall green grass lazy in the wind, growing browner the closer stalks waved near the upward sloping rock.

But even fantasy should be respected. She did not automatically place herself at the top of the volcano; rather, she walked. She picked her way along ledges. She ported when necessary. She allowed herself the luxury of not needing rest, food, or water. There was only movement toward beauty. Each rock under her boots—she'd kept the heavy boots; witches lived on their feet—each rock spoke the language of contours or permanence.

Scrub here and there bolstered thoughts of perseverance, and surrounding everything: the painted sky, but now streaked with umbers and reds among the gold.

Even time seemed to perform beautifully for her, flowing scenically with her thoughts rather than moment to moment. She attained the top of the volcano precisely when she needed to. More than merely being active, the volcano hungered. Not for sustenance. For everything. Every star and grain of sand, nebulas to washbuckets, tea-stained teeth and books, solitude, lips, fire, community, soup, ice, matter, antimatter...

She didn't know where the last two words came from. Matter. Antimatter. Cause. Detrimental effect. Opposites within a contained whole.

Gravity.

And flight.

The rim of the volcano was huge. Too big. She brought it in closer so that seeing the far side didn't take forever. She merely needed it to be a conduit, not her entire universe.

She glanced behind her. Water. Beach. She wasn't even sure at what point the water and beach weren't water and beach. There were few things more elemental than the drive to be something else. To be fantastic.

Even water and sand likely had dreams outside themselves.

She couldn't see Rukkai or the others. She isolated herself from voices in her head. Thoughts of Unina, Maab, Amis, home—gone. She had to be solely and uniquely herself. Untethered. Light enough to float.

Amnandi stood over the furnace, the view absolute darkness, yet heat tore at her. She ignored the heat; she ignored the rightful stench, which was so assaultive it made her hungry to consume it away. She had already drawn the breath that meant there was no undoing the decision. She neither saw nor sensed a bottom but she knew what waited, what called, and what—in calling—

commanded. A dragoon. One that told her not to swim but to fly. She brightened her eyes, tilted forward, and flew.

Wind rippled her loose dress, giving her wings. Even with her eyes at full light, darkness swallowed sight and sound. Only the rustling of her clothing kept her company.

If eternity was dark and soundless, it was very lonely.

Without visual referents there wasn't even a sense of flying or falling. Just passage. Air across fabric and skin. She created an axis in her mind, and on that axis her body angled downward, arms at her sides, neck and legs straight as an arrow. She imagined slowing herself by going in a great spiral, then felt the wind shift accordingly.

The dragoon's call wasn't to her; it was to what she was, a thing within it, a mind aware of it.

She had the distinct impression it did not get very many visitors.

Ahead, a bit of light. An orange ribbon slowly stretching itself outward in all directions as though a stardrop had fallen. Lines grew brighter without adding illumination to the space at all. The lines continued to branch outward, forming roughly the inner shape of a colossal being that went from reptile to humanoid to bird then eel and back again. If magma were lightning and chaos order, its form would be excellent. A root system beyond all reckoning.

Amnandi registered a sense of ground rushing toward her. She answered with a sense of wings.

Her descent slowed. Her feet swung beneath her. From above, it had appeared the lattices were narrow. As she touched down, she saw each was as wide as an ocean, yet the space separating the two she stood between was barely the thickness of a path. Everything was black except the blood orange of the elemental's nervous system on display.

It was easy for Amnandi to forget she existed as anything

other than pure thought.

Is this the source of all magicks? she wondered, eager to test for new expansions to her power.

This, however, was not the time for that.

Focus, girl. Who do you need to be? she asked herself.

I am Amnandi Khumalo.

And why are you here?

I—

She couldn't remember. Others existed outside this space, didn't they? She wasn't everything. If she was everything, she wouldn't need to be here. There wouldn't even be a here or a her.

Others. Existed. She needed to bring those two notions together.

Matter. Antimatter.

Others. My existence.

Them. Me. Us.

There was something very appealing about this empty space.

Plague!

"Erah dies in pieces and bits!" she shouted, rousing herself from eternity's call.

Nothing. No response. The magma oceans flowed on either side of her.

But on the ground, it was hard to tell if there were changes elsewhere.

Fast as a whim, Amnandi knelt low, sprang up, and continued till she was high in the dark.

Without wings, flight required a huge amount of concentration. Concentration was energy, and she would rather not waste either on the intricacies of feathers.

Perhaps when she and eternity merged. Merging seemed... logical. Optimal. Maybe even necessary.

From her original impossibly high aerial vantage, she noted magma flows bursting into tributaries but no distinct changes.

"Erah dies in pieces and bits," she said again, much calmer this time, an entreaty, not a howl of panic. If a witch howled in panic, all was already lost.

An arm's length in front of her, a portion of the darkness deepened, extruded to three dimensions, and formed what looked to be the iris of a huge cat eye.

She had never particularly cared for cats. They argued with her too much.

The iris radiated a cold Amnandi had never felt before, colder than anything she'd encountered on Erah. There were no fires between stars. She was certain this was that type of cold. She instinctively retreated from it. The blackness, like someone rolling in bed and bringing the covers with them, rotated with her. She allowed herself to drift the opposite way.

The hanging eye followed.

A sepulchral, thick voice reached out from the darkness and clung as sticky as tar to every mote of her. BITS AND PIECES. HAS DEATH EVER BEEN OTHERWISE

The question was not rhetorical. It genuinely wanted to know.

She put aside fears of the darkness to answer it. "Here? I don't think so, no. Is it elsewhere? Life?"

THERE IS LIFE

"Harmony?"

THERE IS LIFE

"Then from your responses, it has never been otherwise. That does not mean it cannot be."

HOW

"We will figure it out."

WHAT ARE YOU

Eternity was apparently extremely uncurious about what it contained, and thus unknowledgeable.

"I don't want the world to die in pieces and bits."

IS THAT WHAT YOU ARE

"It is all I am."

Hints of blue spilled through the black iris, which itself was assuming a different shape. A dot of red. Flashes of gold and green, all softly illuminated as though from within. The eye became a smaller version of the blue giant, serenely patient.

I AM YOU, said the goddess.

"No, that is you as well. Everything…is you. The sickness is you."

AND I DO NOT WANT THE SICKNESS?

"No. It eats you in bits and bigger bites."

I AM FINITE?

"Are you pulling words from my mind?"

FROM EVERYONE'S MIND.

"Then you should know your own answers. There should be no questions."

The goddess spoke with her mouth. The red dot bisecting her lips bobbed and dipped. "There were no questions until the first infection of life that decided to be something else."

"You mean people?" asked Amnandi.

"People. Viruses. Bimaiy. Qo'nos. Lichen. Trees. The trees alone scream chaos at us."

"Your sister goddess—"

"Has died. I consumed her. Infection too great."

"But…that isn't how illness works. It's how it spreads. Are you…well?" It had seemed as if the darkness had gotten closer to Amnandi, but it was difficult to tell in all this nothingness. The blue of the goddess's skin warmed her by a hair more than before.

From the dark, the bob of the red again. "You should flee, child." The goddess's eyes, previously unseeable black pits, gradually brightened like coals to match the orange glow of the elemental's nervous system.

Amnandi didn't move. The goddess's colors quivered in strain.

"Child, this is the only place I can disgorge this."

"Did my presence summon you here?" the witch asked.

They regarded one another in silence.

"My family does not run from places we belong," said Amnandi, and prepared herself for the worst.

"Then hold me," said the goddess, who moved so swiftly against Amnandi that the young one barely had time to throw her arms open then close them upon the goddess's back.

The contact burned but also felt like balm. Amnandi's mind shrieked, but when she forced herself to focus on the sound, she heard a song. Her heart beat so fast her skin vibrated. She couldn't draw a breath, because her lungs were too expanded.

The goddess's anguish poured into the witch, whose spirit returned it to the goddess, and twin cries joined the pitch black, traveling no farther outward than the clasped bodies, a constraint that felt wrong, horrid, untenable. Unkind.

The goddess threw back her head and howled. Amnandi did the same.

A witch howling in *despair* meant all was lost. One howling in anger was quite another thing.

It had taken one Mad King to infect the world. Amnandi was sure that on the way home, she would hear tales of mass death, cruelty exalted, and suffering made lawful. One Mad King who had not simply embraced hatred but mated with it, alchemized it to root into the body of the gods, which supported Erah itself. This was beyond theft, want, or need.

She and the goddess howled in disbelief.

In that moment of rage, Amnandi knew she wanted Erah rid of this new disease. She wanted him.

He appeared. Darkness instantly disappeared. It was replaced by the golden beach. The Raven King, trapped mid-transformation half-bird, half-human, cowered in wild panic the same way Amis had when pulled into a place more alien than dreams. About the same height as Amis, as slight as Amis. Nowhere near the innate character of Amis.

The goddess whirled to consume him.

Amnandi, very softly, said no. The power of that solitary syllable halted the entire universe. Death changed nothing. A delay was not a cure. "I think Daoud already killed him," Amnandi said. "Leave him here."

"What of those he's infected?" said the goddess.

"Learn them. Bring them here. Can you?"

"You have shown me how."

"Let them commune in their sickness until they're cured."

"Or disintegrated."

The goddess Amnandi shrugged. Either was acceptable.

"Are you prepared for the consequences of this, witch?"

"I don't know. Do it."

The goddess spoke to her in the old tongue of the ravens. "Thy will be done."

NO GODS, NO HEROES

Most tales do not end. They linger onward. At the backs of minds. In corners. Hidden by boughs or buried beneath leaves. Erah was incredibly old and its tales more intricate than Amnandi could ever unravel. There was no end to certain things, but she had said no to one, and as she walked the radiant sand to the waters, she told herself that would do for now. Rukkai's back broke the surface and returned below. If its wounds didn't heal, she would consider its ailments her fault. Von and Tem surfaced next. They were pacing, waiting for her. The fact that they couldn't sense her meant something had changed in her. She wouldn't worry now on what it was.

The dragoon had disappeared the moment Amnandi rendered sentence, taking the King with it elsewhere. It was funny to Amnandi that the gods needed as much inspiration from humans as humans claimed to receive from them.

She hadn't laughed.

The three backs of the Mer turned to swim toward her when she was a hundred paces from the shore. She didn't pause to greet them. Her boots slapped the water. Her clothing was again the sheaf of protective wraps. She half-submerged. Rukkai extended an appendage to her. She took it. They dove, then swam faster than any of their bubbles could trail.

✳✳✳

When the goddess uses her voice, the whole world hears it, but most immediately return to the soft amnesia of less challenging thoughts. I suspect this is why she usually speaks through dreams and signs. We are comfortable with most things when asleep.

A fire blazes in the cave. We have traveled away from the water and back toward the light but not out of the cold volcano yet. Everyone is asleep, except Daoud, but he does nothing but quietly watch me. Each snap of flame is loud as a broken bone. I heard that phrase from Cedar, who I hope at some point finds the love she seeks. I'm wrapped in a ridiculous amount of blankets while my clothing dries. It feels good to be naked, even my toes. Maab placed me so close to the fire, I can almost see ghosts. I may see ghosts for the rest of my life, but that is likely simply the way of things. I am well. I am more than well. I answered a question, and that is more than many do in all their days.

We'll journey home soon. Maab has said the Bane *promises to deliver us to our loved ones. It will acknowledge no other mission.*

I've tried a lot of things that I've never tried before. I don't know that all of them worked. I don't know that the questions in the goddess's heart actually had answers. But I know the attempts felt right. They were necessary. I will continue to experiment. As for all failures, perhaps I will try them over and over again. Remember how Blessed Grandmother used to tell us, "It is only magick; there is always more"? I'm surprised I remember. I was so young. A witch that makes no effort to protect things, even memories, no matter her age, is no witch at all.

We sail the instant I port us all back to the ship. We are all far too tired to walk, and I know various ways now. Then more time before I return to you. Writing this helps me think, Unina, but the best telling of a tale is face to face. I hope you will be delighted.

❋ ❋ ❋

"Is that what you want to place in a bottle, luv?" said Maab, handing the journal back to Amnandi under the rippling sails of the *Bane* in the frigid air. Just because they had these new engines didn't mean they wouldn't keep the original girl maintained. Amnandi ripped the page out and rolled it tightly.

"It is. Should we not make it, the words will make their way to Afrela's shore. One day."

Maab nodded that she understood. "The only thing that hasn't happened to us is a sea monster ramming amidships," said the captain. "I'm sure your mother hasn't been simply meditating. Likely monumental things of her own." Amnandi handed her the page. Maab dropped it inside a green bottle and sealed it with a waterproof cork. "We'll drop it when we hit warmer climes, though. Don't want it cracking in this. I've had my fill of the cold."

"So have I."

Maab cast eyes around her ship. It functioned as it had before she left. Even the thief performed duties. All the ravens had taken flight the moment everyone exited the volcano. She wouldn't see them again. She would, however, be seeing Daoud for dinner, and there was a chance Barrow would stay on beyond this voyage. The young genius had mentioned it.

Nyim moved as though tied at the hip to Amis, under the appropriate-yet-discreet watchful eyes of Sarantain and Cedar. It wouldn't do to return Amis to her waiting father betrothed or otherwise romanced. Once on the lush grounds of Waterfall, however, was the girl's own story. Nyim could do worse than grow himself in a prosperous trading port.

"Was it a proper quest to you, luv? I know I haven't attended you as well as I could."

"It was," said Amnandi. "I would not have learned otherwise." She stooped to hug Maab fully, something she hadn't done in a long while. "Thank you."

"For?" Maab said into the girl's scarf.

"Permitting me a journey."

Maab scoffed. They pulled apart. Maab's breath plumed upward between them. "Have you had any signs or visions?"

"Nothing," said Amnandi. "Not even in dreams."

"We'll say we did what we needed then."

"Erah is well."

"As well as she tends to be. Come." Maab opened her arms. "Share my warmth." Amnandi stepped into the embrace again. "Save your magick heat; I've enough."

It was true. The day was cold. Maab was warm. It was enough. Maab pulled further back, reached up, brought Amnandi's head to her lips, and kissed her forehead. Amnandi blessed the contact by closing her eyes and whispering, "All feels well."

"And home awaits."

END

The lives of Mother Khumalo
and Amnandi continue in Book Three...

KHUMALO TALES

ACKNOWLEDGMENTS

By the time anyone reads this, I'll be deep into writing the final book in this series. If I can indulge in one last bit of fantasy before then, may I acknowledge you? Can't see or feel you, but you and I have been through two books together. We're invested in these flights of fancy.

I have nothing but thanks for your participation. Like the notion from *It's A Wonderful Life*, maybe when a reader enjoys a book, an author gets unseen wings. Or at least a feather. There've been more than enough kind words, loving encouragement, and exclamations of "Are you done with the next book yet?!" that doing the work often felt like soaring.

Here's to the readers, without whom a book is just diary misspelled. Thank you for flying with me, and for bringing your unique gifts along for the trip.

Thank you to my beta readers, editors, and especially to my sister from another imaginative twister, Claire Cooney, the source of a thousand updrafts and many many words I like today.

If any of you happen to be in the future far enough that you've read all three, here's a feather. Or two.